Recent Titles by Marcia Talley

The Hannah Ives Mysteries

SING IT TO HER BONES
UNBREATHED MEMORIES
OCCASION OF REVENGE
IN DEATH'S SHADOW
THIS ENEMY TOWN
THROUGH THE DARKNESS
DEAD MAN DANCING *
WITHOUT A GRAVE *
ALL THINGS UNDYING *
A QUIET DEATH *
THE LAST REFUGE *
DARK PASSAGE *
TOMORROW'S VENGEANCE *
DAUGHTER OF ASHES *
FOOTPRINTS TO MURDER *
MILE HIGH MURDER *

* available from Severn House

TANGLED R

TANGLED ROOTS

Marcia Talley

This first world edition published 2019
in Great Britain and the USA by
SEVERN HOUSE PUBLISHERS LTD of
Eardley House, 4 Uxbridge Street, London W8 7SY.
Trade paperback edition first published
in Great Britain and the USA 2019 by
SEVERN HOUSE PUBLISHERS LTD.

British Library Cataloguing in Publication Data
A CIP catalogue record for this title is available from the British Library.

ISBN-13: 978-0-7278-8882-2 (cased)
ISBN-13: 978-1-78029-600-5 (trade paper)
ISBN-13: 978-1-4483-0217-8 (e-book)

All Severn House titles are printed on acid-free paper.

Severn House Publishers support the Forest Stewardship Council™ [FSC™],
the leading international forest certification organisation.
All our titles that are printed on FSC certified paper carry the FSC logo.

Typeset by Palimpsest Book Production Ltd.,
Falkirk, Stirlingshire, Scotland.
Printed and bound in Great Britain by
TJ International, Padstow, Cornwall.

GENEALOGY (from the Gr. *yènos*, family, and *λογοs*, theory),
a pedigree or list of ancestors, or the study of family history.

— *Encyclopedia Britannica*, 11th edition, Vol. 11,
Cambridge, England, 1910, p. 573.

ACKNOWLEDGMENTS

My research for *Tangled Roots* began with the obvious first step: I spat into a test tube and sent it off for DNA testing. I spent the weeks before the results came in constructing my family tree on a popular genealogy website and soon, like Hannah, found myself sucked, head-first, down a rabbit hole. Now, nearly a year later, I've reconnected with a long-lost cousin (Hello, Ellen!), discovered that a first cousin in fact wasn't, learned how my great-grandmother actually died, confirmed family legend that I'm directly related to John Hart the Signer, and visited a cemetery not far from the King Arthur Flour Company in rural Vermont where generations of my family lie buried. Some of these genealogical adventures inevitably wove themselves into the fabric of this book.

Although writing is a solitary business, it often takes a family to make a novel.

I'm particularly indebted to my Native American friends who listened patiently, answered countless questions and trusted me to get it right. If I failed, it's my fault, not theirs.

Thanks to my sister, Deborah Kelchner, who helped build our family tree and whose passion for genealogy rivals my own.

A shout-out to my long-time friend, Linda Sprenkle, who knows my characters almost as well as I do. You were totally right about Georgina.

And to my friend and colleague, Sujata Massey, for sharing her neighborhood and favorite restaurants.

Kudos to James A. Earl, whose winning bid at an auction to benefit the Annapolis Opera Company earned him the right to appear as an artist in this book. Since Jim *is* an accomplished artist, no acting on his part was required.

I'm grateful to Tim Keane, winner of a character auction benefitting Lyme Elementary School in Lyme, New Hampshire, where my grandchildren go to school. In real life, Tim runs a biotech firm producing antibodies for cancer research. He's moonlighting as an attorney in this book.

For 'tough love' I appreciate my partners in crime Mary Ellen Hughes, Becky Hutchison, Debbi Mack, Sherriel Mattingly, Penny Petersen, Beth

Schmeltzer and Bonnie Settle of the Annapolis Writers' Group who read every word, sometimes more than once.

Hugs to Kate Charles and Deborah Crombie, dearest friends, confidantes and advisors, who keep me grounded. Your 'two-cents' are always worth a hundred bucks.

And, as always, to Vicky Bijur.

ONE

It started with a phone call. Doesn't it always?

Although my cell phone was resting face down on the patio table within easy reach, vibrating noisily against the glass, I almost didn't pick up. My hands were encased in rubber gloves while I smoothed marine varnish over the sun-bleached teak of our deck chairs. I could tell by the ringtone, however, that Georgina was on the line. I knew from experience that she'd keep dialing my number until I silenced the chimes either by switching the phone into airplane mode or chucking it into the rhododendrons. So, I caved.

I dunked the paintbrush into a yogurt tub filled with paint thinner, peeled off the gloves and used a damp pinky finger to accept the call.

'Hey,' I said as I leaned over the table and stabbed the speaker button. 'What's up?'

I hadn't heard from my baby sister in two or three weeks. It's probably not nice to say, but Georgina usually called only when she wanted something. I braced myself.

'Did you ever send in that DNA test kit I gave you?'

Georgina had been dabbling in genealogy lately, exploring the Alexander family tree. How she found the time between caring for four school-age children and Scott, her high-maintenance, self-employed CPA husband, I couldn't imagine.

'Not yet. Why?'

'I don't know why I even bothered to give it to you, Hannah,' she huffed.

'I'm sorry, sis. It slipped my mind, is all. I'll get to it soon, I promise,' I said as I puzzled over where I'd put the damn packet. At a family picnic a couple of months before, Georgina had given me and our older sister, Ruth, each a test kit. At the time, she'd seemed eager – with Scott egging her on – to join the Daughters of the American Revolution which required tracing our forefathers (and mothers, Ruth had been quick to remind her!) in an unbroken line back to 1776.

'How hard can it be to spit into a tube?' Georgina sighed in exasperation. 'And postage paid?'

'Sorry,' I apologized again. 'Is it important?'

'I don't know,' my sister said, sounding cautious. 'It's just that I think they might have made some sort of mistake when they tested mine.'

'Yeah?'

'The English and Scottish roots I expected,' she continued. 'There was a smattering of Scandinavian and Iberian Peninsula that didn't surprise me, the Vikings and the Romans, you know,' she rattled on, 'but according to Gen-Tree . . .' She paused. 'Are you sitting down?'

'Don't build me a clock, Georgina. Just tell me what time it is!'

'Gen-Tree says I'm twenty-five percent Native American.'

I reached for a chair I hadn't yet painted and sat. How could my fair, green-eyed, red-headed sister, and by extension Ruth and I . . .?

The Alexanders, I knew, emigrated to Virginia from the Scottish Highlands sometime in the mid-eighteenth century, and our mother's family, the Smiths, descended from frugal, Puritan stock, going back – Grandmother Smith always claimed – to 1630 and the Winthrop Fleet. My husband, Paul, used to tease that this explained my propensity to rinse out and reuse Ziploc bags.

'That's nuts,' I said, after catching my breath. 'It's probably a mistake. Got contaminated, or your sample mixed up in the lab with somebody else's.'

'That's what Scott thought,' Georgina said.

'Call them,' I suggested. 'Ask them to re-do it.'

'I did, Hannah, and they're sending me another test kit for free, but it'll take weeks and weeks to get the results! That's why I was hoping you'd sent yours in. I mean, we should be the same, right?'

'As far as I know. Have you checked with Ruth?'

'She flat-out refused to do it. Hutch said he had serious privacy concerns about those testing companies.'

Ruth's husband was an attorney. He always agonized over the fine print.

Frankly, I thought it'd be rather cool to have Native American blood, but I didn't see how that could be possible. Twenty-five percent? I did the math.

If that were the case, one of our four grandparents would have to have been a full-blooded Indian. I'd known my grandparents on both sides – they'd lived well into their eighties. A long-ago Alexander had migrated from Virginia to southern Maryland where he married a sixteen-year-old Catholic girl related to George Calvert, the first Baron Baltimore. I'd forgotten the fellow's name, but the couple prospered, growing tobacco on a Chesapeake County farm not far away from the one now owned by my husband's sister, Connie. She raised cows down there, though, not tobacco.

Stephen and Charlotte Smith had been farmers, too, on a two-hundred-acre spread near Norwich in rural Vermont, now home to a Christmas tree farm run by one of my second cousins. A cemetery not far from the King Arthur Flour Company was chock-full of our relatives. A wedding photograph still sits on my living room mantel: Grandpa Smith, string bean tall, his sandy hair sticking out in tufts from beneath a broad-brimmed hat. Grandma, diminutive, deceptively frail, her peach-colored hair in full bloom around her face.

'Hannah? Are you still there?'

'Sorry,' I said. 'I was just trying to wrap my head around all this. Honestly, I don't recall any one of our grandparents having Native American features, but I'm not sure what I'd be looking for.'

'Maybe Mom or Dad was adopted,' Georgina cut in. 'Or maybe . . .' She paused dramatically. 'Maybe there were shenanigans.'

I laughed out loud. 'Let's wait until our tests come back, OK?'

She giggled. 'OK. Thanks for putting up with me, Hannah.'

Georgina could be a handful, that was certainly true, but it wouldn't help to agree with her. As I watched the varnish in the open paint can start to skim over, I tried to remember where I'd put the darn test kit. Under the bathroom sink?

'Hey!' Georgina was saying when I tuned in again. 'You're

much better with computers than I am, Hannah. How 'bout I set you up as co-editor on Gen-Tree.com? You can check out the information I've entered so far. Do a bit of poking around.'

'Sounds like fun,' I said truthfully. I'd seen the ads for Gen-Tree on television. Click on one ancestry hint – a flapping pennant icon – then another and another, leading back to – potentially – Adam and Eve. It could end up being more addictive than playing Words With Friends. 'Maybe there'll be horse thieves in the family, or moonshiners,' I mused.

'Then again,' Georgina said, 'they could all be totally boring. Like accountants.'

After we said goodbye, I capped the paint can, cleaned the paintbrush with turpentine and trotted upstairs to shower. The Gen-Tree test kit was, as I suspected, under the bathroom sink. After I dried myself off, I put on a fresh top and a clean pair of shorts, grabbed the kit and padded barefoot down to our basement office. I sat down at the computer. While I waited for it to power up, I opened up the packet and read the instructions.

Activate the fifteen-digit code. Check.

Agree that I can't sue the company for DNA results I didn't like. OK.

Receive emails from our business partners? I don't think so.

Health reports? You bet.

I also agreed, in spite of the vagueness of the wording, to allow my DNA to be used for projects to 'better understand the human species'. Why not, I reasoned. It's the closest I'll probably get to doing scientific research.

When I got to the section about DNA matching, I called Georgina back.

'When you sent in your sample, did you sign up for the DNA matching service?' I asked.

'Gosh, no. Scott had a fit when I mentioned it. He even made me check the box instructing them to destroy my sample after they tested it.' She paused, then said slyly, 'But that wouldn't prevent *you* from signing up for it.'

'Of course not,' I said as I checked the box that would allow Gen-Tree to match me up, DNA-wise, with potential relatives in their database, unsurprised to hear that Scott had kicked up a fuss. My brother-in-law left claw marks on the road as his family dragged him into the digital age. He used email in his work now, but still didn't 'do' Facebook or Twitter and had only reluctantly allowed his children to join the scary new world of social media.

Recently, a serial killer had been tracked down by matching DNA left at a crime scene to distant cousins registered in GEDcom, a public genealogy database. I hadn't murdered anyone recently, so adding my DNA to the pool didn't seem a particularly risky decision.

You were instructed to wait an hour without eating, drinking or smoking before taking the test. I figured the meatloaf sandwich I'd had for lunch was long off my breath, so I obediently spit – and spit and spit and spit – into the tube they provided. When the spit reached a black line, I screwed down a cap containing a blue liquid preservative and shook it for the required five seconds. That done, I slid the tube into a little bag, and the bag into a small, postage-paid box.

Ten minutes later, I intercepted the mailman as he strolled from house to house down Prince George Street. I traded the box for a packet of bills and advertising flyers. 'Take good care of that,' I said.

He scrutinized the mailing label. 'There's a lot of this going around.'

I grinned. 'We could compare notes. Maybe we'll turn out to be fifth cousins.'

'My wife found out she has a German half-sister,' the mailman commented as he tucked my precious cargo into a side pocket on his pouch. 'Seems Daddy was a naughty boy while stationed with the Air Force in Ramstein. It's a good thing he's already dead, or Mary's mother would have killed him.'

'I doubt there'll be any surprises,' I said with a smile. 'My family's so conventional they could have starred in a fifties sitcom sponsored by Walt Disney.'

'Well, good luck,' he said, touching the brim on his cap.

'Thanks,' I said over my shoulder as I returned to the house.

According to Gen-Tree.com, it would be at least six weeks before my test results would be ready. In the meantime, I decided to sit down, roll up my sleeves and see what I could discover by exploring their database.

TWO

I spent the remainder of the afternoon in the basement office, fleshing out the Alexander family tree started online by my sister, Georgina. I was new to genealogical research, but I immediately ran into what must be every genealogist's nightmare: a relative bearing the last name of Smith.

We had a Zebulon in the family woodpile, and a great-grandfather married to a woman named Azubah, but otherwise ordinary Johns, Marys, Sarahs and Abrahams appeared in biblical abundance throughout New England, and Mother herself was just plain Lois Mary.

As I explored the Gen-Tree database further, half the population of Vermont seemed to be Smiths, including Joseph Smith, of magic spectacles, golden tablets and Angel Moroni fame. The founder of Mormonism turned out to be, when I clicked down to it, my sixth cousin several times removed, depending on how one calculates those things.

As far as Smiths in my direct line were concerned, however, the closest Native American connection I could find happened on July 18, 1694 during King William's War. On that day, several hundred Abenaki Indians led by two French priests, massacred nearly everyone in my ancestors' village on the Oyster River near present-day Durham, New Hampshire. 'Just think,' I said to Paul, who had been hovering behind me for twenty minutes, kibitzing, insisting that I open intriguing Family Story documents and read them. 'If eight-year-old Mary hadn't scooted out the back door and hid in the woods while her family was being scalped, I wouldn't be here today.'

'Thank you, Mary,' Paul breathed close to my cheek.

Dad's family, the Alexanders, descended from sturdy, Scottish stock. Our dad was a George from a long line of Georges who were fairly easy to track through successive US censuses, not having moved around a lot during the previous three hundred years.

'If you're going to keep interrupting,' I said while typing, adding a trio of siblings to the Alexander line, 'do something useful, like massage my shoulders.'

'Have you run up your grandmother's line on your father's side?' he asked, applying gentle kneading pressure to my aching muscles.

'Not yet,' I said, leaning back gratefully and surrendering to his magic fingers. 'Right now I'm trying to clean up the mess Georgina's made. She's got one of our great-great-grandmothers married to herself and two of the poor woman's children born years before her marriage, which would probably have been a big no-no back in 1820.' I corrected the spousal connection, then clicked off through the database in search of Sam and Maud Alexander's marriage record.

Working on Gen-Tree was as addictive as playing the quarter slots at Atlantic City. I'd just be thinking of quitting and then . . . I'd click on one more pennant. And then, well, OK, maybe one more. Before long, I had followed a promising hint and found myself back in Vermont with the Smiths.

My third great-grandmother on my mother's side, Helen Smith, was one of thirteen children. Four of the poor woman's ten children perished in a typhoid epidemic in 1856 while still in their teens. 'I. Can't. Even,' I muttered, as I linked to a photo of a weather-worn tombstone for sixteen-year-old Abigail that someone had posted on FindAGrave.com.

'That's why they had big families,' Paul offered, not so helpfully.

'Some simply can't manage it,' I said, indicating an icon of a sorrowful angel. Back in 1876, baby Richard lived for six hours, and his mother died the following day.

I'd lost a baby sister, Mary Rose, to crib death, and even after all these years, the memory still stung. 'Vermont keeps terrific records,' I said, moving on quickly before I could tear up, 'but some other states, not so much.' Baby Richard's father had remarried, but I lost track of him after the 1880 census. The entire US census for 1890 had been destroyed in a fire at the Commerce Department in Washington, DC, and by the time the 1900 census rolled around the guy had disappeared.

'What are you looking for, exactly?' my husband wanted to know. 'I can't see how tracking this dead boy's father is going to get you any further along on the Native American question.'

I clicked on my own icon – my senior yearbook picture from Oberlin College, the one where I was rocking the Dorothy Hamill wedge – and displayed my immediate family tree. My parents, four grandparents and eight great-grandparents lined up in rows of tidy boxes. 'If I am one-quarter Native American, it stands to reason that it happened in this generation here,' I said, indicating the row of boxes representing my grandparents.

Although my mother had died fairly young of congestive heart disease following decades of smoking, the four grands had lived long and happy lives, until – as one death certificate had put it – 'a surfeit of years' had carried each of them away. Earlier, I had uploaded family portraits of each of them. 'Nobody looks the least bit Native American,' I pointed out.

Paul leaned closer to the screen, adjusted his reading glasses to better study the images. 'I'd have to agree.'

'I wish I could ask Mom some questions,' I told him.

'You can't assume it's on your mom's side of the tree,' Paul said. 'Could be your dad. He's still alive and kicking. Why don't you ask him if he remembers anything?'

'I plan to,' I said, 'but he's been away. When I talked to Neelie the other day, she mentioned he's off in Florida tweaking some component on a SpaceX guidance system.'

Cornelia 'Neelie' Gibbs was my father's long-time girlfriend. Why they hadn't tied the knot, I couldn't say, although I suspect it had something to do with the retirement benefits from Neelie's late husband which, I gathered, had set her up for life as long as she didn't remarry. It didn't trouble me that Daddy was 'living in sin' with Neelie, but it had been an issue for Georgina's husband, Scott Cardinale. A 'recovering Catholic', he dragged his family off every Sunday to an evangelical mega-church just outside the Baltimore beltway, where he served as Treasurer, taught Sunday School, and led a Wednesday night Bible study class. 'I called Dad's cell and left a message for him to call,' I said. 'But I didn't say exactly why.'

Paul pulled up a chair and sat down next to me. 'Meanwhile, since you don't have your test back, and just for the sake of argument, let's assume that Georgina's results are accurate.'

'OK.'

'First scenario. Your DNA is relentlessly North European and Georgina's adopted.'

'Impossible. I remember when she was born. Mom was so pregnant she couldn't fit behind the wheel of a car.'

He held up two fingers. 'Second scenario. Your dad's in the Navy, on active duty. Maybe your mom had an affair while he was deployed?'

I punched him in the arm. 'Shut your mouth! That is totally out of the question.' I thought for a moment. 'Besides, when Mom got pregnant with Georgina, we were living in San Diego. Dad had a desk job at the Naval Sea Systems Command, doing . . .' I paused to think. 'Developing something that had to do with landing planes on aircraft carriers.'

Paul shuddered. 'Those guys are gods.'

I had to agree. Anyone who could land a plane at full throttle on a moving target no larger than a football field in the middle of the ocean deserved respect.

'So, one of these,' Paul said, indicating my grandparents, 'is full-blooded Native American.'

'So it would seem.'

'Or, perhaps two of them were half Indian?'

I shot daggers. 'You can be exasperating sometimes, you know that, darling?'

'Or one-eighth and three-eighths,' he continued with a grin. 'Or, three-sixteenths and five-sixteenths, or . . .'

'That's enough for today,' I said, cutting him off before he could lob more fractions my way. I logged off the website and shut down the computer.

Paul rose from his chair and rested a hand on my shoulder. 'Maybe Georgina's test was wrong and all this is for nothing.'

'Oh, not for nothing,' I said. 'Aren't you the least bit curious to know why a Vermont death certificate lists great-great-great-grandmother Smith's death at age eighty-three as "suicide by hanging"?'

'The one with thirteen kids?'

'Ten,' I corrected.

'I rest my case.'

'Go away,' I said. 'Isn't it your turn to cook dinner?'

For our thirty-fifth wedding anniversary, our daughter Emily had given us a three-month subscription to a popular meal delivery service. Turns out, Paul enjoyed the service more than expected, throwing himself into meal preparation like, well, a mathematician. His small dice of green peppers – precisely six by six by six millimeters – had to be independently verified using a specially-marked cutting board he'd bought for himself from a company called Obsessive Chef.

It was agonizing to watch.

'Besides,' I said, 'how else would I know that I'm related to Lovey Bean, whose descendent, Leon Leonwood Bean, founded L.L. Bean?'

'Think that will get you a free pair of duck boots?'

I put a hand flat on his back and shoved him out the door ahead of me. 'A gal can dream.'

THREE

Not long after Paul and I had crawled into bed, Dad returned my phone call. 'Did I wake you up?' he asked to my groggy hello.

'No, no,' I said while squinting at the bedside clock. 10:42. I propped myself up on one elbow. 'I had to get up anyway. The phone was ringing.'

Dad chuckled, deep and gravelly. 'Sorry to be calling so late, but I was out to dinner with some of the team.'

I heard ice clink against glass – my father's nightly tonic and lime ritual. 'Papa Vito's,' he said, adding in his best Valley Girl accent, 'the cheese bread is to die for. I may never have to eat again.'

'Where *are* you, exactly?' I asked.

'If I told you, sweetheart, I'd have to kill you.'

'Seriously, Dad!' I really wasn't in the mood for jokes.

'Florida.' The ice clinked again.

'Neelie said it had something to do with SpaceX,' I said.

'Tangentially,' he said. 'What goes up must come down, at least that's the idea. Sideways spoils everyone's day.'

'When do you get back?'

'Back' would be to the two-bedroom condo he shared with Cornelia Gibbs at Calvert Colony, an upscale retirement community that sprawled grandly along the banks of the Chesapeake Bay just outside of Annapolis. It was adjacent to Paradiso, the day spa owned by our daughter, Emily, and her husband, Daniel Shemansky, or Dante as he preferred to be called. Just plain Dante, like Elvis, Madonna or Cher. The spa had been a dream of my son-in-law ever since he dropped out of Haverford College a year before graduation and eloped with our daughter. Somewhere I had a photo of the happy couple posing in front of a wedding chapel in Las Vegas. Not an auspicious start to a life-long relationship that now included three adorable children.

'Next week,' Daddy was saying. 'Neelie's signed us up for a Road Scholar trip to Cuba. Thirteen days of birdwatching.'

'I didn't know you were interested in birds.'

'I'm not, but Neelie's passionate about her feathered friends. According to the brochure, there are twenty-five avian species unique to Cuba. She hopes to add some of them to her life list.'

Tramping around all day in hot, humid, tropical rainforests didn't appeal to me one bit, and I said so. 'I'd rather hang out with artists and musicians in Havana.'

'What? And miss the opportunity to spot a rare Gundlach's hawk?'

'Tragic,' I said.

Next to me, Paul stirred, opened an eye and said, 'What's going on?'

I flapped a hand at him and whispered, 'Sorry. Just talking to Dad. Go back to sleep.'

After another sip of his drink, Dad said, 'It's wonderful to hear your voice, Hannah, but I got the impression from your message that there was something on your mind.'

I scooted up in bed and rearranged the pillow between my back and the headboard. 'I wanted to give you a heads-up on something. And also pick your brain.'

'Sounds ominous. Do I need to add some gin to my tonic?'
This was a joke, and I knew it. Dad was a recovered alcoholic.
He'd earned his ten-year medallion from Alcoholics Anonymous
and was proud of his hard-won sobriety. And so were we.

'You know those DNA test kits Georgina handed out a while
back?' I asked.

'If you're calling to nag me about sending it in . . .'

'No, it's not that,' I said, gathering my nerve, stalling for
time, 'but, uh, did you?'

'Did I what? Take the test?'

'Yeah.'

'Forgot all about it, sweetheart.'

That didn't surprise me. He'd accepted the test kit from
Georgina reluctantly. She'd flounced off in a snit after he referred
to the commercial testing company she'd chosen as 'recreational
DNA'. He'd made no secret of his disdain for the industry either,
lumping it together with pseudosciences like aromatherapy and
homeopathy. I thought he was overreacting.

I forged on. 'You know the fine print, where they warn you
to be prepared for identity-disrupting surprises?'

'Uh huh,' he said cautiously. 'Cut to the chase, Hannah.'

'Georgina's test just came back. According to Gen-Tree DNA,
she's one-quarter Native American.'

A long, low whistle came down the line, then silence.

'That means that either you or Mom—'

He cut me off. 'I know what it means. And it's nonsense.'

I explained that Georgina had demanded a re-do from the
company and was still waiting for results. I told him I'd sent
my test kit in, too.

'So the jury's still out,' he said.

'Yes, but . . .'

'But, what?'

'I've done a good bit of reading since Georgina called with
the news, and Gen-Tree's quality control is convincingly solid.
Because each company uses a different database, results may
vary from one DNA company to another, even between identical
twins, but specimen contamination and out-and-out mix-ups are
rare.' I paused to take a breath. 'I'm proceeding on the assumption that Georgina's test results are accurate.'

Daddy let the remark pass. 'Did the test identify a specific tribe of Native Americans?'

'The science is confusing, Dad, at least to me. Apparently they can link you to one of five broad mitochondrial DNA haplogroups but they're unable to pinpoint a particular tribe or even a particular combination of tribes,' I told him. 'The database is too small. I read while I was poking around that forty-four percent of Native Americans belong to haplogroup A.'

'What was Georgina's haplogroup, do you know?'

I confessed that I didn't. 'I'm waiting to see how my test results turn out before digging any deeper. I don't intend to become the world's foremost authority on Native American mitochondrial haplogroups unless I have to.'

'When will you know?' Dad asked.

'I waved goodbye to my saliva this morning,' I said, 'so five or six weeks. I hope the suspense doesn't kill me.'

After a moment, Dad said quietly, 'Hannah?'

'What?'

'I don't want you to lose any sleep over this. It doesn't change who I am or who your mother was.'

I puffed air into the phone. 'I know that!'

'There's nothing you can do to change the past,' he added gently.

'I know that, too,' I said, but there was something in his voice – was it a hint of apology? – that made me think Dad knew more about our family tree than he was admitting.

After we said goodbye, I lay flat on my back staring at the ceiling, listening to Paul's gentle snoring. Shadowy leaves hopscotched over the striped wallpaper, cast by a full moon shining through the branches of a tulip poplar just outside our bedroom windows.

I closed my eyes, slowed my breathing and concentrated on repeating the mantra I'd been given – *hirim, hirim, hirim* – but my thoughts kept drifting.

DNA. Fractions.

All along, I'd been focusing on one of my grandparents. But as Paul had pointed out before dinner, there were other mathematical possibilities. Despite everything I believed I knew about her, had my mother been unfaithful?

FOUR

'In the nucleus of every cell,' I read aloud to Coco, 'there are twenty-three pairs of chromosomes. Twenty-two of these matched pairs are called autosomes, while the twenty-third pair – either X or Y – determines your sex.'

My daughter's chocolate-colored Labradoodle cocked a shaggy brow and considered this information with eyes of liquid gold. Her tongue lolled as if to say, 'And dogs have *thirty-nine* pairs of chromosomes, did you know that, Hannah? Neener, neener, neener!'

'Smarty pants.' I patted the dog's head and continued reading.

Autosomal DNA is inherited equally from both parents – I remembered that from college biology – and includes contributions from previous generations in ever lessening fractional degrees: your grandparents, great-grandparents, great-great-grandparents and so on. It's a genetic snapshot of what makes you uniquely you. By comparing the bits we have in common with our mutual predecessors, Gen-Tree's DNA test can match us up with relatives, both known and unknown.

The frustrating part at this early stage of the process was the realization that the test couldn't pinpoint exactly where on Georgina's family tree that the Native American match occurred. No wonder she had encouraged everyone in the family to get tested; it would help narrow down the field.

But Mom was no longer with us, Dad seemed reluctant and Ruth openly hostile, having told Georgina to ask her again when someone developed a test that could tell who you were in a previous life. It seemed to me that good, old-fashioned research might be the way to go.

I'd spent a significant portion of my professional life commuting from Annapolis to Washington, DC, getting my ticket punched along the way until I made it to the top – a high-paying job at Whitworth and Sullivan as head of archives and records. All was going well until a quality management team somewhere on the tenth floor began throwing darts at the accounting firm's organizational chart and twenty-five percent of middle-level management, including yours truly, found ourselves tossed out on K Street, dazed and blinking, clutching our dress-for-success briefcases.

Frankly, I had mixed feelings about being RIFd. I'd been recovering nicely from a mastectomy and chemo-from-hell, thinking that there was nothing like a cancer diagnosis to give me the permission I needed to ditch the punishing long-distance commute and seek part-time work closer to home. With the decision out of my hands, I registered with a local agency and worked on and off as a temp in libraries, insurance agencies and even for Spa Paradiso when I could spare the time. Paul was a tenured professor, so we didn't really need the money, but no sense allowing my brain to grow rusty.

Fast forward. Me, sitting in our basement office, refreshing my research skills by reviewing census records for 1920 and 1930 that placed my grandparents firmly in Vermont and southern Maryland, respectively. Although Indian tribes inhabited both states during English colonization, they had either been forced onto reservations further west or been assimilated into local populations by the time my grandparents were born.

Genealogical research should come with a warning. I linked to a photograph of my grandfather Smith's tombstone in Tunbridge Village Cemetery in Vermont. It was like getting sucked, head first, down a rabbit hole into a parallel universe entirely populated with dead people.

For several days, I worked on expanding our tree, adding supporting documents – birth and death certificates, city directory listings, high school and college yearbook photos – until the tree looked fleshed out and attractive when displayed on the screen, but I was no closer to an answer. Eventually, when Gen-Tree ran out of hints and I'd exhausted the search engines of the historic newspaper databases, I had a brainstorm and decided to call my father again.

'What happened to the storage boxes that were in the attic when you and Mom lived in Providence?' I asked, naming the upscale community on the Severn River where my parents had lived before Mom's final illness. I hadn't thought about those gray Tupperware tubs in years. The last time I'd pawed through one of them I was looking for *Tiger Tales*, my high school yearbook, when I volunteered for the reunion committee. Mother had saved everything – ancient report cards for my sisters and me, school pictures, immunization records, juvenile artwork and essays. There were boxes containing nothing but loose photographs, I recalled, and at least two dozen fully-loaded Carousel slide trays.

'Aren't you putting the cart before the horse?' Dad wondered.

'Maybe,' I admitted, 'but it occurred to me that somebody ought to sort through all that stuff. Organize it. And who better than I?'

Daddy laughed. 'You planning to digitize it, Hannah?'

'Maybe,' I said. I'd actually given some thought to digitization of the family archives, but in my saner moments, worried I'd be exchanging one obsolete form of technology for another. I had a five-and-a-half-inch floppy disk reader somewhere in the basement, for example. One never knew when you'd need to find that letter you wrote back in 1982 that was pure genius, although the *New York Times* foolishly failed to print it.

'Remember our family trip to the Outer Banks?' Dad asked.

'How could I forget?' I said, wondering why he'd segued in that direction. Our first day at the condo, ten-year-old Georgina had scattered complimentary peanuts from American Airlines on the deck and we'd spent days fighting off scavenging seagulls.

'How many pictures of seagulls does one need?' Dad asked.

I laughed. 'Point well taken. Someone needs to do a proper culling. I'm not sure I'm up to wading through boxes of gap-toothed photos of myself with untamed curls and ineffectual hair bows.'

'Times three,' he said, meaning Ruth, Georgina and me. After a moment, he added, 'When we moved, I put most of what didn't sell at the garage sale in a self-storage facility on Route 2, near the South River, along with the big chest freezer and your grandmother Smith's bedroom furniture. Pop-pop's roll top desk is down there too,' he added. 'There's a complete inventory back at the condo if that will help.'

'Since I don't know exactly what I'm looking for, *anything* might help,' I said.

Since my father hoped to wrap up his business in a couple of days, I agreed to wait until he returned to Annapolis and could lay hands on the inventory, rather than send Neelie off on a wild goose chase through Daddy's records. Besides, I might be hearing back from Gen-Tree any day. If Georgina's results turned out to be a fluke, I'd have spent days spinning my wheels for nothing.

Except a perfectly gorgeous online family tree.

FIVE

Four weeks later, my feet were soaking in warm, sudsy water at Spa Paradiso while Wally Jessop worked wonders on my nails. I'd just set the chair's remote to gentle massage and melted into the buttery leather when my cell phone dinged.

Wally's emery board paused its see-sawing motion. If he'd had any eyebrows, he would have raised them. 'You need to get that?'

Even if my phone hadn't been stuffed in the handbag hanging from a decorative wall peg more than six feet away, I knew Wally too well to bother. 'It's only an email,' I told Wally. 'It can wait.' I waggled my fingers. 'Besides, it would be criminal to ruin my manicure.'

'You got that right.' Eyebrowless Wally of the gleaming scalp and multiple piercings flashed a smile that let me know I'd made a wise decision. One of Dante's original hires, Wally was a card-carrying perfectionist. It was rumored he used a thermometer to make sure the water in the pedi-spa was maintained at a perfect 143 degrees. I had no reason to doubt it.

'What color?' he asked a few minutes later. His voice seemed to drift in from a long way off.

'Hmmm?' I managed.

'What color rings your chimes today?'

Earlier that morning I'd had one of Garnelle's famous, deep-tissue massages and I still felt like a boneless chicken. Before

sitting down for my mani-pedi, I'd half-heartedly selected two
bottles of polish – My Solar Clock is Ticking, an in-your-face
red, and a rosy pink shade called Aurora Berry-alis – but I still
couldn't make up my mind. 'Surprise me, Wally.'

So he did.

Turn On the Northern Lights is a deep, dark purple. After
I'd lived with it for a while, Wally assured me, I'd adore it as
much as he did.

I'd arranged to meet my daughter for lunch in the spa cafe.
Emily was late, as usual, so I ordered iced tea with extra lemon
for both of us and decided to kill time by checking my email.

As I expected, there was a lot to delete. Junk mail from
political candidates I'd never vote for in a million years.
Invitations from sexy Asian women simply dying for a date. A
notice that our Volvo was due for its sixty-thousand-mile checkup. My purple-nailed index finger was swiping messages into
oblivion so quickly that I nearly missed it: a notice from
Gen-Tree.com that my DNA test results were ready.

I pressed the iPhone to my chest, closed my eyes and tried
to steady my breathing.

Emily found me like that. She pulled out a chair but stopped
short of sitting down in it. 'Mom? Are you all right?'

I lay the phone down on the marble-topped table, carefully
avoiding a puddle caused by an errant ice cube. 'Of course,' I
assured her, stalling for time. I had no idea with whom Georgina
had shared information about her initial test results, but until
the results were confirmed, I had seen no reason to discuss
them with anyone other than Paul and my father.

Emily sat down, looking relieved. 'Order the fish taco,' she
advised. 'It's today's special, and François is a genius with the
baja sauce.' She flipped her single blond plait over her shoulder
and squinted across the table at me. 'There's something on your
mind, I can tell.'

I took a deep breath and let it out slowly. 'I had my DNA
tested at Gen-Tree.com, and the results are in.'

Emily flashed a grin. 'Quick! Somebody call *The Washington
Post*!'

Our eyes locked. I scowled. Emily's grin vanished.

'I don't want to be alone when I open up the results,' I said at last.

Her eyebrows disappeared under a fringe of professionally trimmed bangs. 'Why? You can't be worried about skeletons in the family closet . . .' She paused and frowned. 'Can you?' She leaned across the table and lowered her voice. 'Honestly, Mom, nobody gives a shit about that sort of thing these days.'

I was saved from providing an answer by Chef François, who materialized at our table dressed in full chef regalia. He'd come a long way since Haverford College days where the name on his transcript read Frank Lesperance. François dipped his head in deference to Emily, then turned to me. 'Welcome, Mrs Ives. It's been a while since we've seen you.'

'I'd show up every day, if I could,' I told him truthfully. 'Honestly, I don't know where the summer's gone. You commission the Firsties in May and ship them off into the Fleet, and before you know it, here comes July and the Plebes are being sworn in. Paul and I haven't even had time to squeeze in a mini-vacation.'

'You need a Spa-cation,' he suggested, 'and what better place . . .?'

'I'm working on it,' I said, displaying my freshly manicured nails, 'but Paul has an aversion to hot tubs. Just had a massage, though. Garnelle's hands should be insured by Lloyds of London.'

We chatted a bit about his family – a pregnant wife and young son – and after he left with our order for fish tacos, Emily said, looking serious, 'You're not worried about the test turning up some weird genetic disease, are you?'

This made me laugh. 'No, no, not that. I didn't pay extra for that sort of test.'

'Well, that's a relief.' Emily opened a pink packet of sweetener and stirred it into her iced tea. After she'd taken a sip, I explained about Georgina's earlier test results.

'Wow, just wow!' Emily flopped back in her chair, almost as if I'd punched her. 'That would mean . . .'

'Exactly.'

'So you've taken the test, too.'

I tapped my iPhone. 'And the results are in.'

Emily waved our server over. 'Will you bring our lunch to
my office, please?' She stood, picked up her glass of tea and
indicated that I should do the same. 'Follow me, Mom.'

A few minutes later, I was seated at my daughter's desk in
an ergonomically-correct chair, my feet planted firmly on an
ergonomically-correct adjustable foot rest, powering up her
environmentally-friendly, twenty-seven-inch iMac. After the
Gen-Tree website appeared, I logged on and clicked the pull-
down DNA menu, waiting impatiently for the 5K retina screen
to refresh.

A world map appeared, centered on the Atlantic Ocean.
Colorful blobs indicated the geographic origins of my
ancestors.

And there it was.

> 56% England and Wales.
> 25% Native American.
> 15% Ireland.
> 4% Norway.

I didn't realize I'd been holding my breath until I let it out.
'Well, that's it, then.'

Emily laid a hand on my shoulder. 'Freaking awesome!'

'I'd say so.'

'That means I'm one-eighth Native American.'

'Presumably.'

'And the kids . . .'

'One-sixteenth.'

'What side did it come from, Mom?' Emily asked, her blue
eyes wide. 'Your mom's or your dad's?'

'I don't know,' I told her, 'and neither does my father. I've
been building our family tree on the Gen-Tree website, but I'm
no closer to an answer than I was when Georgina first told me
about it.'

'Wait till I tell Dante,' Emily hooted. 'He'll be totally
psyched.'

'And I'd better telephone Georgina,' I said.

My call to Georgina was unexpectedly short.

'Shit,' she spat when she learned of my results. Hers had not yet come in.

'What's the big deal?' I asked.

'They warn you,' she said, 'right on the damn website. But did I listen? Nooooh!'

'What are you talking about, Georgina?'

'They said the test might contradict prior assumptions and lead to distress.' She paused, then yelled into the phone so loudly I had to pull the device away from my ear. 'Well, I'm distressed! Dammit!'

'But, Georgina, you just said you knew it was a possibility when you sent in your first sample, when you gave them permission to analyze it.'

'I can't deal with this right now, Hannah.'

'OK,' I said, 'but when *would* be a good time to talk about it?'

'I'll let you know.'

And the connection went dead.

I stuck my tongue out at the screen. Georgina was treating me like a telephone solicitor for an Ocean City timeshare, and I didn't appreciate it.

Feeling thoroughly put out, I called and left a message for my father, then went home to wait for Paul.

SIX

A round nine o'clock that evening, Dad returned my call. They'd had unexpected delays on his top-secret project, so he was still being held captive in Florida.

I waded right in. 'I'm twenty-five percent Native American,' I told him. 'No doubt about it at all.'

'Well, that's settled then,' he said.

'I don't think it settles anything at all,' I whined. 'I'm dying to figure out where the DNA came from.'

'I can solve part of the mystery,' my father said. 'After we talked, I drove out to Sam's Club and bought a test kit from

23 and Me. I'd planned to call you tonight anyway, because my results are in.' He paused so long I could hear him breathing.

'Don't you *dare* keep me in suspense,' I said. 'You're as maddening as one of those makeover shows on HGTV. "We've decided to . . ." then they cut to the ads before saying whether they'll Love It or List It.'

'It has to be on your mother's side,' he said, taking pity. 'I'm English, Welsh and Irish, with a bit of Norwegian thrown in. Nothing unexpected.'

I let the significance of his results sink in. One massive branch of the family tree – the Alexanders – had instantly been eliminated from the DNA equation.

'That's cut my work in half,' I said with relief. 'Now I'll just have to explore further up the Smith family tree.'

'Why?' he asked.

'Why?' Daddy's question had me stumped.

'What difference can something that happened almost a century ago make to you or to us now?'

'Don't you want to know?' I asked, hardly believing what I was hearing. My dad was a scientist, an engineer. He dealt with facts.

'Not particularly.'

'How could it hurt?' I reasoned. 'Everyone directly involved is already dead.'

On the other end of the line, I could hear his television tuned to the *Rachel Maddow Show*. It was a while before my father spoke again. 'Be careful what you wish for, Hannah. You might just get it. Old Chinese proverb.'

'Ha!' I scoffed in a good-natured way. 'Sounds more like the inside of a fortune cookie.'

'Georgina can be fragile,' Dad said. 'Be careful with her.'

'Kid gloves,' I said. 'I won't cause any trouble.'

One day, I'll learn to keep my big mouth shut.

SEVEN

I was on my hands and knees weeding the herb garden when my back pocket trembled. I stripped off my gloves, wiped my sweaty hands on my jeans and checked the phone.

U home?

It was a text from Julie, my niece, Georgina's seventeen-going on eighteen-year-old daughter.

Sup? I texted back.

Can U come up?

'Up' would be Baltimore's Roland Park neighborhood, to Scott and Georgina Cardinale's lovingly restored Craftsman near the end of Colorado Avenue.

Ask your mom?

Just U & me.

??

I'm grounded for life.

I located the Edvard Munch 'scream' emoji and hit send.

Sucks, she replied.

So I show up, casual like?

I wasn't sure what was on my niece's mind, but I was a good listener. When she was fourteen, Julie had been drugged and assaulted on a cruise ship. Her parents had been overprotective ever since; Scott was particularly inflexible. I didn't know what crime had merited a life-long grounding but it wouldn't be the first time Scott had made a federal case out of a parking ticket.

Besides – if she didn't cut me dead – it would be an opportunity to discuss our DNA test results with Georgina. Dad had telephoned her about it, too, I knew, but I hadn't talked with my sister since.

However, our older sister Ruth had embraced her new-found heritage. Being part Native American had flipped her 'no way' to a 'hell, yes' now that *her* actual DNA wasn't drifting around the Webosphere. She'd beamed like a celestial body when I told her about it at lunch over Irish tomato-whiskey soup and crab cakes at Galway Bay. Ruth owned Mother Earth, a funky shop on Main Street in downtown Annapolis where she sold a variety of New Age gizmos. After we hugged goodbye on the sidewalk outside the popular restaurant, she probably rushed straight back to Mother Earth, where I pictured her combing through catalogs looking for kachina dolls, orca spirit boxes and beaded mandalas to add to the dreamcatchers already in her inventory.

The day I decided to drive to Baltimore, the traffic was mercifully light. I merged off 295 onto the MLK expressway and zipped around Camden Yards in record time. Fifteen minutes later, I turned the Volvo around in the cul-de-sac at the bottom of Colorado Avenue and found a parking spot not far from the Cardinales' home, heading uphill.

Georgina stood in her front yard, attached to a pair of ear buds, attacking the hawthorn hedge with clippers of medieval proportions. Her long hair – gleaming in the sun like buttered sweet potatoes – was twisted into a knot high on her head and secured with a turquoise claw. If the ragged results of her hedge trimming efforts were any indication, Georgina's work was less a matter of hedge containment and more an act of anger management.

I stood on the sidewalk and watched the clippings fly, waiting for her to notice me.

Two minutes later, she did. She dropped the clippers, yanked out the ear buds and frowned.

'Sorry,' I said. 'Did I catch you at a bad time? If it were me, I'd welcome any interruption from trimming the hedge.'

'No, you surprised me, is all. Why didn't you tell me you were coming?'

'I'm meeting a friend for lunch at Jimmy's,' I lied. 'It's restaurant week and they're offering a twenty-dollar prix-fixe special.' I shrugged. 'So, thought I'd pop in for a minute.'

'Oh,' she said, wiping sweat off her brow with the back of her hand, looking worried.

'You OK?' I asked.

'Of course I am, Hannah. What would make you think I wasn't?'

'It's just that when I called the other day, you hung up on me.'

'I can't talk about it,' Georgina said, cutting me off again.

She glanced around the yard, almost as if she was afraid of being overheard. There was nobody within earshot, at least as far as I could see, but she lowered her voice anyway. 'Scott wants me to forget the whole thing.'

This surprised me. 'Wasn't Scott the one who insisted you send the test in to begin with? To verify your Revolutionary roots?'

Georgina flushed. I didn't think it had anything to do with the August heat. 'It accomplished that all right,' she said. 'I'm cross-matched straight back to old Enoch somebody-or-other who was a Minuteman at Lexington and Concord. Scott's already filled out the paperwork for the DAR and sent it in.'

'Then what's the big deal, Georgina?'

'Scott won't admit it, but I think he's worried about his stupid men's club. They have a couple of Jewish members, I know, but if you're black, brown, yellow or red, forget about applying.'

I knew about the Cosmopolitan Forum, a league of local businessmen so far to the right on the political spectrum that they made the Tea Party look like flaming liberals. The smear ads the forum had sponsored during the previous presidential campaign made me cringe. As a result of this affiliation, family visits could turn ugly in an instant, so I tended to avoid my brother-in-law whenever possible. I hadn't seen him since last Easter dinner where . . . well, riffs in the family might be more easily repaired than my vintage Imari earthenware platter. More than once, I wondered why my sister stayed with the pompous jerk, particularly now that the children were older. There had to be more to a marriage than financial security and, as Georgina had once confided, fantastic sex.

Tears glistened in my sister's eyes.

'Talk to me, Georgina,' I urged.

She drew a deep, shuddering breath. 'He yelled at me, Hannah. He called me a squaw!' She spread her arms wide. 'Honestly, do I look like an Indian to you? *Do* I?'

It's a good thing Scott was nowhere in the vicinity or I would have slapped him six ways into Sunday. What century did he think we were living in? Georgina began to sob.

I gathered my sister into a hug, stroking her back, soothing her like a child. A half-dozen anti-Scott remarks perched on the tip of my tongue, but I knew from past experience that if

I let fly, Georgina would bristle and begin making excuses for her husband, so I held back.

She didn't disappoint. 'A lot of Scott's business is driven by social contacts,' she whimpered into my shoulder. 'He can't afford to lose clients because of me.'

I took Georgina by the shoulders and held her at arm's length. 'Have you looked at yourself in a mirror lately?'

'That's my point, Hannah! I don't look like an Indian, so why would I want to *be* an Indian?'

I could think of several reasons, although I hadn't dug into the matter too deeply. Tribal membership might mean a share in casino profits, oil and gas revenues, free health care, college scholarships. As far as tribal membership was concerned, the more Indian blood you have the better, but you'd have to be descended from a federally recognized tribe and be able to prove it. Short of divorce, it seemed certain Georgina had no interest in pursuing the tribal membership route, so I let the subject drop.

'Is Julie here?' I asked. 'How about Colin and the twins?' I quickly added Julie's siblings to cover for my niece. 'I haven't seen them in ages.'

Using the hem of her T-shirt, Georgina dried her cheeks. 'Sean and Dylan are at swim club today, keeping an eye on Colin. Julie's around somewhere.' She managed a smile. 'In the meantime, I'd kill for a glass of iced tea. I just brewed a fresh pitcher. Interested?'

I smiled back. 'With extra lemon?'

She nodded.

'Sold.'

EIGHT

Georgina and I were perched on stools at her kitchen island discussing their vacation plans – a week at Bethany Beach, Delaware at the end of the month – when Julie breezed in. 'Aunt Hannah! Gosh, what a surprise!'

I sent Julie a glance that said: *Chill. Don't overplay your hand, missy.*

Julie opened the fridge, eased a Coke out of the door dispenser and popped the top. She made a beeline for a vacant stool, sipping noisily along the way.

'I'm meeting a friend for lunch,' I told her. 'Just popped in.'

'Uh huh,' Julie said, feigning boredom. 'How long can you stay?'

I checked the wall clock, a Route 66 gas pump reproduction that echoed Georgina's retro 1920s décor. If I manufactured a late lunch, I'd have a better chance of getting Julie alone. 'We're meeting at one,' I said.

Georgina refreshed our tea from a frosty, ice-filled pitcher, then went on to brag about how the twins would be starting grad school at Johns Hopkins in the fall. 'The acceptance rate is only ten percent,' she boasted. 'Even with three point eight GPAs, it was by no means a sure thing.' She leaned sideways and lowered her voice, as if sharing a confidence. 'And they won $10,000 scholarships. Each!'

'Big deal,' Julie snorted. 'It still costs the earth. I hope food stamps are still around when we need them.'

Georgina's glare would have stopped a charging rhino in its tracks. 'Don't you have something you're supposed to be doing, young lady?'

Julie slid off her stool, Coke in hand. 'I'm supposed to be memorizing the Maryland driver's manual. It's pretty lame.'

'Are you taking drivers ed this summer?' I asked.

'Nah. Took it at school last year, but you have to get in sixty practice hours. Dad's been my coach.'

I'd rather learn to drive from Jabba the Hutt, but thinking about Julie's need to clock in some practice hours gave me an idea. 'Would you like to take me for a drive, Julie?'

Julie beamed, bouncing on her toes. 'I'd *love* to! Mom? It's OK, isn't it?'

'I don't know . . .' Georgina began.

'Please?' Julie was channeling *Les Miz* starving orphan full-on.

'I'm sure Hannah has better things to do, Julie.'

'No, I'd like that.' I smiled and turned to my niece. 'I'm not taking my life in my hands, am I?'

Julie giggled. 'I've had *almost* sixty hours of driving experience, Aunt Hannah. You can check out my practice log if you don't believe me. Dad says I might be able to take the driving test next week.'

'Julie is . . .' Georgina began, then paused. I suspected she had started to mention something about Julie's restriction, but thought better of airing the family's dirty linen. Instead, she flapped a hand. 'It's fine, Julie. Just don't make your aunt late for her lunch.'

We agreed to take my Volvo. As I settled into the passenger seat and strapped in, Julie took her place behind the wheel. 'Ahhhh,' she sighed, running her hand affectionately over the gear shift knob. 'Automatic transmission. I think I'm in love.'

After she adjusted the seat and fastened her seatbelt, I handed over the keys.

'Dad's making me learn to drive stick,' she said, slotting the key into the ignition. 'That's the way he learned, so he expects me to suffer, too.'

'Builds character,' I suggested. 'Plus, what'll you do if there's an emergency and the only vehicle available is equipped with standard transmission?'

She looked at me, wide-eyed. 'That's exactly what my mom says!'

'That's because our mom said it to us when we learned to drive stick.'

Julie released the parking brake and eased the car forward. 'Do you have any idea how hard it is to up shift on this stupid hill with a clutch?'

When we got to the top of Colorado, Julie turned right on Roland Avenue and demonstrated her parallel parking skills in front of Eddie's Supermarket. 'Well done!' I said, genuinely impressed.

She accepted the compliment with a self-satisfied grin, then turned off the engine.

I wasted no time. 'Now, tell me. Why are you under house arrest?'

'I hacked into my mother's laptop,' she confessed.

'No wonder you're in trouble,' I said.

'It was super easy,' Julie said, as if that made it OK.

Before I could comment, she said, 'I know about the DNA test, Aunt Hannah. About being part American Indian.'

'Ah, I see.'

'Even if I hadn't seen it with my own eyes, I'd have to be deaf not to. Dad was yelling so loud that they probably heard him on Mars.' She turned sideways in her seat and looked directly at me. 'I don't get him, I really don't. This is twenty-first-century Maryland, for heaven's sake, not the wild, wild west.'

'How do you feel about it, Julie?' I asked, reaching across the center console to squeeze her hand.

'I think it's awesome, don't you?'

'I do, but I don't see how it's going to make any difference in my day-to-day life. It's just an interesting fact that I know about myself.'

'But only if you decide that's how it's going to be, Aunt Hannah. Being one-eighth Native American may not sound like a lot, but it's more indigenous blood than most people have in them. I think it means I have a responsibility to my people.'

Her people? According to Gen-Tree, I was four percent Norwegian, but I wasn't stocking up on pickled herring, lutefisk and krumkake. Then again, I was a generation older than Julie and far more jaded.

We sat quietly for a moment, watching shoppers pass in and out of the popular grocery, carrying bags laden with Eddie's signature Gourmet to Go.

'The DNA isn't able to link you to any particular tribe,' I reminded her gently.

'I know that,' she said. 'That's why I need your help.'

Somewhere in the recesses of my brain a brass band was tuning up, ready to launch into 'Ya Got Trouble (Right Here in River City)'. You'd think I'd heed it. But, no.

Genuinely curious, I waded right in. 'In what way?'

'When I hacked Mom's account, I noticed some DNA matches. Second and third cousins. That's pretty close, isn't it?'

I agreed that it was. But something was puzzling me. 'Your mom told me she hadn't signed up for the genetic matching.'

'Then she lied.'

'Julie!'

'Well, maybe that was the truth second test around, but not the first. Dad was printing out data for that DAR form he was filling out when he caught me snooping. It's all gone now, of course. He deleted the Gen-Tree account.'

Of course he did. Typical Scott.

'I still can't believe you hacked your mom's account,' I said. 'Wasn't it password protected?'

'Of course it was password protected, Aunt Hannah!' she said as if I were a particularly slow and difficult child. 'But Mom's passwords are easy to guess. Besides, she keeps a list of her accounts on her computer saved under the file name "Passwords1". Yeah, stick a one on the end. That'll really throw hackers off.'

I had to laugh.

Maybe she took my laughter for assent. 'So, you'll help me?'

'That depends,' I said.

'It's really important to me,' she said.

'OK,' I said. Then, 'Maybe,' I clarified. 'But you have to promise that you'll quit hacking your mom's computer.'

Julie rolled her eyes, sighed theatrically, then nodded. 'I promise.'

'So,' I said after several beats of silence. 'What's the deal?'

'Can you keep a secret?'

'As long as you haven't murdered anyone, yes.'

'I sent in my own test kit.'

I sat back in surprise, wondering where she'd gotten the money to pay for it. Scott and Georgina were fairly well off, but Julie didn't work a part-time job, and I didn't think she could afford ninety-nine-dollar DNA test kits on her weekly allowance, even with a twenty-percent-off coupon.

'Aunt Ruth gave me hers,' Julie explained, as if reading my mind.

'Don't you have to swear that you're eighteen years of age or older?' I asked, having read the fine print on the test kit I sent in.

'So, call the cops,' she said. After a moment, she reverted to a more reasonable tone. 'I'm seventeen and ten-twelfths, Aunt

Hannah. Close enough, it seems to me. Besides, I'll turn eighteen by the time the test comes back.'

Based on my Gen-Tree turnaround experience, that was certainly true.

'So, what do you want *me* to do?' I asked.

'Be there for me, serve as a resource, help me out if I need it.' She took a deep breath. 'Dad's confiscated my laptop until further notice, so I may not be able to manage this on my own. I can't count on my parents to help, I just *can't*!'

I thought carefully before answering. 'Julie, you can always talk to me. I don't guarantee that you'll like what I have to say, but we're family. I'll always have your back.'

It was lunchtime. Customers were starting to double park in front of the market, jealously eyeing our parking space. 'Aunt Hannah?' Julie said as she fired up the Volvo and pulled out into the street.

'What?'

'Thanks.' Then, a few seconds later, as if the previous discussion hadn't even taken place, 'I'll bet I can guess your password.'

'Go for it,' I said as she swung wide right and headed down Deepdene Road.

'123456?' she suggested.

'Nope.'

'Admin?'

'I'm not that stupid!'

'Letmein?'

'Ha ha, but no.'

'How about Cocodoodle?'

I swiveled in my seat. 'Julie! You *are* a witch!'

Then it was my niece's turn to laugh. 'Not today!'

'Then how did you guess . . .' I began.

She brought the car to a jerky halt at the corner of Summit and Colorado, leaned forward and looked both ways before easing the car into the intersection and turning left. 'Last time I visited, you had it written on a Post-it stuck to your monitor.'

With the engine still running, Julie set the parking brake and climbed out of the car. I walked around and took her place in the driver's seat. As my niece stood on the sidewalk, smiling and waving goodbye, I made a mental note to change my password the minute I got home. Family or not, I wasn't sure the little minx could be one hundred percent trusted.

NINE

Following sage advice I read on the Internet, I created a new system password that earned a 'highly secure' rating from Doctor Google. 'Make up a phrase you can easily remember,' Google advised, 'like "Christopher Columbus discovered America in 1492", then use the first letter of each word plus the number as your password.'

Now that I seemed to be closely related to Native American people, I decided to give old Christopher Columbus, a latecomer to the New World if there ever was one, a pass. After considerable thought, I decided on: Sacajawea guided Lewis and Clark across the Rocky Mountains to the Pacific Ocean in 1805.

Sglacatrmttpoi1805, I typed a few minutes later, testing it out.

While I was at it, still feeling cyber-vulnerable, I reset the security questions on my bank and credit card accounts.

Credit card companies seem to have a thing for pets and grandmas. 'Mother's maiden name' and 'city of your birth' were popular, too, information readily available in public records such as the ones I'd been scrolling through recently on Gen-Tree. 'High school attended' and 'name of favorite movie' were equally risky, easily figured out by any hacker – like my renegade niece – with access to my Facebook friends or Twitter feeds.

Where were you on New Year's 2000? my bank, BB&T wanted to know. The question got points for being un-guessable, but it gave me the heebie-jeebies. On December 31, 1999 I'd been racing around Annapolis during gala First Night celebrations, trying to stop a maniac from shooting my daughter. I didn't think that was any of BB&T's business and scrolled on.

Who was your least favorite boss? That was easy. *Fran,* I started to type, then paused. What if there were a massive data breach like what happened at Yahoo? Would it help Fran to learn that she was universally despised? I tried again.

Where do you want to retire? BB&T asked. Maybe it would be safer to lie. *On Mars*, I wrote, smiling, hoping I'd remember if ever called upon to provide the correct answer.

BB&T's security questions were less quotidian than most, but I was thinking that if companies were truly serious about protecting their clients, how about asking *What Monopoly game piece is your older sister's favorite?* or *Who did your maternal grandfather vote for in the 1964 presidential election?*

Better yet, what could be more private than our sex lives? *What was the make, model and year of the car in which you first lost your virginity?* for example.

I'll never tell.

Several weeks later, I decided to tackle the online accounts I had with Amazon, eBay, Home Depot, Best Buy and numerous department store chains. I was giggling to myself and filling in the usual 'boyfriend' and 'first grade teacher' – Ron and Mrs Grieg, respectively – for Macy's when Julie telephoned, two days after she turned eighteen. Scott and Georgina had celebrated this milestone in their daughter's life by taking the immediate family not to Bethany Beach as planned, but on a week-long holiday to Disney World in Orlando, Florida. Julie suspected the trip was more about ten-year-old Colin than her but confessed to having a good time anyway.

'I passed my driver's test,' she announced breezily.

'I had every confidence you would,' I said. 'Congratulations.'

'Now I can drive down to see you.' She paused for a moment. 'If they let me have the keys to the Subaru.'

Was Julie speaking figuratively, I wondered, or fishing for an invitation?

'I thought you were under house arrest,' I said.

Julie laughed. 'I babysat Colin the whole week. Went with him on all the rides that made Mom barf, so Dad sawed off the leg irons.'

I chuckled at the image. 'You can come visit me any time, Julie, but call first to make sure I'll be home.'

'How about tomorrow?' she asked before I could draw breath.

'I'd like that,' I said. 'Want me to arrange a spa day?'

'That would be awesome, Aunt Hannah, but I don't think I'll have time for that.' She paused. 'There's something serious I want to talk to you about.'

'Can you give me a clue?'

She ignored the question. 'Ten o'clock OK?'

I said that it was.

'Cool,' she said, and the line went dead.

Using the house key I'd given Georgina in case of emergency, Julie let herself in the front door a little after ten the following morning. 'Aunt Hannah!'

'I'm in the kitchen,' I called.

Julie breezed into the room, slipped a backpack off her shoulder and let it drop to the floor. She made a beeline for the fridge and helped herself to a cold Coke. 'Do you mind?' she asked as she ripped off the metal tab.

'Too late for minding,' I said with a laugh.

Ignoring the Coke for a moment, Julie took a deep, exaggerated breath. 'God, it smells good in here!'

'I'm baking chocolate chip cookies,' I said, reaching for an oven mitt. 'This is the last batch.' I pointed to the cookies already cooling on racks on the counter, then opened the oven door. 'Help yourself.'

Using her free hand, Julie stacked three cookies on top of one another, then carried them over to the kitchen table. After I'd turned off the oven and racked up the remaining cookies, I poured myself a cup of coffee, grabbed a warm cookie and joined her.

'So,' I said, getting straight to the point. 'What's on your mind?'

Julie pressed her hands, palms down, on the tablecloth. 'I've decided to take a gap year.'

This announcement surprised me. Julie had seemed excited about starting her freshman year at Towson University in the fall. She'd even gone to Target with Georgina, shopping for the mini-fridge and microwave oven every college student seemed to require these days, as well as stocking up on cartons of ramen noodles.

'What about Towson?' I asked.

'Everybody's taking gap years,' she said. 'Even Malia Obama.'

Presidential daughters aside, I doubted that *everyone* was delaying college by a year to go off on some extra-curricular, horizon-expanding adventure, but decided not to challenge her.

'Towson's totally cool with it,' she added.

'How about your parents?' I asked, thinking that Scott was rarely totally cool about anything that didn't fit in exactly with his plans.

'Even they know I'm not a mental giant like Sean or Dylan,' she said with a ladylike snort.

'So instead of hitting the books at Towson, what *will* you do?'

'I'm not really sure,' she admitted. 'That's why I wanted to talk to you. *Before* I talk to my parents.'

Swell, I thought.

'Look,' she said, leaning closer across the table. 'I'm in my prime! When else will I have no job, no significant other, no kids to hold me back? The answer is never!'

I simply stared, letting the truth of what she said soak in, but Julie was just warming up. 'I can travel to new places, make new friends! I want to volunteer somewhere, Aunt Hannah. Make my life count for something!'

'I don't want to dampen your enthusiasm, Julie,' I said with a smile, 'but becoming a global citizen might require a bit of money.'

She dismissed my concern with a flick of her hand. 'I know that! That's why I'm looking at VISTA. It's kind of a domestic Peace Corps. They give you a modest living allowance.' She paused. 'And health care.'

'Don't you have to be a college grad for VISTA?' I asked.

She shook her head. 'According to their website, you have to be at least seventeen.'

I felt Julie's eyes on my back as I carried my coffee mug over to the sink, rinsed it out and inverted it over a peg in the dishwasher.

'You think I'm crazy, don't you, Aunt Hannah?'

I turned to face her. 'I don't think you're crazy at all, Julie.

But I know your parents fairly well, and I suggest you do your research very thoroughly before springing this idea on them. Is there a guidance counselor at Poly you can talk to?' I asked.

Baltimore Polytechnic Institute, located at the corner of Falls Road and Cold Spring Lane, was one of Baltimore's highly-ranked magnet schools, specializing in STEM: science, technology, engineering and mathematics. Julie's grades at Poly, while not stellar, had been solid.

'I emailed for an appointment this morning,' she said. 'So stay tuned.'

I assured her that I would.

'Oh!' Julie said, suddenly leaping to her feet and retrieving her backpack. After unzipping the front pouch and rummaging inside, she produced what looked like a novelty key chain. She held it in front of me where it tick-tocked like a pendulum: a miniature Yoda from *Star Wars*. 'Here,' she said, handing it over. 'I almost forgot.'

'Cute,' I said, 'But what is it?'

'A flash drive,' Julie said. 'You pop off his head.'

I wrapped my fingers around the tiny Jedi Master.

'I thought it might help,' she said in what turned out to be the understatement of the year.

I looked up. 'Help with what?'

'It's my raw DNA data. I downloaded it at the public library when my test results finally came in.' She shouldered her backpack and turned toward the door. 'But don't tell Dad. He'll go ballistic.'

I squeezed Yoda a bit tighter.

'Take good care of it,' Julie said. 'Dad's got this crazy hang-up.'

'So I gathered,' I said. 'I'll try to upload it this afternoon.'

'Do or do not,' Julie quoted. 'There is no try.'

'Funny girl,' I said. 'Did you keep a copy?'

Julie shot me a dismissive blink that made me feel like an idiot.

I was quick to catch on. '*Duh*, right?'

Julie tapped her forehead with an index finger. 'But I deleted my Gen-Tree account. Just in case Dad asks me . . .' She paused. 'He can always tell when I'm lying. Best not to take chances.'

TEN

After a hasty lunch – cream of mushroom soup and a peanut butter sandwich – and with Yoda curled in my hot little hand, I traipsed downstairs to our basement office and powered up the computer.

For everything to work properly, I'd need to set up an account separate from my own to hold Julie's data. And if Scott were as All-Wise-and-All-Knowing as his daughter feared, I'd need to protect her identity. After some thought, I chose her initials and birth year: JLC2000 and linked the account to a Gmail address I sometimes used for Internet purchases. Then I uploaded Julie's test kit data.

Julie would also need a family tree. I'd already built an extensive one for the Alexander-Smith side of the family. Fortunately, the Church of Jesus Christ of the Latter Day Saints had developed GEDCOM – GENeaological Data COMmunication files – that enabled one to share genealogical data from one software program to another. Creating a family tree for Julie was as simple as downloading the Alexander-Smith GEDCOM from my account and uploading it to hers, then linking Julie's individual family tree record to her test kit. While Julie's DNA was out there, I kept her family tree strictly private. If anyone should inquire about possible matches, they'd have to go through me.

It would take a few hours, I knew, for Gen-Tree to verify, process and crunch the new data, so I spent the afternoon reorganizing our bedroom closet, making a pile of gently used clothing I intended to donate to Purple Heart.

My head was deep in the closet, my hand reaching for a pair of prehistoric brown and green plaid trousers when Paul, home early from the Academy, breezed into the bedroom.

'Don't you dare throw those away!' he barked.

I dropped the hanger and pressed a hand to my chest. 'And don't you dare sneak up on me like that! You scared me half to death.'

'Those are my lucky pants,' he explained.

'You weren't even born when these pants were popular,' I said.

'Don't be silly.' He stooped, picked up the hanger and smoothed the trousers gently over it. 'I rocked that plaid in the seventies.'

'I'll bet they don't even fit,' I said.

Paul checked the label inside the waistband and flashed a sheepish grin. 'You're right, but I'd hate to see them go. I shot a hole in one at Oakmont while wearing those pants.'

'You don't even play golf anymore, darling.'

'There is that,' he admitted.

'And you gave your golf clubs to Dennis a couple of years ago,' I reminded him.

'I wonder if he's using them?' Paul mused as if contemplating a quick snatch-back from his sister Connie's husband.

I gave him the evil eye.

'OK, you win,' Paul said, tossing his lucky trousers onto the donation pile. 'But if the Ravens don't advance to the Super Bowl this season, it will be all your fault.'

'I'll try to live with the shame,' I said.

Paul sat down on the edge of the bed and unlaced his shoes. 'So, what did young Julie want?'

I explained about the gap year.

'Oh, oh,' he said. 'That spells trouble.'

'I'm not so sure,' I said. 'While I was strolling down memory lane in the closet just now, it occurred to me that Scott might be strapped for cash. Sean and Dylan are starting graduate school in the fall, and Georgina mentioned that Colin was transferring to Friends. Tuition at Friends is almost twenty-eight thousand. I looked it up.'

'For a fifth-grader?' Paul whistled. 'And we thought putting Emily through Bryn Mawr College was a financial stretch.'

'I don't think Scott would want to deny Julie a college education,' I said, 'but Towson runs about twenty-two thousand. Scholarships and loans go only so far. He might welcome a year's respite.'

Paul stretched out on the bed, propped his hands behind his head and eyed me speculatively. 'Interesting that he seems to have no trouble shelling out for the boys.'

'Don't get me started!' I said, and quickly changed the subject before I could launch into a fruitless, anti-Scott rant. 'Julie brought me another surprise.'

'Oh?'

I told him about Yoda and Julie's test kit. 'I'm waiting for her kit to process now.'

'What do you hope to learn from Julie's test results that you don't already know from your own?' he asked.

I flashed him a toothy grin. 'That Scott is mostly Hispanic or Asian? That would be positively delicious.'

Paul laughed out loud. 'You have an evil mind, Hannah Ives.'

'Thank you,' I said.

As it turned out, Scott was in no danger of being blackballed from his snooty club. Based on the DNA he'd handed down to his daughter, Scott's pedigree was as Italian as his name, Cardinale, would suggest. And Julie's Native American ancestry was also confirmed.

I texted Julie with the news:

Italy	30%
England/Wales	28%
Native American	13%
Ireland	10%
Greece	10%
Sicily	7%
Norway	2%

A few minutes later my niece got back to me with a thumb's-up icon, followed immediately by a smiley with its mouth zipped shut.

I replied with a heart and the 'speak-no-evil' monkey, then returned to my research.

I logged on to my family tree, rather than Julie's, reasoning that I was one generation closer to my grandparents than she. Because I'd linked both of our data to the DNA matching service, I was ridiculously relieved to see that the first thing that popped up when I clicked on 'DNA Matches' was that Julie and I were 'Close Family'.

I had no first cousins that I knew of. My mother had been an only child and my father's only brother had died childless. But the list of possible second, third and fourth cousins that followed Julie's listing made me gasp. I scrolled through the list, looking for familiar names, but most people, like Julie, were identified by cryptic screen names.

Concentrate, Hannah. Think.

Charlotte Drew Smith was my grandmother. In order to share Charlotte with me, a person would have to match at the first cousin level. But no first cousins were listed. That didn't mean that no first cousins existed, just that they weren't part of the Gen-Tree database.

A second cousin, then, with a shared great-grandparent.

I began a methodical search down the list of possible second cousins, clicking on each entry and examining our relationship. If the person were linked to a family tree, Gen-Tree's 'Shared Match' function made the task simple. I eliminated several Alexander and Collinson cousins on my father's side that way.

If no family tree had been linked to a person's DNA results – maddeningly often – or if that person's family tree was set to 'private', the only option was email.

So I emailed potential matches, keeping it short and simple.

Hello, cousin! My name is Hannah Ives. According to Gen-Tree, we share a common ancestor. Would you be willing to give me access to your family tree so I can learn how we are related? I'd be happy to share my tree with you, too.

Around four-thirty, Paul came downstairs to check on me, carrying two glasses of chilled Pinot Grigio. 'How are you doing?'

I accepted the glass, clinked his in a toast and took a grateful sip. 'Relatives are multiplying like guinea pigs left to their own devices with unlimited access to sugar.' I took another sip and gestured at the monitor with my wine glass. 'When a three-times great-grandmother has ten children, the cousins that accumulate at the bottom of the family tree can number in the thousands.'

'What's that?' Paul asked suddenly, leaning in so close I could tell he'd eaten an Italian sub for lunch.

'What's what?' I asked.

'That.' He tapped the monitor where a miniature pennant was flapping over the box labeled Paul Everett Ives.

'It's a hint for you,' I explained, moving the mouse until an arrow hovered over the pennant. 'I thought I'd checked out all the hints yesterday, but it looks like we've got a few new ones.'

When I clicked the mouse a single suggestion appeared. 'This looks interesting,' I said, clicking again. A page from a high school yearbook materialized on the screen. Several dozen fresh-scrubbed youths, dressed in band uniforms, sat in a semicircle holding their instruments. I adjusted my reading glasses and squinted at the screen until I could read the list of names underneath the picture. 'I didn't know you played the trumpet in high school!' I said.

'Very badly,' Paul said with a grin.

'I'm saving *this* record for posterity,' I said as I added the entry to my husband's Gen-Tree profile.

A second flapping pennant caught my eye, this time for my grandfather, Stephen Axford Smith. Holding my breath, I clicked. According to the state of Vermont, a Congregationalist minister in Randolph had joined Stephen Smith and Charlotte Drew in holy matrimony on October 15, 1932. I added the record to my grandfather's profile, linked it to my grandmother's, then flopped back in the chair. 'Whoa!' I muttered, as the significance of the date sank in.

'When was your mother born?' Paul asked, although I suspected the question was rhetorical. Paul knew very well when my mother was born.

'May 25, 1933,' I reminded him.

I didn't need to count on my fingers to figure that out.

When her great-granddaughter Chloe was born, tipping the scales at ten pounds, my mother, citing herself, had quipped that hefty babies ran in our family. If these genealogical records were correct, Lois Mary Smith, my mother, had been a nine-pound-fourteen ounce, seven-month preemie.

ELEVEN

Behind my eyelids it was summertime. The honk of a car horn, the slap of a screen door and Grandma Smith – all flowered aprons, broad smiles and damp, cinnamon-ginger hugs – waiting for me on the stoop. Now it seemed disrespectful to be counting backwards on my fingertips, trying to determine exactly when my mother had been conceived. A full-term pregnancy was, what, approximately forty weeks? Back in high school biology class, persnickety, prune-faced Mrs Garfield had glossed over human gestation periods.

According to Professor Google, the average length of human gestation is two-hundred-and-eighty days from the first day of the woman's last menstrual period. I sagged in my chair; like I'd know when that was for Charlotte.

Somebody should invent a reverse conception calculator, I thought as I typed in the terms on the Google search bar. To my surprise, a website named babyMed had, saving me from having to count backwards on my fingers. When I plugged my mother's birth date into their online calculator, it estimated that she had been conceived on September 1, 1932 and that Grandmother's last period had begun on the eighteenth of August. Only four percent of babies are born on their estimated delivery day, the website cautioned, but for my purposes, early September was close enough.

Where had Charlotte Drew, just turned twenty, been living in September of 1932? In Vermont, I presumed. When she married Stephen Smith there the following month, she would have missed only one period. Had she even known she was pregnant?

There had been Indian tribes in New England for centuries before the colonists came. By the 1600s most had moved west, into Canada, or had been assimilated. Every school child knew that. According to Wikipedia, though, remnants of the Abenaki, Mohican and Pennacook tribes were scattered throughout the state of Vermont to this day, but none of these groups were federally recognized. Was a young man from one of those tribes our Native American connection?

With renewed determination, I launched the Gen-Tree website and pulled up my grandmother's record. No pennants were waving to attract my attention to a new fact. I stared at Charlotte's image for a long time, as if willing her to explain everything to me. I'd uploaded several family pictures to her gallery, but for her icon, I'd chosen the photo from her wedding day. The bright blue eyes, the plump lips, the rosy glow – had Charlotte been the quintessential radiant bride, or simply a pregnant one?

I slapped my own cheek. *Behave yourself, Hannah!* The two were not mutually exclusive.

Since Gen-Tree had no suggestions for me, I decided to do a deep dive into early twentieth-century US census records. Using the Advanced Search option, I selected Charlotte's father, my great-grandfather Josiah Drew, and requested the 1920 census for Vermont. I found the Drews almost immediately living in South Royalton on Chelsea Street. Josiah, head of family with Jane, his wife, and Charlotte, age eight. A son, Adam, was also listed, age five.

Using the same search criteria, I requested the 1930 census. Josiah and his son Adam, now fifteen years old, were still living on Chelsea Street, but Charlotte – who would have been eighteen at the time – was not listed. Neither was Jane.

The question of what happened to Jane was answered easily enough. Under 'marital status', Josiah was listed as 'W' – a widower. Sometime between 1920 and 1930, then, Jane had passed away. I made a note to search for her death certificate.

But what had happened to Charlotte?

Using my grandmother's full name, I did a broader search across the whole US census for 1930. I spent the better part of an hour scrolling through more than seven hundred results spanning the continent from sea to shining sea. I eliminated the Charlotte L. in Nashville (too old), the one in Kansas (dead) and the one in Cleveland who was only a Drew by marriage. Several dozen others seemed promising, but none turned out to be a positive match for my grandmother.

I sat back in my chair, feeling defeated.

What next?

Small town newspapers, I'd found, were a treasure trove of information and, thanks to digitization, almost as easy to read as if strewn across my coffee table. In the halcyon days before Facebook, Twitter and Instagram took over our lives, newspapers reported on town meetings, social events, and land sales; on births, deaths and weddings. You learned who was visiting whom, both in and out of town, and why. Whose sheep had escaped and were roaming freely on the green. Umbrellas lost and pocket watches found. Police reports and personal notices often revealed facts about our ancestors that they'd rather have been kept shrouded in mystery.

As it turns out, my subscription to Newspapers.com would have been cheap at twice the price. Among the dozens of historic newspapers in rural Vermont, I found the announcement for Charlotte's wedding, titled Smith-Drew, fairly easily. It had taken place on a day when frocks with 'pep' were two dollars ninety-eight at J.C. Penney, a pound of Maxwell House coffee cost thirty-three cents, Miss America smoked Lucky Strike (It's toasted!) and Rinso was so easy on the hands.

I shot from my chair and yelled upstairs for my husband. 'Paul! Come see what I found!'

His voice, drifting down from the living room, was muffled. 'I'm watching the game! Can it wait?'

'No, dammit!' I grabbed my laptop and trundled up to join him.

According to the *Bethel Gazette* for Thursday, October 20, 1932:

> *All the brilliant tints of autumn in branches of the changing foliage adorned the residence of Mr and Mrs H.H. Westerly for the wedding of their niece, Miss Charlotte Louise Drew of South Royalton, Vermont who was united in marriage Saturday morning to Stephen Henry Smith of Randolph, in the presence of sixteen relatives and intimate friends of the contracting parties.*

At eleven o'clock the bride and groom descended the stairway and entered the parlors, attended by the maid of honor, Miss Ida James of South Royalton and the best man, Charles Keane of Baltimore, a friend of the groom.

Very lovely was the bride in her wedding gown of white crepe de chine with lace and pearl trimmings. For ornaments she wore a watch, the gift of the groom, and a pearl necklace that had once belonged to her mother, and she carried a beautiful shower bouquet of white carnations. The maid of honor was prettily gowned in pink messaline. Among others in attendance were the groom's mother, Mrs Jacob Smith of Randolph, and the bride's grandparents, Mr and Mrs Asa Drew of South Royalton, the former having reached the age of eighty the 29th of August and the latter attaining to fourscore the 29th of September, and being now in the 59th year of their married life.

After the service came an elegant wedding breakfast in a dining room decorated in pink and green with spruce, sweetpeas and asters.

I sat in the living room with my laptop on my knees, reading the article to Paul in the plummy tones of an old-time radio announcer. I glanced up from the screen to see if he was paying attention. 'Small town newspapers are gems. This is like the Rosetta Stone.'

Paul was half listening to me and half watching the Yankees get trounced by the Orioles on ESPN. 'In what way?'

'In addition to the birthdays of my Drew great-great-grandparents, I can also calculate the year of their marriage.'

Paul silently pumped his fist, not to recognize my brilliance but as Mancini homered to center.

I ignored him. 'Also, reading between the lines here, Charlotte's mother and father must have passed away by October of 'thirty-two. Stephen's father, too, or they all would have been attending the wedding.'

Paul leaned closer to the television, sending positive *mojo* to Nunez who had just stepped up to the plate. 'Uh huh.'

'And I picked up a couple of relatives I never knew about.'
Paul risked a glance my way. 'You did? Who?'

'An aunt and uncle I've never heard of, the Westerlys. I
wonder if she's a Drew or a Smith?'

'I thought you said her name was Westerly.'

'*Mr* H.H. is the Westerly,' I explained. 'Before her marriage,
Mrs H.H. must have been either a Drew or a Smith if Charlotte
is her niece.' I paused. 'My guess is Mrs H.H. is standing in
for her late sister, Jane.' I sighed. 'Back in the day, a woman
lost her identity upon marriage, at least as far as the social
columns in newspapers were concerned. I'll have to do some
digging through the census files for Mrs H.H.'s first name.'

Paul leapt to his feet as Nunez singled to center, sending
Joseph sliding into third. 'Yes! That's what I'm talking about!'

'You're hopeless,' I said. With two players on base, getting
my husband's undivided attention was mission impossible.

While I jotted down some dates on the back of an old *New
Yorker* magazine, Joseph managed to score on an infield single
by Valera, giving the Orioles a safe six-point lead and Paul
permission to go for a beer. At the door to the dining room he
turned and said, probably as an afterthought, 'You want anything?'

'Maybe later,' I said, glancing up from my notes. 'There's
more to the article, if you're interested.'

'The anticipation is killing me,' he said.

I reached behind me for a pillow and tossed it at his head.
'You haven't heard one word I've said!'

Laughing, Paul batted the pillow away. 'Oh, yes I have.'

I gave him a hard side-eye.

'There's one thing I really have to know,' he said.

I set my laptop to one side and looked up. 'Yes?'

'What's messaline?'

When Paul returned to the game carrying his beer and a steaming
bag of microwave popcorn, I described the fabric to him.
'Messaline's a lightweight silk, with a textured finish, like twill.
I don't think they make it any more.'

I helped myself to a fistful of popcorn. 'There's more to the
article,' I said, chewing thoughtfully.

'Read on, Macduff,' Paul said.

'Very punny, Mr Shakespeare.' I reached for the laptop. 'There's more about fabrics, you'll be pleased to hear,' I said, paging forward and continuing to read where I'd left off.

The bride having donned a traveling gown of green broadcloth with a hat to match, Mr and Mrs Smith left in a cloudburst of confetti for Boston and after November 1st will be at home on the Smith family farm in Randolph. The bride was last year studying nursing in Pierre, South Dakota. For the past month she has been staying with relatives in South Royalton.

'South Dakota?' I nearly fell off my chair. All that time spent trolling through the census files and the answer was in the newspaper all along. 'What's in South Dakota?'

'A school of nursing, I presume,' Paul said.

'But why go all the way to South Dakota to attend nursing school?'

'Maybe she got a scholarship,' Paul suggested. 'Money could have been an issue. Didn't you say her parents were dead?'

'According to the census, her mother died sometime before 1930, but her father was still alive then. There could be another reason he didn't attend the wedding.' I made a note to check the 1940 census to see if Josiah and his son Adam still appeared, chiding myself for not doing it earlier.

TWELVE

Pierre, South Dakota, has a population of 14,000, according to the Pierre Chamber of Commerce. The state capital was described as a friendly community whose 'tree-lined streets, historic downtown and lush green parks give way to rolling hills and steep bluffs as the county spreads east into the state's expansive plains'.

But that was today.

Back in the thirties, it must have been the wild, wild west, and only George Washington's carved granite head would have greeted tourists visiting Mount Rushmore. Pierre, then as now, was located in the heart of Sioux Indian territory, not far from the Lower Brule and Rosebud Indian Reservations.

I had to be on the right track.

Armed with the information I'd learned from the *Bethel Gazette*, I called up the 1930 US census data. This time, I limited the search to 'South Dakota' and 'Charlotte Drew'. When I studied the search results, I saw immediately why I'd missed Charlotte in my earlier, much broader attempt to find her. When the census taker knocked at the door back in April of 1930, whoever answered his questions had given Grandmother's name as 'Lottie'.

I'd never known my grandmother to use that nickname. Grandfather always called her 'Buttercup' after the heroine in his favorite Gilbert and Sullivan operetta, *H.M.S. Pinafore*. 'Lottie' was definitely my grandmother though – the age was correct, as was her place of birth, Vermont. In 1930, Lottie Drew had been living with seven other 'boarders' at a house on North Huron Avenue. Her occupation: student.

The census also answered another question – how Charlotte happened to find herself in South Dakota.

Another boarder in the house on North Huron was Charles Keene, her future husband's good friend, the one he'd chosen for best man at his wedding. Charles's occupation? Doctor. One other doctor, two nurses, a stenographer and a drayman also shared the house, which was headed by Bertha Lumley, age fifty-one. With all that medical horsepower close at hand, where better to be struck by a car in Pierre, South Dakota, I mused, than the middle of North Huron Avenue?

If proximity were any guarantee, Charles Keene was a likely candidate for my biological grandfather. I imagined a smart, ambitious Native American lad, the first of his family to attend medical school, returning home to care for his people after completing training at a university back East.

A search of online yearbooks put the kibosh on that theory. Charles Jameson Keene had been a graduate of Johns Hopkins University, class of 1926, transferring from Middlebury College in Vermont in 1922, majoring in Pre-Med. His picture in the

Hullabaloo for that year showed a blond, blue-eyed poster child for a Finnish health spa, his curls marcelled into a swirl on top of his head, like a cone from a soft-serve ice cream machine. Chuck also ran track his first two years and had been a member of the Musical Club.

I'd peppered my research with periodic updates to Paul, who finally gave up on the ball game, switched off the television and perched on the ottoman next to my feet.

'"Chuck" had some great loves,' I read aloud from the yearbook entry, 'but not for girls. They are for vases, flowers and paintings, in fact for anything old and interesting.'

'I'm old and interesting.' I studied my husband over the tops of my reading glasses. 'He would have loved me.'

Paul snorted. 'Sounds like your good friend Chuck might have been gay.'

I gave him a soft kick in the thigh.

Chuck's craving for old things was illustrated by the mention that he'd recently purchased a second-hand flivver and, reportedly, broken all speed records in Towson over the summer. 'However,' the entry continued, 'it is hard to imagine Chuck dissecting a "stiff" or, worse still, performing an operation on an honest to goodness human being.'

'Joy riding around town in an old Model T Ford?' I said. 'I think I would have loved this dude.'

Doctors and nurses had to be working somewhere nearby, I reasoned. Almost reluctantly, I clicked away from Chuck's colorful yearbook entry and brought up Google. A search for hospitals in present-day Pierre came up with only one, now owned by Avera, a health care conglomerate with more than 300 locations in South Dakota, North Dakota, Nebraska, Minnesota and Iowa. Before it became part of a sprawling, for-profit enterprise, though, the hospital had been simply called St Mary's.

I navigated to the Avera St Mary's website and clicked on the 'history' tab. Back in 1882, I read, a doctor named D.W. Robinson who planned to practice medicine out in California, found himself stranded at the end of the railroad line in Pierre. Out of funds, he began to support himself by caring for patients in the old Park Hotel there, operating on kitchen tables, ironing boards and even the floors.

In 1899, ten years after South Dakota became a state, five Benedictine Sisters took over the old Park Hotel. It had been deserted for several years by then, the only guests being animals and birds, and was so filthy from critters and river sand that the Sisters couldn't even determine the color of the woodwork. Their intention was to clean it up for use as a school, but the city fathers convinced them that health care was an even greater need than a school. The Sisters immediately changed their plans, opening a hospital and a training school for nurses. Mary Woods was the first white baby born in the hospital on December 9, 1899 and the first operation was performed a little more than a month later on a proper operating table donated by the afore-mentioned Dr Robinson.

The enterprise thrived. By the time Charlotte and Charles arrived in Pierre nearly thirty years later, the hospital had been accredited and a new facility was being built with one hundred beds.

'No wonder they needed doctors and nurses,' Paul said. 'They were expanding.'

I smiled. 'Imagine how a staunch Congregationalist like Charlotte must have chafed under the yoke of the Benedictine Brides of Christ. I'm old enough to remember when John F. Kennedy, a Catholic, was running for president. "We can't have a mackerel snapper occupying the White House!" Grandmother would rant. "He'll answer to the Pope, not the American people!" What she'd say about the far-right religious wingnuts who seem to be calling the shots in politics these days I can only imagine.'

It seemed clear that an invitation from Charles Keene had drawn Charlotte to a professional training opportunity in South Dakota, almost two thousand miles from her home. I wondered if she had grown homesick out on the Great Plains, so far away from the lush, Green Mountain state.

Nowadays Charlotte would have texted: School sux. Send $$. Had she written letters to her father and little brother back home?

A hundred years before her great-great-grandchildren's every move would be chronicled on Facebook and Instagram, had Charlotte kept a diary?

A search of the storage facility mentioned by my father just moved closer to the top of my To-Do list.

'Do you know what happened to Charles after he attended your grandparents' wedding?' Paul asked.

'Not yet, but stay tuned.'

A search of Fold3, the military database, turned up Charles's World War Two draft registration card. According to the Cuyahoga County draft board, Charles was working as a surgeon in Cleveland, Ohio, had blond hair and blue eyes, was five foot ten inches tall, weighed one hundred and eighty pounds and had a slight scar on his forehead. 'After the attack on Pearl Harbor in December of 1941,' I reported, 'Charles shows up on Navy muster rolls as a Lieutenant in the Medical Corps. He must have been deployed somewhere in the Pacific theater.'

'How do you know that?'

'He's got a fleet post office address in San Francisco,' I said. 'If they'd shipped him out to Europe, it would be FPO New York.'

Paul squeezed my big toe. 'I'm going for more wine. Refill?'

'You bet,' I said, handing over my empty glass.

While Paul was fetching the wine, I logged on to the newspaper database and searched Ohio newspapers for Charles's name. A short obituary in the *Cleveland Plain Dealer* provided chilling details: Lieutenant Charles Keene had been killed in action on Tarawa, November 23, 1943, when the field hospital where he was operating was hit by enemy fire.

On FindAGrave.com, I found an image of Chuck's tombstone at Greenmount Cemetery in Burlington, Vermont. I stared at it for a long time, thinking about my grandmother's friend, feeling desperately sad that his, and so many other young lives, had been cut short by war. I didn't realize until tears dripped onto my keyboard that I'd started to cry.

Paul appeared at my elbow, holding a glass of wine in each hand. 'What's wrong, sweetie?'

'He died,' I sniffed.

Paul's eyebrows shot up. 'Who died?'

'Charles Keene, my grandfather's best man.'

Paul set the wine glasses down on the end table. 'Hannah, he would almost certainly be dead by now anyway.'

'I know, but I wish I had known him, is all. He was only thirty-eight years old when he was killed.'

Paul sat on the ottoman, looked into my face and swiped an errant tear away with his thumb. 'You're very good at this, you know.'

I swallowed hard. 'Good at what? Weeping at the drop of a hat?'

'Research.'

'Just shut up and get me a tissue,' I snuffled.

'How about a pizza?' Paul asked when he returned. 'I don't think either of us feels like cooking.'

I snatched a tissue from the box he held out to me and blew my nose. 'With mushrooms?'

'With whatever toppings you want.'

'I don't want to go out. Let's have it delivered.'

Paul picked up the wine glasses and handed one to me. 'Your wish is my command.'

We clinked the rims of our glasses together and sipped.

'You know,' he mused after a few moments of companionable silence. 'When you finish with this family project, maybe you can find Amelia Earhart.'

THIRTEEN

I had plenty of research pending on my To-Do list before charging off on fruitless searches for Amelia Earhart – or Jimmy Hoffa or D.B. Cooper, for that matter.

After checking my email for responses to my DNA matches – nothing heard – I went looking for information on my maternal great-grandmother, Jane Drew, and her son, Adam, the great uncle I never knew.

Fortunately, the state of Vermont keeps meticulous vital records. Since 1779, town clerks were required by law to record all marriages, births and deaths. Most of this data appears on handwritten index cards, images of which can be found online.

When my great-grandmother married Josiah Drew in 1910, her maiden name was listed as Jane Gillette, daughter of William Gillette and Susanna Cook of Rutland, Vermont. Jane's age at the time was nineteen, so I calculated she had been born around 1891, which was confirmed by another card recording the birth of a daughter named Jane to a William and Susanna Gillette on October 18, 1891.

Jane and Josiah's daughter Charlotte blessed the happy couple in 1912. Before Charlotte's brother, Adam, came along in 1917, there had been another child, a boy named Josiah Drew after his father, but the lad died in the winter of 1915 when the poor thing was only three months old. No cause of death was recorded.

Jane's death, however, was fully documented. She passed away on December 22, 1926 of rheumatic heart disease, a complication, according to the doctor who signed her death certificate, of infantile scarlet fever.

If only penicillin had been discovered earlier, I mused sadly as I updated my family tree with this new information.

But what had happened to Charlotte's brother, my great uncle Adam Drew? After crawling around my databases for an hour, I gradually drew a picture of his life. Adam had graduated from Dartmouth College in 1938 with a degree in engineering. While in college, he rowed crew and sang in the glee club. When 1940 rolled around, he was living with his widowed father, Josiah, in Rutland, Vermont and working as a mechanic, although the census didn't say where. He'd enlisted in the Navy in October 1942, where he served as a MoMM2c. Motor Machinist's Mate Second Class Drew had shipped out to Europe on a destroyer, the USS *Gleaves*, which had been named, I was fascinated to find out, after an 1877 Naval Academy graduate who invented ways to improve the accuracy of torpedoes.

Adam Drew had survived the war – he was granted an honorable discharge in 1945 – but after that, his online record turned grim. In 1947, two days after his thirtieth birthday, Adam committed suicide by shooting himself in the head with a revolver. The *Rutland Evening Dispatch* carried the story in blunt, no-nonsense terms:

*On Monday, during the forenoon, Mr Drew purchased a
revolver. Returning to his father's house, he seated himself
at a table and wrote a brief note, wherein he stated that
people were talking falsely about him, etc., and then,
without rising from his chair, placed the muzzle of the
revolver to his right temple and fired. The ball passed
through his head, killing him instantly. Temporary aber-
ration of mind is assigned as the cause of the fatal act.*

Swell. Like red hair, did mental illness run in the Drew family?
More likely, I chided myself, young Adam had been suffering
from post-traumatic stress disorder, which was called shell
shock back then. If this kept up, I'd either have to start taking
anti-depressants or give up genealogical research altogether.

Hoping to uncover uplifting news, I went in search of the
mysterious Mrs H.H. Westerly, the woman who had hosted my
grandmother Charlotte's wedding. What facts I discovered did
nothing to lighten my dark mood.

According to her obituary in the *Bethel Gazette*, Mrs H.H.
turned out to be my grandfather's younger sister, Mina Smith.
I'd never known my great aunt Mina; like Charles Keene,
she'd died in the early years of the Second World War, or so
I'd been told. According to family lore, she'd taken a train
to Boston for dental surgery and never returned, succumbing
in 'Beantown' to a fatal reaction, perhaps an overdose of
anesthesia.

I created a record for Mina and connected it to her husband
Howard Harrison Westerly. When the screen refreshed, a pennant
on Mina's icon began flapping, and when I clicked on the
pennant, there it was: an image of Mina's death certificate from
the state of Massachusetts. My eyes were first drawn, as they
always were these days, to 'cause of death'.

Ovarian tumor?

Damn! I flopped back in my chair. Years back when I was
diagnosed with breast cancer, I'd claimed with confidence, when
interviewed by the doctor, that there was no history of cancer
in my family. None. And yet, there it was, typed out in black
and white on an official Massachusetts death certificate: the Big
C, a diagnosis too embarrassing to talk about back then.

I felt like everything I thought I knew about my family was tumbling like dominoes.

What next?

Unlike Adam, who was single when he died, Mina left Howard with four youngsters to raise. He'd remarried within a year and moved to Denver where, according to the census for 1940, he worked as a mining engineer. At that point, we'd lost track of that branch of the family. I figured that some of the cousins I'd recently matched may well have descended from Mina's line. But in spite of the emails I'd sent out, no one had responded. I was beginning to grow impatient.

The first nibble came a week later in the form of an email alerting me to a message waiting in my Gen-Tree account. I was at Whole Foods picking out some pork chops for dinner, but as soon as I got home, I stuffed the groceries in the fridge, bag and all, then rushed downstairs and turned on the computer.

Dear Hannah Ives, the message began. *My name is Nicholas Ohanzee Johnson, born in 1996 on the Pine Ridge Indian Reservation in South Dakota. I am Ogala Lakota, and I may be the connection you are looking for. Please write back and tell me more.*

When my hands had stopped shaking, I emailed Nicholas back, telling him what I knew about my grandmother, Charlotte Drew, concluding with:

Although our Native American ancestry came as a complete surprise, we are delighted to learn of it and hope you can help us fill in the blanks in our grandmother's early life. She was living in Pierre studying to become a nurse and would have come into contact with your family sometime between 1929 and 1932. Do you know where Charlotte might fit into your family tree?

Hoping to speed up the conversation, I added my private email address and hit send.

I'll ask my Great-Great-Aunt Wasula, Nicholas replied almost at once. *She might know. She just turned 102 but has a Wikipedia-like memory. Back to you soon.*

But I didn't hear any more from Nicholas for a maddening three days. I lit candles at St Catherine's Church for great-great-aunt Wasula's continuing good health, praying she hadn't

suddenly passed away, taking all that valuable knowledge along
with her.

In the meantime, I met up with a group of like-minded
political activists at a real estate office on Old Solomon's Island
Road. Fueled by coffee and donuts, we manned the telephone
banks and hand-addressed postcards (the personal touch!) to
everyone in our precinct, urging them to vote in November.

In my spare time, I read up on the Pine Ridge Reservation.
Located in the southwest corner of South Dakota on a border
it shared with Nebraska, the reservation was about the size
of the state of Connecticut and was, according to Wikipedia,
the eighth largest Indian reservation in the United States.
Several years before, Pine Ridge had been in the news when
tribal members joined with other Native American activists
on the Standing Rock Indian Reservation to protest the 1,172-
mile Dakota Access crude oil pipeline that runs through North
and South Dakota, Iowa and Illinois and has a capacity to
move 500,000 barrels of oil per day. The pipeline cuts across
huge swaths of native ancestral land. 'It's like constructing
a pipeline through Arlington Cemetery or under St Patrick's
Cathedral,' a lawyer for one of the tribes stated. And where
the pipeline crosses the Missouri River, it becomes a real
threat to the drinking water supply.

In truth, the Lakota Sioux had been 'troublemakers' ever
since Custer made his Last Stand at the Little Big Horn in
1876. That same year, perhaps in retaliation for Custer's defeat,
the US Congress decided to open up the Black Hills to development, putting 7.7 million acres of Indian land on sale to
homesteaders and private interests. In 1889, what remained
of the Great Sioux reservation was divided into five separate
reservations, one of which was Pine Ridge.

Needless to say, none of this set well with the Sioux. Nerves
were on edge, and when US troops descended upon Wounded
Knee in order to relieve the restive Lakota of their rifles, a
scuffle with a tribesman named Black Coyote – who refused
to give up his rifle because he'd paid a lot of money for it –
resulted in a massacre. At least one-hundred-and-fifty men,
women and children were murdered, and fifty-one more
wounded.

Almost ninety years later, in 1973, Wounded Knee was back in the news, receiving widespread media coverage as American Indian Movement (AIM) and Ogala Lakota activists – petitioning for restoration of treaty rights – staged a seventy-one-day stand-off with US law enforcement that resulted in gunfire and several deaths. The stand-off ended, but the violence continued. In 1975, an armed confrontation between AIM activists and the FBI resulted in the Pine Ridge Shootout and the death of one activist and two FBI agents.

Nowadays on the Pine Ridge Reservation, eighty percent of the residents are unemployed; forty-nine percent live below the federal poverty line; the infant mortality rate is five times the national average; obesity, diabetes and heart disease are epidemic; and 4.5 million cans of beer are sold annually in White Clay, Nebraska, just over the border from Pine Ridge. That's 12,500 cans of beer a day. The reservation itself is dry.

Golly. Why would anyone voluntarily live in such a place? Did Nicholas live on the reservation now, I wondered, or had he escaped to a better life?

'When are you going to tell your sisters about Nicholas?' Paul asked me as we were eating dinner several days later.

'When all the facts are in, I think. I don't want to confuse things. Ruth is pretty solid, but I'm worried about Georgina. One minute she's nagging us to take the DNA tests, the next, forget about it, so sorry I asked.' I gnawed thoughtfully on a raw carrot. 'Scott's got something to do with Georgina's crazy about-face, you can bet on that.'

'Julie certainly seemed keen,' Paul remarked.

'Emily, too,' I said. 'But Emily's less likely than Julie to go off half-cocked.'

'Half-cocked?'

'Oh, like painting her face, braiding feathers into her hair, hopping on a bus to South Dakota and spending her gap year on the reservation.'

Paul laughed, then his face grew serious. 'From how you describe it, the reservation could use all the help it can get.'

'I know. Maybe there's something we can do.' I lay my fork down on my empty plate. 'But, dammit! Why doesn't Nicholas get back in touch? I don't even know him and he's already driving me crazy!'

'That proves he's family,' Paul said.

FOURTEEN

As if to illustrate a cosmic connection between us, I received an email from Nicholas the following morning, time stamped 20:18, sent exactly when Paul and I had been finishing dinner.

'Hi, cousin! Can we FaceTime?'

Taking this as a sign he had information to share, I emailed back, 'Of course! Name a time.'

At seven p.m. EDT, with Paul hovering behind me, I powered up the computer, launched the FaceTime app and waited for Nicholas to call.

In preparation for the session, I'd washed and coaxed my unruly curls into submission with a generous squirt of styling mousse, then fluffed them out around my face in a casual, beach-blown way. Lipstick and a judicious application of eyeliner kept me from looking like a washed-out hag, or so I hoped. No use scaring the kid.

The computer began to ring.

Suddenly nervous, I looked back at Paul who smiled, nodded encouragingly and said, 'What are you waiting for?'

I clicked *Accept*, and in less than a second Nicholas's image filled my screen.

'Hi, cousin,' he said.

'Hi,' I said back, feeling tongue-tied and stupid.

Nicholas's strong brows arched over dark eyes set handsomely into a round face. His straight nose and full lips would have looked right at home on a Roman statue. He wore his jet-black hair trimmed close on the sides and long on top, swept back in an iconic quiff. A tendril had escaped whatever hair product he used to tame it, dangling fetchingly over one eye. As I pondered what to say next, a young woman swam into view behind him, as stunningly beautiful as he was handsome. Her blue-black hair was parted on the side and cascaded loosely over her shoulders. She waggled her fingers at the camera.

'Hi,' she said.

'This is my sister, Mai. We're twins.'

'Twins run in the family,' I said. At least on my side of the continent, the ice had been broken.

I was going to introduce Paul, but he scooted his chair aside and waved me off, letting me know that this was my show, not his.

'I won't keep you in suspense,' Nicholas said. 'I talked to my aunt, and she remembers your grandmother. She says Lottie was one of the nurses who came with the doctor to treat patients on the rez.'

I pressed a hand to my chest in a futile attempt to slow my racing heart. 'Does your aunt know how we might be related?'

'Auntie had two brothers, Matoskah and Tahatan, although your grandmother might have known them by their English names, Joseph and Henry. Tahatan, Henry, was our great-grandfather.

'They were cowboys,' Nicholas continued. 'Both of them died before I was born, so I never knew them.'

Cowboys? I must have looked puzzled because Nicholas went on to explain that Joseph and Henry had been Lakota cowboys active on the rodeo circuit.

'Does your aunt Wasula think Henry was my grandfather?' I asked.

'It's hard to know what Auntie thinks, Hannah. When I explained about the DNA, she listened quietly, but she stared out the window the whole time I was talking to her. She didn't say anything for two whole days, so I thought maybe she didn't believe me, but then she called me into her room. She wants to talk to you.' He paused. 'Annapolis is near Washington, DC, right?'

Although I couldn't figure out why he was asking, I agreed that it was. 'About thirty miles.'

'It's total coincidence, but next week we're coming to Washington for the big Native Lives Matter March. I'm hoping we'll be able to meet you then. Will you be home?'

'I will, and I'd like that very much,' I said. 'I'll come to your hotel. Where will you be staying?'

Nicholas laughed. 'Not in a hotel. Dad's driving us down in the RV. We plan to stay for a week or two at a campground in College Park, Maryland. Cherry Hill. Perhaps you know it?'

'I do,' I said.

Situated in a tree-lined park just north of Interstate 495, Cherry Hill was one of the Washington area's premier campgrounds, offering cottages, cabins, tents and hookups for a gazillion RVs. They had a restaurant, swimming pools, hot tubs, a dog park and recently had gone even more upmarket by adding yurts for glamping.

'Cherry Hill's not far from IKEA,' I added. 'Unless I leave my credit cards at home, I can get into a lot of trouble at IKEA.'

Nicholas chuckled. 'Tell me about it. That's how I furnished my dorm room.'

'Where do you go to college?'

'Went,' Nicholas corrected. 'I graduated from Marquette last spring with a major in Finance. Mai and I were luckier than most. Dad's a security officer at Prairie Wind Casino, so the tuition for Red Cloud High wasn't a stretch. I got a full ride at Marquette, and Mai . . .' He paused and looked over his shoulder. 'Here I am hogging the computer, you tell her, Mai.'

Mai gave her brother a friendly swat on the head and leaned into the camera. 'I went to Creighton in Omaha. It's a Jesuit-run school, too, just like Red Cloud was, and Marquette.'

'What was your major, Mai?'

'Marketing. Nicholas and I, both of us, are working at the casino, at least for now. I'm a floor attendant in the Bingo hall. The pay sucks, but I'm getting experience. Nicholas's a slot technician, but he won't be happy until they put him in charge of the auditing department.'

Nicholas grinned at his sister. 'Mai's helping out with the casino website, too. She's aiming for something in the promotions department, but if that doesn't work out, I think she'll move on.'

'You mentioned your father . . .' I began.

'Everybody calls him Sam, but his Indian name is Chaska

which means "Eldest Son". My mother's name is Wachapi. Star.'

Nicholas grabbed a piece of paper and held it up, closer to the camera. From the boxes and lines hand-drawn on the page, I could tell it was a family tree, but Nicholas's writing was too small to read. 'It's complicated, so I've drawn a family tree.'

'Is your family tree online?' I asked. 'It might be easier for me to see it that way.'

'We didn't upload our tree,' he said. 'Just the DNA. Dad was reluctant even to do that, but one of his sisters needs a bone marrow transplant and nobody on the rez is a match.'

I quickly volunteered to be tested, then asked, 'What issues did your father have with the DNA testing?'

'It's the fear of appropriation,' Nicholas explained. 'Historically, our land, artifacts and even our ancestors' remains have been taken away, shared and studied. That was beginning to happen with our DNA, too.'

This was ringing a bell. 'Ah, I remember reading an article in the *New York Times* about a Grand Canyon tribe who successfully sued Arizona State for using their genetic samples to conduct research outside the purpose of the original study.'

'The Havasupai, yes. They settled for seven-hundred-thousand dollars, I think.'

'Could you scan that page and email it to me, Nicholas?'

'Sure. Or I can bring it when we come.'

'I'd like to study it ahead of time, if you don't mind. It might answer a few questions.'

'No problem. I'll take care of it as soon as we hang up.'

'When do you think you'll arrive?' I asked.

'Hard to say, but we're aiming for Thursday, weather and traffic permitting.' He paused. 'Tell you what. I'll text you after we get settled so we can set up a time to get together. Aunt Wasula goes to bed crazy early, so it'll probably be in the morning.'

'Your aunt's coming, too? Didn't you tell me she's one hundred and two?'

Nicholas laughed. 'Try telling Auntie *not* to do anything. She lives in an oil and gas area and there's oil flares and pipelines everywhere. She had two horses drop dead from the fumes.

They just started kicking, then keeled over. I'll be pushing her wheelchair, but she'll be carrying the "Keep Calm and Frack Off" sign.'

I had to laugh. 'I can't wait to meet her.'

FIFTEEN

Nicholas was as good as his word. Half an hour later I had the Johnson family tree in hand.

While I waited impatiently for Thursday to roll around, I spent time getting acquainted with the ancestors on his, and probably my, family tree. If my suspicions were correct and I had descended from either Joseph or Henry Johnson, my maternal great-grandparents would have been John Otaktay (Kills Many) and his wife, Mary Ehawee (Laughing Maid).

In addition to the family tree, Nicholas had included a helpful note:

> *Hannah: Sometime before their son Joseph was born in 1911, Otaktay and Ehawee chose the last name, Johnson, as their surname. To facilitate land transfers after the Dawes Act of 1887, the purpose of which was to break up the reservations, assimilate the Indians and turn them into land-owning farmers, the Commissioner of Indian Affairs in 1890 ordered that all Indians living on reservations be given an English Christian name. They would retain their surname but translate it into English and shorten it, if necessary. Thus Otaktay officially became John Kills Many. The Indian agent was not happy with Kills Many, my Aunt Wasula says. He gave her father a choice between Washington, Adams, Jefferson or Monroe, but Otakay picked Johnson, naming himself after the agent. There must be a story behind that! – N.*

I didn't know how large the Johnson's RV was and I didn't want to overwhelm the family with newfound relatives, but I didn't want to meet them alone, either. Paul sensibly suggested I give right of first refusal to blood relations, but Ruth and her husband were on a Viking river cruise to the Baltic and Georgina was avoiding the topic like small pox.

I called Emily and invited her to join me, but she demurred. 'You should take Julie,' Emily advised. 'Her mom's the one who started the whole thing, and Julie's totally into it. She'll never forgive you if you don't.'

'I'm not sure her father would approve,' I said.

'What's the worst that will happen?' Emily said. 'Scott will never speak to you again? Sounds like a win-win to me.'

'Don't be naughty, Emily.'

'It's my job, Mom.'

'Thanks,' I said with a laugh.

'And Mom?'

'What?'

'Take pictures.'

'If I don't ask, they can't say no,' Julie said when she presented herself at my house on Thursday morning. She'd driven herself there in the Cardinale family Subaru. 'We're shopping,' she said. 'You're buying me a suitcase.'

'What happens when you come home without one?' I asked.

Julie tossed her car keys on my kitchen counter, shrugged and said, 'I couldn't find one I liked? I'm notoriously picky.'

Remembering the words of Admiral Grace Hopper – *It is often easier to ask for forgiveness than to ask for permission* – and against my better judgment, I went along with Julie's plan.

From the moment we hit Route 50 outside Annapolis to the time we merged with the Washington beltway, Julie chattered non-stop. I'd told her about my FaceTime session with Nicholas and Mai, emphasizing their academic achievements, hoping they'd serve as a shining example to someone who was about to step off into a gap year of the Great Unknown. Sadly, I'd miscalculated. Julie seemed more interested in hearing about their casino jobs. 'I wonder how much training you need to be a blackjack dealer?' she mused.

I handed her the Johnson family tree. 'Shut up and read,' I said.

Fifteen minutes later, we took exit twenty-five toward College Park and followed Cherry Hill Road as it wound back north, passing under the beltway.

'There it is!' Julie bounced in her seat, the family tree forgotten. 'There's the sign!'

I swung the wheel left onto Jayrose Drive and entered the park.

'The Johnsons are expecting us,' I told the guard at the security gate. 'Site number four-seventeen.'

'You can park over there,' he said, gesturing to his right. 'Near the bus station. It's a short walk from there.' He handed me a map of the campground. Site 417 on Crater Lake Vista was circled in pencil. I passed the map to Julie and thanked him as the turnstile rose up to let us pass.

I'm no expert on recreational vehicles, so when Nicholas told me to look for an Allegro 31 motor home, I had to look it up on the Internet. The RV was bigger than I expected from the online photograph. It was the size of a school bus, with maroon, silver and black Nike-style swooshes painted along the side. A hand painted wooden sign hung from a hook on the door: *Cikala Inipi*. I wondered if that was Lakota for "Welcome".

I'd texted Nicholas from the parking lot, so he and Mai were expecting us, sitting outside the RV in canvas lawn chairs under a green and white striped canopy. When we ambled around the corner, they leapt to their feet, arms outstretched in welcome.

Julie lunged forward, hugging her newfound cousins as if she had known them all her life. 'I'm so excited!' she said, as if we couldn't guess.

I extended my hand. 'I'm so pleased to meet you, Nicholas.'

'Please,' he said while handing me off to Mai. 'We're family. Call me Nick.'

'Father!' Mai called out. 'They're here.'

Their father, I saw now, was crouched at the rear of the RV, his head deep into one of the undercarriage compartments. As I watched, he hauled out a barbeque grill, set it on the ground, unfolded his six-foot-something-inch frame and stood.

Cousin Samuel 'Eldest Son' Johnson was about my age. He wore a black T-shirt belted into slim-fitting jeans, and a pair of expensive, handcrafted leather boots. His black hair was worn long, fastened at the nape of his neck with a loop of braided leather. He whipped a yellow bandana out of his back pocket, used it to wipe sweat off his forehead, returned the bandana to his pocket, then stepped forward to greet us.

'Welcome,' he said, taking my hand in both of his.

'Nick has explained Lakota names to me,' I said. 'But it's still a bit confusing. Shall I call you Chaska, Eldest Son, or Samuel?'

He smiled, revealing a row of dazzling, slightly crooked teeth. 'Sam will do fine. Let's go inside where it's cool.'

Sam held the door open while Julie and I stepped into the RV.

I couldn't stifle a gasp.

The inside of their motor home was larger than some New York City apartments. We found ourselves in a bright, living room-dining room-kitchen area, fully carpeted and beautifully furnished with rich, buttery leather upholstery. In the cab to my right, the driver and passenger seats, equally plush, sat before a dashboard cluttered, at least to my mind, with screens, knobs and buttons like the bridge of the Starship Enterprise.

'It's roomier than it looks from the outside,' I commented as I eased sideways into a kitchen equipped with stainless steel appliances, including a full-size refrigerator, more up-to-date than any in my kitchen at home.

'We have two slides,' Sam explained, indicating the bedroom where the foot of a queen-sized bed covered with a Navajo quilt was just visible. 'Once we get parked and leveled, the bedroom and the living-dining room areas pop out.'

'Do you live in the RV year round?' Julie asked. She seemed to be admiring the flat-screen television built into the wall. Underneath the television, incredibly, was a gas log fireplace. I must have been ogling the fireplace because Sam smiled and said, 'It gets cold in South Dakota.'

Turning to Julie, he said, 'My wife and I live on a farm near Oglala. Aunt Wasula still lives in the house my father and I grew up in. Nick and Mai have moved in with her temporarily.'

Julie glanced around the living area, her brow slightly furrowed. 'But where do you all *sleep*?'

I'd been curious about that, too.

If Sam found the question rude, he gave no indication of it. 'Mai shares the queen bed with her aunt, I sleep on the pull-out sofa and Nick . . . wait, I'll show you.' Sam strolled into the cab, released a couple of pins, reached overhead and pushed a button. A bunk bed began to emerge from the ceiling over the cab. He let the bed descend about a foot before sending it back up where it came from. 'The seats fold back at night,' he explained, 'so the bed can be fully deployed.'

I was beginning to wonder whether Aunt Wasula had actually made the trip when a door next to the television slid open and a stooped, elderly woman emerged from what I assumed was the bathroom. This had to be Wasula.

Her hair, still predominately black but evenly streaked with gray, was parted in the middle and had been freshly-braided. It hung over her shoulders in double plaits almost to her waist. She wore an ankle-length, cotton skirt splashed with flowers, and in spite of the August heat, a red cardigan buttoned over a yellow blouse. As she shuffled toward us, the smallest pair of Birkenstock sandals I'd ever seen on an adult peeked out from beneath her skirt.

Sam took his aunt gently by the arm and steered her toward a seat on the L-shaped sofa. 'T'unwín-la, this is Hannah and her niece Julie, the cousins I told you about.'

Wasula beamed, accentuating her already deeply-creased smile lines. She nodded, saying nothing but looking incredibly wise. Once seated, hands folded in her lap, she commanded the room. I found it hard to look away.

There was a bit of friendly chatter while Mai directed everyone to a seat, and then – silence – as one by one we noticed that Wasula had raised her hand.

Something extraordinary was about to happen.

'I have many names,' she began. 'The Indian name given to me by my parents, their first gift to me, is Wasula. Wasula means Hair Storm, because I was born with a full head of black curls.' She stroked one of her braids and smiled wistfully.

'My Christian name is Miriam,' she continued, 'given to me by the missionaries after the sister of the great prophet Moses. Since I left the day school, I have not used that name, but if

I ever want to travel abroad it will be the name on my passport.

'Chaska Eldest Son – Samuel – calls me T'unwín-la, father's sister.'

She leaned back and closed her eyes, her small frame seeming to melt into the cushion. For one long minute, Wasula said nothing and I thought she might have dozed off, but then she opened her eyes and looked directly at me.

'Before me, Hannah, came my two brothers. They were named Matoska and Tahatan, born two years apart. From the time Tahatan learned to walk, the boys competed over everything. Who could shoot the arrow the farthest, whose sled reached the bottom of the hill first, whose horse was faster, who got to eat the last piece of molasses bread.' She leaned forward. 'But when it came to races, it was Matoska's horse that usually won.'

Wasula's dark eyes flashed. She turned her head toward Julie who sat rigid with attention in one of the dinette chairs. 'The Lakota are the best horseback riders in the world. Did you know that, Julie? My brothers were cowboys. Horses were all they knew. Raising them, training them, riding them, raising and selling cattle. They worked the rodeo circuit, too, using their Indian names, White Bear and Hawk. Roping, branding, bronco riding, steer wrestling – there was no competition my brothers could pass up. And for Hawk it was always a good day when he bested his older brother.

'Lakota cowboys were like rock stars,' she continued, inclining her head toward me. 'When our father, Otaktay, was a young man, some Lakota left their farms and joined Buffalo Bill's Wild West Show, travelling all the way to England to perform for Queen Victoria.' Wasula took a deep breath. 'It must have been a spectacle. Father's friend, a Lakota named Blue Horse was one of the performers. They billed him as chief of the Shoshones.'

'All Indians looked alike,' Nick interjected.

Wasula smiled indulgently. 'The English had never seen anything like the Wild West Show. Crowds thronged the streets to catch a glimpse of the cavalcade. Blue Horse told me that they travelled with eight hundred performers, nearly two hundred horses, eighteen buffalo, ten elk, five Texas longhorns and two deer.'

'They re-enacted Custer's Last Stand only ten years after it occurred,' Sam added. 'Remarkable, while reprehensible. It goes without saying that the Indians were portrayed as savages. Attacking wagon trains, stage coaches and settler's cabins until Wild Bill Cody and his troops rode triumphantly into the scene.'

Wasula smiled. 'It was a little bit more low-key in my day. We had the annual Pine Ridge Sioux Rodeo to look forward to, of course. It was a big tourist attraction. And cowboys like my brothers often left the reservation to compete in tournaments in other cities.'

As I waited for her story to continue, hardly daring to breathe, Wasula paused and closed her eyes. Were long-ago events scrolling past her eyelids? After a moment she raised a hand, as if reading my mind. 'You will want to know how our families met.'

'My grandmother was a nurse,' I said. 'I'm guessing it was in that capacity.'

'You are right. About once a month, there was a doctor from Pierre, I do not recall his name, who would drive to our clinic in an old Model T. Sometimes there would be another doctor with him, too, but he always brought a nurse.

'Matoska, White Bear, had gotten into a disagreement with a Brahma bull and the bull won. Just broken fingers, I was told, but Nurse Lottie helped the doctor patch White Bear up. The next month, White Bear reported for a checkup, and the next month, too, even though his hand had healed.

'After that, whenever the Model T was spotted coming down the road he'd show up at the clinic, offering to help out around the place. I was only thirteen, but even I knew it wasn't the doctor White Bear wanted to see.

'When Hawk informed Mother about his brother's interest in the nurse, I think he expected Mother to forbid such a relationship, but that didn't happen. Everybody respected Lottie. Besides, it wasn't all that unusual for a Lakota man to marry a white woman. Our day school teacher came from Chicago and married a Lakota. They had two children together.

'I do not know if Lottie returned White Bear's affection. She smiled and was kind to everyone. She brought flour for the women, tobacco for the men, books and candy for the children. They honored her with the Indian name, Mika, which means Clever Raccoon.' Wasula circled an eye with her index finger. 'Lottie wore round eyeglasses with tinted lenses. The children had never seen sunglasses before.'

I remembered those eyeglasses. Grandmother had kept them in a beaded case on her dresser, next to a bottle of Shalimar perfume.

'Julie?' Wasula patted the empty spot on the sofa next to her. When Julie joined her, Wasula turned and took both of my niece's hands in her gnarled ones. After a moment, she reached up to touch Julie's cheek. 'You look very much like her, Granddaughter.'

I choked back a sob.

'After White Bear died,' Wasula continued, still holding one of Julie's hands, 'Lottie never came again. I was fourteen then, and heartbroken. Lottie would bring me lipstick. She taught me how to French braid my hair. She gave me movie magazines.'

She grinned mischievously. 'I was obsessed with Claudette Colbert. I confessed to Lottie that I wanted Claudette's eyebrows, so the next time she came, Lottie brought tweezers and showed me how to use them. The clinic had closed, but the doctor had to wait while she finished doing my Hollywood makeover.' Wasula laughed. 'I didn't care that the older girls made fun of my war paint.' She lowered her voice. 'I think they were jealous.'

'Tell me how White Bear died,' I said. 'He was so young!'

'They said he was trampled to death by a horse,' Wasula said matter-of-factly. 'Father found him in the horse trailer, slumped against the wooden slats. They loaded him into a wagon and drove him to the hospital in Pierre, but he died two days later.'

'Massive head and internal injuries,' Sam supplied. 'Liver, spleen, intestines.'

Wasula's face clouded. 'Wakinyan could *not* have done that.'

'Wakinyan?' I asked.

Sam answered for his aunt. 'White Bear's horse, Thunder Spirit.'

'White Bear raised him from a colt,' Wasula said. Her eyes, unwavering, caught mine. 'I do not know who beat my brother to death, but it was not his horse.'

SIXTEEN

Wasula sagged, her eyes closed. I glanced over to Mai with alarm.

'She's just exhausted,' Mai said with a smile. 'It's been a long and interesting morning. Stuff I never knew.' Mai gently stroked Wasula's arm. 'Nap time, T'unwín-la.'

While Mai was helping her aunt get settled in the bedroom, we relocated to the patio where Sam had arranged a half-dozen canvas chairs in a semi-circle under the shade of a sugar maple tree.

'What does the sign mean, Nick?' Julie asked as we were taking our seats.

'Cikala Inipi?'

Julie nodded.

'Mai's idea. It means Little Lodge.'

'Nick carved the sign when he was in high school,' Sam added. 'It used to hang in our old Airstream trailer.' After a moment he pointed toward an Igloo picnic cooler and said, 'I've got cold beer and soft drinks in the cooler. Can I get anyone anything?'

I'd never developed a taste for beer, besides, I was driving. 'Coke for me, please, if you have one.'

As we were making our selections, Mai emerged from the RV carrying a box of sugar cookies.

Julie selected a cookie to go along with her Coke, then turned her green eyes on Nick. 'Can I ask you something, like, personal?'

Nick seemed to flush. 'Sure.'

'I don't want to step on any toes, so I'm wondering what, um, the indigenous people of the Americas prefer to be called. Indians? Native Americans?'

'Speaking for our tribe,' Nick said, 'we use the term LDN Peoples – Lakota, Dakota and Nakota.'

'I'll bet that has some people scratching their heads,' Julie said. 'Trying to figure it out, I mean, like LGBTQ or something.'

Sam laughed out loud. 'Tell me about it!'

'Julie probably mean Indians in general,' Nick offered.

Julie nodded.

'"Indian" is the term we've known for generations. The term Native American is relatively new. Like African-American, it arose in the sixties and seventies out of political-correctness concerns of the civil rights era.'

'Not too long ago somebody took a survey and asked Indians that same question,' Mai cut in. 'Fifty percent said they preferred American Indian, thirty-seven liked Native American and the rest had no preference.'

'So Indian is good?'

'It's good.'

I angled my chair so that it faced into the sun and adjusted my sunglasses, hoping to make my Vitamin D quotient for the week. 'Tell me about the Native Lives Matter March,' I said. 'Is it about police brutality? I read in the *New York Times* or somewhere that Native Americans are being killed by police at a higher rate even than African-Americans and are three times more likely to be killed by police than white people.'

Nick rested his beer can on his knee. 'Organizers are taking a page from the Black Lives Matter movement, sure, but the fact of the matter is that you can't have a legitimate conversation about racism, about institutionalized racism in particular, or about white supremacy without inviting native peoples to the table. At Pine Ridge, though, we're focused much more broadly. Lack of housing is our number one concern.'

'Then there's poverty, unemployment, struggles with substance abuse,' Sam added, gesturing with his beer can. 'It's all related.'

Mai's face grew serious. 'Two of my friends from high school committed suicide last year. There were twenty-three youth suicides in 2015. It's an epidemic.'

'I'm so sorry, Mai,' I said.

But Mai was just getting wound up. 'This country gives away *billions* and *billions* in foreign aid to countries most people have never even heard of. Our nation was built on two horrors.' She ticked them off on her fingers. 'One. The genocide of

indigenous peoples and, two, the enslavement of Africans . . .'
She paused. 'We want politicians to listen to us. They just *have*
to do better!'

Considering the current occupants of Capitol Hill, there was
vast room for improvement.

Julie plunked her empty soda can down on a folding end
table. 'OK, you talked me into it. I'm coming to the march.
Where do I sign up?'

I shot a warning glance her way, but if Julie noticed, she
ignored it.

Nick and Mai exchanged glances, then Nick turned to Julie
and grinned. 'We're assembling at Judiciary Square at ten. The
first stop is the Government Accountability Office at 4th and G.'

Mai shot from her chair. 'I'll get you a printout,' and
disappeared into the RV.

'GAO?' I asked. 'The waste, fraud and abuse agency? What
does GAO have to do with Indian affairs?'

'That's where the Bureau of Land Management has their
offices.'

'Ah,' I said, thinking pipelines and fracking.

'Then we march down 7th Street to the FBI, and from there,
on to the White House. We'll end up at the park in front of the
Department of Interior, at 18th and E. That's where the Bureau
of Indian Affairs hangs out.'

I'd worked in Washington, DC for years and was familiar
with the route. 'That's a long walk,' I said. 'I hope the weather
cooperates.'

'According to Alexa this morning, it's supposed to be sunny.'

'Here's the information.' Mai was back.

She handed me two sheets of paper. One was a black and
white map of the parade route, the other a list of instructions:
*So You're Going to Join a Protest March: Health and Safety
Tips*. My eyes scanned the list. I'd need to have $100 in my
pocket, in case I was arrested, and leave my contact lenses at
home because of tear gas. Swell.

Maybe it was the ominous advice about writing the telephone
number of your lawyer on your arm in Magic Marker that made
me turn to Julie and say, 'Julie, you will absolutely have to ask
your parents for permission to do this.'

'Why? I'm eighteen.'

'But you're living at home,' I said reasonably. 'Unless you're planning to move out, they still get to call the shots.'

She scowled. 'Can I tell them you'll be coming with me?'

Mai and Nicholas stared at me expectantly.

I looked at Julie. Her face wore that obstinate you-know-I'm-going-to-do-it-anyway look I'd seen hundreds of times before on my own daughter Emily. Somebody had to watch out for the kid. 'How can I refuse?' I said.

SEVENTEEN

6:30 a.m. I had just begun to enjoy my first cup of coffee when Julie texted with a last-minute change of plans. Rather than driving herself down to Annapolis, she would be catching a Baltimore Light Rail train at Cold Spring Lane. Could I pick her up at the BWI airport station?

An hour and a half later, I cruised past the International Air Terminal and pulled into the 'no standing' zone in front of the light rail station, but the platform was practically empty. A uniformed guard scowled and waved me away, forcing me to exit the airport and circle around. When I pulled into the station again, I was relieved to see that the guard had moved on. As my car idled, I checked my iPhone to see if Julie had left a text message.

Someone rapped on my car window. Thinking it was the guard back to scold me for the second time, I dropped the phone onto the passenger seat, shifted into drive and prepared to pull away.

But it wasn't the guard. Julie's Baltimore Poly T-shirt filled the passenger side window. I popped the lock. She opened the door, tossed her book bag on the floor and slid into the passenger seat.

'What have you done to your hair?' I gasped, although the answer was perfectly obvious. Julie had dyed her hair flat, shoe-polish black and arranged it in a single braid, the end wrapped with a yellow and red woven band. No wonder I'd missed seeing her on the platform.

'I'm embracing my heritage,' she explained.

'But . . .' I began.

'My parents hate it, too,' Julie said, as if reading my mind. 'Dad had an absolute fit. That's why I'm car-less again.'

'Seatbelt,' I said, and waited until my niece was strapped in before driving away. 'It's not your best look.'

'It'll wash out,' she said. 'Eventually.'

'I always wanted red hair,' I confessed as I merged onto US 1 heading south toward DC. 'You and your mother seem to have cornered the red hair market in our family. You should show more respect for such a gift.'

Our older sister, Ruth, had been fair-haired as a girl but had gone prematurely white, courtesy (I always felt) of her first marriage to the womanizing Eric Gannon. My curls were the same mousy brown they'd always been, although these days streaked with more gray.

'So, who do you think your grandfather was?' Julie asked, wisely steering the conversation in another direction. 'If what Aunt Wasula told us is true, it has to be either White Bear or Hawk.'

'It certainly seems so,' I said. 'She may be one hundred and two, but memory-wise she's still playing with a full deck of cards.'

'I'm hoping it's White Bear,' Julie said. 'He seemed, I don't know, nicer? Always helping out at the clinic and stuff.'

'Your great-grandmother was very attractive,' I said. 'I'm not surprised he hung around.'

'Wasula believes that White Bear was murdered, doesn't she?'

'It certainly looks that way,' I said.

'Two juniors got suspended from Poly last year for fighting in the restroom,' Julie said. It seemed like a non sequitur until she added, 'One didn't like that the other was taking Maryanne Grayson to see *Despicable Me 3*. What anyone sees in that stuck-up little bitch is beyond me.'

I shot a scowl sideways.

'Tramp?' Julie amended.

'How about floozy,' I suggested with a grin. After a minute

I added, more soberly, 'You may be right. Lovers' triangles sometimes end in tragedy. Think about Julius Caesar, Marc Anthony and Cleopatra.'

'Or John Mayer, Taylor Swift and Katy Perry,' she said.

I had no idea who Julie was talking about: two generations separated by a common language.

By the time we pulled into the Greenbelt Metro parking lot (only two dollars all day Saturday!) Julie had concluded that White Bear and Charlotte had been romantically involved and someone had killed him in a jealous rage. Julie's alternate theory, in which Charlotte, the attractive visiting nurse, had been raped and gallant White Bear had had a confrontation over it, was put on the back-burner. 'Nobody wants to be the product of rape,' Julie said reasonably. 'So until evidence surfaces to the contrary, I'm going with the first story.'

'You read too many romance novels,' I teased as Julie and I headed for the ticket machines. 'Ever heard of Occam's Razor?'

Julie slotted a ten-dollar bill into the machine and topped up her SmarTrip card. 'Help me out, Aunt Hannah.'

'*Entia non sunt multiplicanda praeter necessitatem*,' I quoted. 'All things being equal, the simplest explanation is usually the correct one.'

'You mean White Bear's horse got spooked and trampled him to death?'

'It could have been that simple,' I said as we passed through the turnstiles.

From two steps above me on the escalator, Julie looked back and said, 'I like my theory better.'

My niece and I rode the Green Line into the city and got off at Gallery Place where we flowed in the direction of the escalator, joining an ever-increasing river of high-spirited, poster-carrying protesters. In such close quarters, I was thankful that Nick and Mai had volunteered to bring the protest signs. I had no idea what mine would say but prayed it wouldn't embarrass me if in the future I lost my mind and decided to run for political office.

Hoping to avoid the larger crowd that I knew would be assembling at the police memorial at Judiciary Square, I'd suggested we meet the Johnson family on the southwest corner

of 5th and F Streets. By the time we got there, however, the
crowd was already surging down F, heading for the memorial,
carrying us along like trees uprooted in a flash flood. 'Stay
close, Julie,' I said as we bobbed on tiptoe, like prairie dogs,
scanning the crowd for our new-found family.

'No worries.' Julie leaned against the wall of a fire station,
eased her cell phone out of her back pocket, woke it up and
tapped the Find My Friend app. 'Almost here,' she announced,
turning the screen so I could see the map. Nick's icon was
moving east along H Street, rapidly closing the distance
between us. 'They must have gotten off at Metro Center,' she
said, her thumbs darting about the keyboard as she sent her
cousin a text.

While being jostled right and left, Julie and I had a hard time
staying put, but eventually we spotted the real Nick rounding
the corner at 5th and G. Nick was skillfully steering the wheelchair with Wasula in it through the crowd which parted before
them like the Red Sea.

Julie waved both arms overhead and shouted, 'Over here!'

As he drew closer, Nick caught sight of her, his face puzzled.
'Don't ask,' Julie said, gently shoving him aside and taking
charge of Wasula's wheelchair. 'Yesterday I thought it was a
good idea.'

Mai giggled and linked her arm through Julie's. 'Whatever,'
she said. 'Dye or rinse?'

'Rinse,' Julie said. 'I wasn't *that* brave!'

'Shall we wait for your father?' I asked, thinking that Sam
had somehow gotten lost in the crowd.

'Worst luck.' Nick frowned. 'The air con in the RV's conked
out. He's waiting for the repairman. If it weren't so hot . . .'
His voice trailed off.

'C'mon, Nick!' his sister said.

Wasula, I noticed, was in charge of the picket signs, stowed
as they were in a bag hung over the back of her wheelchair.
She was dressed in the same outfit she'd been wearing when I
first met her but had swapped the cardigan for a multi-colored
shawl that matched the beaded circle earrings that dangled from
her ears. Wasula's green ball cap made me smile: MAKE
AMERICA NATIVE AGAIN.

Nick did the honors, handing me a handmade sign that said, 'INDIGENOUS RESISTANCE SINCE 1492.'

'I like it,' I said. 'Very much.'

'Dibs on this one!' Julie said, grabbing another of the signs he'd fanned out in front of him. She waved it in a few practice arcs over her head: TWEET NATIVE AMERICANS WITH RESPECT.

Carrying a sign that said, HONOR THE TREATIES, Mai charged ahead leading Julie, Wasula and the wheelchair. We followed close behind. Soon our family cluster became engulfed by a crowd that pitched and heaved, amoeba-like, along the entire length of the street between the General Accountability Office and the Pension Building.

At ten o'clock precisely, a Native American I took to be the leader of the demonstration mounted the steps in front of the soulless, block-like building and took charge. Dressed in a fringed white leather jacket and wearing a magnificent feathered headdress, he aimed a bullhorn at the protestors.

'Irresponsible decision . . .' the bullhorn spit and crackled. 'Future generations . . .'

'What's he saying?' I shouted into Julie's ear.

'Who knows?' she shouted back. 'Isn't this fun?'

'Suffer the consequences . . .' the spokesman continued. 'Risking natural resources . . .'

Wasula tugged on Nick's arm. 'Isn't anyone from the Corps of Engineers going to come out and speak to us?'

'It's Saturday, T'unwín-la. They're probably at home, grilling burgers in the back yard.'

'Cowards,' she muttered. 'We're here. They should be, too.'

'Who's the guy with the bullhorn?' I asked Nick.

'Spotted Dog,' he said, 'One of our sub-chiefs.'

'Water is life, water is life, water is life!' Spotted Dog chanted into the bullhorn.

As he no doubt intended, the protestors picked up the cry: 'Water is life, water is life, water is life!' as we followed Spotted Dog west, marching to the hypnotic beat of a half-dozen native drums and waving tribal flags and protest signs.

At 7th Street the exuberantly noisy crowd flowed south, heading for the crumbling J. Edgar Hoover Building where the

FBI still had its headquarters. I warned our group well away from the building, recently swathed in construction netting to keep chunks of it from falling on the heads of passersby.

A Native American girl I took to be around ten climbed up on one of the concrete planters and, borrowing a protest song from the early days of the civil rights movement, launched into 'We Shall Overcome' in a clear, high soprano. Several thousand voices strong, we joined in while continuing west on Pennsylvania Avenue. Spotted Dog stopped short in front of what used to be the old Post Office Building, now converted into the controversial Trump International Hotel.

The singing gradually died. Boos and catcalls ensued. No surprise. Donald J. Trump was the president who had signed an executive order, reversing an earlier Obama administration stay, that allowed construction of the Dakota Access Pipeline under Lake Oahe to resume. 500,000 barrels of crude oil per day now flowed under the reservation's main water supply.

'Too bad it's not dark,' I said. 'There's a renegade multimedia artist who sometimes shows up with a projector to beam messages over the entrance, like "Emoluments Welcome: Pay Bribes Here".'

Mai's eyes widened. 'Doesn't he get arrested?'

'I don't think the guy's breaking any laws,' I said. 'He's got the projector hooked up to his laptop on a rolling battery-powered cart, and he's not blocking the sidewalk or anything.'

'It's totally hysterical,' said Julie. 'Remember when Trump was calling Africa and Haiti shithole countries?'

Nick, who had been releasing the brake on his aunt's wheelchair preparing to move on, looked up with interest. 'Yeah?'

'The guy projected "This place is a shithole" over the door.'

Nick and Mai laughed.

I wasn't sure Wasula was following our conversation until she gave a big thumbs up.

As we marched up Pennsylvania Avenue in the direction of the White House, I took over wheelchair duties, while Nick, Mai and Julie ambled slightly ahead, their protest signs and three dark heads – Julie's dye job still had the ability to shock – bobbing along together. Every once in a while Nick would glance back, presumably to make sure he hadn't lost the geezers.

The heat was intense and it was only eleven o'clock. I was grateful for my hat, but my nose stung; I wore no sunscreen because, according to Mai's brochure, it would cause tear gas to stick to your skin.

At the street corner by the Willard Hotel, we were confronted by a band of anti-protesters, carrying signs: THE ONLY GOOD INDIAN IS A DEAD INDIAN and GO BACK TO THE REZ.

'I wondered how long it would take before the likes of them showed up,' Wasula grumbled.

The ragtag band – about ten in number – danced at the periphery of our march, just out of fist-fight range. The police presence, I noticed, had increased, too. Uniformed officers – DC Metro by their insignia – lined both sides of the street. As we spilled into Lafayette Square Park, those officers were supplemented by US Park Police, some wearing green Day-Glo vests over their summer uniforms.

Even before the terrorist attacks of 9/11, cars had been banned from the block in front of 1600 Pennsylvania Avenue – heavy, steel crowd-control barricades and strategically-placed concrete bollards made sure of that. I was busy positioning Wasula next to one of the bollards and as far as possible from a row of ripening porta-potties, when the anti-protestors made their move. Whooping like back lot Indians in a Grade B western, they began to taunt the marchers by twirling 'scalps' in the air. One of the scalps – a long, blond fright wig no doubt dug out of a Halloween costume box – brushed Julie's face. Julie started, touched her cheek in surprise, then lunged in the jerk's direction.

I gasped. Before I could let go of the wheelchair and sprint after her, Nick grabbed Julie from behind by both arms and drew her back out of harm's way.

As the youngsters rejoined us, I mouthed a silent thank you. At least someone in this crazy family group was level-headed.

'Is the president in residence?' Mai asked, shouting over the counterfeit war cries intensifying behind us.

'It's Saturday,' her brother snorted. 'What do you think?'

A woman standing next to Nick and holding a miniature helium-filled Trump Baby balloon by a string had apparently overheard. 'He's at one of his goddamn golf clubs, don't you think? Attending to urgent business.'

'Hah!' Wasula muttered.

Soon, the anti-protestors' taunts were drowned out by native drums and rhythmic chanting as half a dozen Lakota teens, dressed in shirts and trousers decorated, not with feathers, but fringe, began swaying from side to side in time to the beat.

'Grass dance,' Wasula explained.

'It celebrates our relationship with Mother Earth,' Mai added.

The anti-protesters were still whooping it up, but they were soon outnumbered by a group of Japanese tourists, iPhones held aloft to capture the dancers or fastened at the end of selfie sticks in order to put themselves in the scene.

'God, it's hot,' Mai said. 'You'd think Mother Earth could send us a breeze.'

'Water?' I dug a few bottles out of the compact cooler stowed under Wasula's wheelchair and offered them around.

I untied the lightweight jacket I hadn't needed from around my waist, spread it out on the warm pavement and sat down, cross-legged, to sip my water. Protected by Wasula on one side and a wall of marchers on the other, I closed my eyes, hypnotized by the warmth of the sun and the rhythmic pulsing of the drums.

I was dozing, blissed-out, when a familiar chant muscled its way in, so out of place that my eyes flew open. 'Hell no, we won't go!' it began, transporting me instantly back to my Oberlin days and to campus demonstrations against the war in Vietnam.

'Hell no, we won't go!' echoed down the corridor of years. 'Hell no, we won't go!'

We'd made life hell for the Army recruiters visiting campus. In the excitement of that moment, I'd helped overturn one of their cars. With the guy still in it.

But, why were they chanting it here, and now?

Sweat dripped down my neck and trickled between my breasts. I took a generous swig of water, shook my head in an attempt to clear my vision. Wasula's wheelchair was gone.

I struggled to my feet and looked around. I seemed to have lost my family. The crowd roared and surged forward, moving closer to the iron fence that separated us from the White House grounds.

'Hell no, we won't go!'

Sirens pierced the air. An ambulance, I wondered? Had someone been injured?

More sirens. The Park Police who had been standing off, closed in, wearing helmets and carrying batons.

'What's happening?' I asked the woman holding the Trump Baby balloon.

'They're ordering us to disperse!' she shouted.

Two policemen appeared in front of us. 'Move along, now,' one of them said. 'Time to go.'

Move along? Our next stop, according to Nick, was the US Department of the Interior, just two blocks further west. I aimed myself in that direction and, to my great relief, caught sight of Julie less than ten feet ahead, walking backwards, waving her arms to attract my attention.

'Here,' the balloon lady said, thrusting her arm in my direction. 'Hold this for me a minute, would you, while I text my husband?'

I grabbed the string and followed after Julie with Trump Baby bobbing over my head.

'MAGA, MAGA, MAGA,' somebody hissed in my ear. I turned to see who it was. A gap-toothed anti-protestor wearing a red *Make America Great Again* ball cap had infiltrated our ranks. He snarled and made a grab for the balloon. Instinctively, I jerked my arm away and watched in dismay as Trump Baby floated off, drifting over the bronze, outstretched arm of Major General Comte Jean de Rochambeau.

'Sonofabitch!' Balloon Lady yelled, looking directly at me. 'I paid twelve bucks for that!'

I shrugged and pointed an I'm-not-guilty finger at Mr Make America Great Again who was doubled over, laughing like a demented hyena. Balloon Lady got the picture immediately. She balled up her fist and let the guy have it.

'Bitch!' he yelled, clutching his upper arm.

She grabbed his MAGA cap by the bill, cocked her arm and sent the hat sailing, like a Frisbee, into the park. 'Now we're even!'

He lunged, sandwiching me between them as they flailed away. I dropped to my knees in self-defense, covering my head with my arms. A boot missed its intended mark and landed hard against my thigh. I'd have a world-class bruise there in the morning.

Seconds later, when I dared to look up, I was relieved to see a Park Police officer looming over me. Before I could thank her for breaking up the fight, she said, 'Stand up. You're under arrest. You have the right . . .'

As she rattled off the familiar litany, I glanced around in bewilderment. Balloon Lady and Mr MAGA Hat had vanished.

'But . . .' I started to protest, but then wisely clammed up.

Rules, remember the rules. *Don't argue with the police*, we'd been instructed. *Do exactly as you are told.*

'Yes, ma'am,' I said as I staggered to my feet, rubbing the sore spot on my thigh. 'May I ask with what I'm being charged?'

My impeccable grammar didn't impress her in the least. 'Failure to obey,' she grumped as she secured my hands behind my back with plastic zip-tie cuffs. With a gentle but firm hand grasping my upper arm, she began to lead me away.

Piercing in its urgency over the roar of the crowd was Julie's voice, 'Hey! Hey! Where are you taking her?'

EIGHTEEN

'Where' turned out to be a white police minibus parked on 15th Street near the Willard Hotel. The arresting officer escorted me to the door and after the driver opened up, waited until I climbed inside. 'Sit anywhere,' she said rather pleasantly.

I slid into a window seat behind the driver and struggled to get comfortable, an impossible task with hands tied behind your back. Meanwhile, my cell phone vibrated frantically in my back pocket. When I didn't answer after three attempts, it began to ping. Once I got my hands on it again, I knew I'd find a zillion frantic text messages from Julie.

I rested my head against the window and closed my eyes. I could still hear the distant chanting and the drums as the protestors moved on without me. Where were Julie, Nick, Mai and Wasula now?

When I opened my eyes again, the minibus – which I estimated could accommodate sixteen people – was nearly full. I was impressed with my fellow passengers – seven women and five men, so far – a veritable United Nations of gender, race and ethnic diversity that, unlike a great many things these days, made me proud to be an American.

Moments before the door was shut and secured, a fair-skinned woman, her dark blond dreadlocks semi-contained by a bandana, plopped down in the seat next to me.

'Hey,' she said.

'Where are they taking us?' I whispered.

She grinned. 'First time?'

Not counting the terrifying weekend I once spent in Baltimore as a guest of the US Marshalls, I said, 'Yes.'

The woman, who I took to be in her mid-thirties, twisted in her seat. Her lips moved in what I guessed was a silent head count. When she turned back around she said, 'Good thing we're fourteen.'

'Why's that?'

'If it was just you and me, less than ten or eleven anyway, they'd take us to the Central Cell Block for processing.' I felt her shiver. 'That hellhole ought to be on the black list of Amnesty International.'

'Good to know,' I said. 'I'm Hannah, by the way.'

'Katherine Emily Tuckerman hyphen Dutton,' she said, 'but you can call me Kit.'

Kit's last name rang a bell. 'Tuckerman-Dutton, as in Tuckerman-Dutton Development Corporation?'

'My grandfather,' she said.

Tuckerman-Dutton had been responsible for the revitalization of countless Baltimore neighborhoods following the deadly race riots of 1968. I whistled softly. 'I'm impressed.'

Kit shrugged a richly-tattooed shoulder. 'I'm somewhat of a disappointment to my family, as you probably guessed.'

'So, where *are* we going?' I asked after a bit.

'It's the DC police motor pool. A big parking garage, anyway. Down in southwest.'

'You sound like you've done this before?'

She nodded. 'Three times, maybe four.'

'So, why should I be glad I'm not going to get intimately familiar with the inside of the Central District Cell Block?' I asked.

'Ever been to the pound?' Kit asked.

'Stray dogs, you mean?'

'Like that. Stainless steel cages, inside and out, so you can hose them out, I suppose. Can in the middle . . .'

'Can?' I cut in.

'Toilet.'

'Ah.'

'Last time I had to stay overnight. Didn't sleep a wink. Spent the whole night stomping roaches.'

Now it was my turn to shiver. 'Gross.'

'Tell me about it! And the bologna sandwiches . . .' She imitated a cat coughing up a hairball.

I had to laugh.

Twenty minutes later I was relieved to see that Kit had been correct about our destination. According to the street signs I read through my window, we were somewhere in southwest DC – K and Half Streets, SW, I would learn later, at the Capitol Police's Vehicle Maintenance facility, directly across the street from DC's Motor Vehicle Inspection Station.

The minibus idled for several minutes on Half Street waiting for an intimidating black garage door to roll up. Once the bus was safely secured inside the building, we were invited to disembark. Still handicapped by handcuffs, we followed one of the officers, like obedient ducklings, into a large, empty room where we were ordered to line up against a stark white wall.

Despite Kit's nonchalance, I began to hyperventilate. Breathe in, Hannah. Breathe out. In . . . and . . . out.

'Feels like a firing squad, doesn't it?' Kit quipped.

I exhaled, shook the tension out of my shoulders and said, 'Maybe the white paint makes it easier to clean the blood off the walls?'

'Ha!' Kit said. Then quickly added, 'It usually doesn't take too long, unless somebody's cranky.'

After cooling our heels for ten minutes or so, I was beginning to worry that Captain McCrankypants was definitely in charge when two officers showed up to relieve us of our handcuffs.

Shortly thereafter, a woman in uniform appeared, identified herself as Sergeant Susan Wilson and read aloud from a laminated card. We were, all of us, being charged under 18DCMR 2000.2 with Failure to Obey a Lawful Order, a misdemeanor. Apparently we hadn't moved along quickly enough when ordered to do so by the police.

I wanted to wave my hand and shout, not guilty! If a lawful order had been given, I surely hadn't heard it, but then I'd been caught in the middle of a feral squabble over a Trump Baby balloon and a MAGA hat and hadn't been paying proper attention. Recently uploaded YouTube videos with Japanese subtitles might even acquit me in a court of law.

'You will be booked, fingerprinted, photographed and searched,' Sergeant Wilson continued.

I sucked in breath, let it out slowly. Not for the first time, I flashed back to the nightmare of being arrested by the FBI for the murder of Jennifer Goodall. The charges had been dismissed, of course, but yet I worried. Were my fingerprints still in the database? When they fingerprinted me here today, would lights flash and an alarm whoop-whoop-whoop until burly, grim-faced officers charged in to cart me away?

When I tuned in again, Sergeant Wilson was explaining how I could end my case immediately – hallelujah! – by paying a $100 fine. Should I decide to take the 'Post and Forfeit' option, she said, in two years' time if I kept my nose clean, the arrest would be sealed.

'If you want to go to court . . .' Wilson continued.

I glanced sideways at Kit, who frowned and shook her head.

I relaxed, grateful for the advice. My lawyer's phone number was inked on my forearm, but I was glad I wouldn't have to use it. Murray had already earned enough gray hairs – and money – on my account.

'Why go to the trouble of arresting us in the first place?'

I whispered to Kit after Sergeant Wilson finished addressing the troops.

'Gets us off the street, I guess, not to mention lining the government's pockets with cash.' She waved an arm, taking us all in. 'This sting is worth thirteen-hundred dollars. Imagine how much they netted after the march against the Trump administration's immigration policy.'

I'd followed that particular protest with interest. According to the *Washington Post*, over five hundred protestors had been arrested that day. I did the math. 'I see what you mean,' I said. 'Enough to buy a new police cruiser, you think?'

Kit nodded, her dreadlocks bobbing. 'Post and forfeit. It's the only way to go.'

Take my advice: always listen to a pro.

A massive bit of paperwork and two crisp fifty-dollar bills later, I was released to the corner of Half Street and K with only vague instructions on how to find my own way home to Annapolis.

Although I certainly hadn't planned it that way, according to Google Maps, I was only six blocks from the Navy Yard-Ballpark Metro station on the Green Line. If I caught the Metro, it would take about thirty-five minutes to be reunited with my Volvo.

But first, I'd need to check in with Julie.

I began scrolling through her messages:

OMG! Where are you? They won't tell us ANYTHING!!

Who do you want me to call? I won't call anyone UNLESS YOU TELL ME TO!

Don't worry, it's OK. I'm going home with Nick and Mai!

I sighed with relief and had started to text back, 'Stay put. I'll pick you up soon,' when the phone began to ring. 'Julie?' I said.

'Not Julie. It's Nick. Where are you?'

'I'll explain when I see you, but the short story is I paid a fine and the police let me go. I should be able to pick up Julie in about an hour.'

'Didn't she text you? Julie's not here.'

I swallowed my rising panic. 'But Julie said . . .'

'Oh, she *was* here,' Nick said, 'but she got an upsetting call from her mother, so we put her in an Uber and sent her home.'

'Upsetting? In what way upsetting?'

'She seemed worried, is all. And since we didn't know how long you'd be in police custody, we thought it best to get her home.'

'Thank you, Nick. That was exactly the right call. How much do I owe you for the Uber? That ride must have been expensive.'

'Forget about it,' he said. 'Are you sure you're OK?'

Was I? Loitering on a street corner, in an unfamiliar light-industrial neighborhood, in southwest DC, across from a vehicle inspection station and a post office? 'The Metro's nearby,' I reassured him. 'I'm heading there now.'

'Call us if you need anything,' Nick said, sounding sincere.

'How much longer will you be in town?' I asked. 'I'm hoping to introduce you to more of the family.'

'A while. Until we get the air-con fixed, anyway. We'll stay in touch, right?'

'You can count on it, Nick.'

NINETEEN

At first, I thought I'd reached a wrong number. All I heard was heavy breathing.'

'Julie?'

Her response was breathless, garbled.

'Slow down, Julie. I can't understand a word you're saying.'

Julie gulped. 'Dad didn't come home last night!'

Last night seemed an entire lifetime ago. 'I'm sorry, but I'm confused. I thought you said you saw him this morning.'

'No,' Julie whimpered. 'I left home around seven. Dad was still asleep, or so I thought.'

'What does your mother have to say? Surely she would have missed your father before this morning.'

'Colin was being a little asshole yesterday.' Julie sniffed, her voice steadied.

I was about to ask what Colin's behavior had to do with Scott going missing, when Julie continued, 'He bought a thousand dollars' worth of virtual coins on TikTok. Said it was by accident. Mom called to get the money refunded, and Apple was being shitty about it. He is sooo grounded.'

Confiscating Colin's cell phone would be one solution, I thought, and docking his allowance, maybe forever, but it didn't seem like a good time to offer pro tips on parenting. 'Yikes,' I said.

'Mom ended up with a migraine,' Julie rattled on breathlessly. 'She took some Imitrex and crashed early, so I made chicken fingers for dinner.'

Georgina had been plagued by migraines since her late teens. For the past several years she'd been seeing a chronic migraine specialist. Medication and a diet regime had dramatically reduced the number and frequency of her headaches, but the pills, I knew, could knock Georgina out cold. Zoned out on Imitrex, she could sleep through the Zombie Apocalypse.

'When was the last time anyone saw your father, Julie?'

'Mom saw him just before noon yesterday. He had a lunch meeting or something. When he wasn't home by two, she figured the meeting ran over, so she didn't actually miss him until she got up this morning.'

'Can I talk to your mom?'

'She's pretty fuzzy. You know how she gets on the pills.'

'Have you tried calling your dad's cell phone?'

'Of course I did, Aunt Hannah! And it goes straight to voicemail.'

Scott worked from home, in an office carved out of a space in their former attic. If he had a lunch meeting it could have been just about anywhere. 'Did you check his desk calendar?'

'He keeps it on his cell phone,' Julie said.

Of course he did, I thought. The phone that was missing.

'Can you help me, Aunt Hannah? Mom's a mess.'

'I'll be there as soon as I can,' I promised. 'But where are your brothers?'

'At Cape May for a week. One of their friend's parents has a condo on the beach.'

'You need to call them, Julie.'

'Mom won't let me. She says it might be a false alarm. School starts soon and she doesn't want to wreck their vacation. If he's not home by tomorrow . . .' Her voice trailed off.

I sighed. Dealing with Georgina could be exhausting, and not something easily accomplished over the telephone.

'I'll be there as soon as I can,' I repeated.

'I love you,' Julie said, and ended the call.

I made a snap decision: the hell with the Metro. I tapped the Uber app, requested a car then watched the screen as the icon representing Tamara in a Red Ford Taurus inched along Maine Avenue, heading in my direction. While waiting, I called Paul and told him what I was doing. I didn't mention my arrest. That would need to be a steak dinner, home fries and bottle of fine, red wine discussion sometime in the future.

Twenty-two minutes, twenty-seven dollars and a three-dollar tip later, Tamara reunited me with my car in Greenbelt.

In Baltimore, Julie greeted me at her front door, her eyelids red and puffy. She wrapped her arms around me, squeezed tight, and buried her face in the crook of my neck. 'Thank God you're here.'

I reached up to smooth her hair, her ridiculous hair, with my hand. 'Where's your mom?'

'In the kitchen,' Julie said. 'She's telephoning hospitals.'

'Has she called the police?'

Julie nodded. 'She actually went to the station on West Cold Spring. They told her to file a missing persons' report, but when she saw a copy, she freaked.' She lowered her voice. 'They want a description and a picture, you'd expect that, but they also want the name of his dentist.'

I shivered. 'That would freak me out, too.'

'So she's phoning hospitals instead.'

'Let me handle your mother,' I told her. 'Where can I find you later?'

'I'm supposed to be in the basement doing laundry,' she said.

'As good a place as any,' I said. 'Off you go.'

I found my sister perched on a stool at her kitchen counter, a printout lying open in front of her, a cell phone pressed to her ear. 'Well, thanks for checking,' she was saying as I walked in.

'Georgina,' I said.

She glanced up, flicked the pages. 'Do you have any idea how many hospitals there are in Baltimore? I'm only halfway there.'

I crossed the room and wrapped her in a hug. Her body sagged, and she began to sob. 'What could have happened to him?'

I let her cry for a bit, then offered her a paper towel, soaked in cool water and squeezed out. She pressed it to her eyes.

'Has Scott ever . . .' I began, weighing my words carefully. 'Has he ever stayed out all night before?'

'Gosh, no, Hannah. I get where you're going though.' She blew her nose on the towel, then looked up at me. 'But you don't have to stay somewhere overnight to, you know, have an affair.'

Something in my sister's voice made me ask, 'Do you think Scott was cheating on you?'

'I honestly don't know. It's just that he spends a lot of time at the church, and when I ask him about it, he claims he's working on the books.'

'But, he's church treasurer, right? So that makes perfect sense.'

Her green eyes flashed. 'Well, it didn't used to take up so much of his time.'

Filling out the personal income tax forms for the Ives family didn't used to take so much time either, I thought. It's just that our finances, and the tax laws, had grown more complicated over the years.

'Church of the Falls membership has doubled, hasn't it?' I reasoned aloud. 'I imagine Scott's workload has doubled right along with it,' I added, surprising myself by making excuses for Scott.

Georgina's mouth formed an obstinate line. I could tell she wasn't buying that argument. 'His wallet's gone, and so are his car keys, but the car is still in the driveway.'

'Maybe his lunch date picked him up?'

'Colin had a dental appointment yesterday morning, then I took him to Pepe's for pizza. When I came back, Scott had already left for lunch and he'd taken the car. He was meeting somebody at the church, that's all I know.'

'If the car's in the driveway now,' I said reasonably, 'then he must have returned at some point.'

'Well, somebody brought it back.'

Grown men had been known to run away from home before, I thought. Go out for a carton of cigarettes and ten years later they're found living in Arizona with a new wife and two adorable kids. But no matter how many ways I looked at it, Scott didn't seem like the deserting type. He'd stuck with Georgina through some tough times, back when the children were young and she'd come completely unglued. I couldn't see him walking out on her now.

'What about his cell phone?' I asked gently.

'It goes straight to voicemail,' she said. 'He must have it with him, because it's not in the house. I've looked everywhere.'

'Have you tried using Find My iPhone?'

Georgina's eyes widened. 'You can do that?'

'If Scott set it up that way.'

Georgina's face clouded. 'Well, he changed all his passwords after that incident with Little Miss Smarty Pants, so now, because of Julie, I guess we're screwed.'

Knowing my clever niece, I wasn't so sure about that. I walked over to the basement door, opened it and yelled down. 'Julie, can you come up here a minute?'

When her head appeared at the top of the stairs, I asked, 'Do you have access to your father's computer?'

Julie scowled. 'I can't believe you're asking me that, Aunt Hannah. No. He changed his passwords.'

I slumped. 'I was hoping he'd set up Find My iPhone.'

Julie's face brightened. 'Wait a minute!'

Without another word, she bolted through the kitchen, slamming the basement door behind her. I could hear her clump-clump-clumping up the stairs that led to the second floor, followed by a moment of silence, then more clump-clumping up the next flight of stairs to her father's office.

A minute later she reappeared, brandishing an iPad. 'Tah dah!'

Julie pulled out a stool and sat down at the kitchen island next to her mother. 'Dad fixed his computer, Mom, but maybe he forgot about his iPad. He hardly ever uses it.' She opened the black leather case. After several seconds she said, 'Damn! Battery's dead. Where's the charger?'

Georgina pointed to the kitchen counter. Julie hopped off her stool and plugged the device into a cord dangling from an outlet it shared with the toaster. For what seemed like hours, with the clock tick-tick-ticking overhead, we waited for Scott's iPad to revive.

'It's got fingerprint ID,' Julie said when the login screen finally materialized, 'but you can use the access code, too.' She tapped a few numbers, shook her head, backspaced and tried again.

'We're in!' Julie beamed at her mother. 'He's using your anniversary date, Mom.' To me, she confided softly, 'One of his faves.'

Georgina smiled, but blinked back tears.

I watched over Julie's shoulder as the screen refreshed and populated itself with Scott's personal icons. Julie swiped sideways, located the Find My iPhone app – a green radar screen icon – on the third swipe. She tapped the icon, and a map appeared with symbols for each of her father's devices on it: the iMac, the iPad and the iPhone.

Julie turned to her mother, eyes wide. 'Jeesh! His phone's in the backyard, Mom.'

Georgina shot from her chair, heading for the kitchen door.

'Stop!' I caught up with her and grabbed her arm, guiding her gently back to the stool. 'Was Scott working in the yard yesterday, Georgina?'

'He mentioned he might finish clipping the hedge I started, but from the looks of it, he never got around to it.'

'I'll go look for the phone,' Julie said.

'No!' Georgina shouted.

'But . . .'

'Don't argue with me, young lady!'

'I'll go,' I said. I extended my hand, palm up. Julie got the message and handed Scott's iPad over.

'I'm coming with you,' Georgina said.

'Are you sure, Georgina? What if he's . . .'

'Don't you even think that, Hannah.' And with a freezing sit-stay look at Julie, she shot out the door with me following, carrying the iPad.

TWENTY

Once we'd stepped off the flagstone patio, the neatly-manicured Cardinale lawn sloped gently down to the alley that separated the Colorado Avenue backyards from the backyards of the houses on Deepdene. The hedge Georgina had been tending was on the left – scraggly tendrils indicated where she'd left off – and a trampoline popular with the boys sat at the head of the driveway on the right.

Scott's cell phone signal seemed to be emanating from a shed in the back left corner of the yard, one that Paul had helped Scott assemble from a prefab kit purchased at Home Depot. The shed was approximately eight by twelve feet, in a classic farmhouse style, and the door was secured with a keypad combination lock.

Georgina cupped her hands around her eyes and peered into one of the windows that flanked the door. 'I can't see anything.'

'We'll need to go inside, Georgina.'

She turned a worried face in my direction. 'I'm afraid to look.'

'Scott could simply have left his phone in the shed.' I didn't sound convincing, even to myself. I considered the lock, suddenly filled with dread. 'Do you know the combination?'

Georgina nodded, punched in the code, pushed down on the handle and pulled the door open. I reached out to hold her back, but she was too quick for me. She stepped into the shed, froze, and started to scream.

My brother-in-law lay sprawled on the concrete floor, his head resting on a bag of mulch that had been slashed open, spilling its contents.

Before I could stop her, Georgina rushed to her husband's side and knelt in a pile of rich, dark soil.

'Don't touch anything!' I yelled, hoping she could hear me over her own anguished cries.

It was obvious from all the blood and Scott's open, sightless eyes that there was nothing we could do to help him now. I fell to my knees next to my sister and wrapped her in an embrace while she shook with sobs.

'He's dead, isn't he? Isn't he, Hannah? Who . . .?'

I didn't know the who but the how seemed clear. The garden shears I'd seen Georgina working with earlier in the week had been discarded nearby, their blades darkly stained with a substance that had to be blood, and Scott's head . . . I closed my eyes for a moment, swallowing the bile that rose in my throat.

Gathering courage, I felt Scott's neck, hoping for a pulse, but there was none. His skin was cold.

'We need to call the police,' I said, all the while urging my sister to her feet.

'I can't, I can't just leave him alone,' she stammered.

'There's nothing you can do for him, sweetie. C'mon. The sooner the police get here, the sooner they'll find whoever did this to Scott. Our being here will just make their job more difficult.'

I guided my sister reluctantly, step by agonizing step, back across the lawn and into the kitchen.

Julie, obedient for once, still sat on her stool, texting with someone on her iPhone. When she caught sight of our faces, hers crumpled. 'Did you . . .? What? He's . . .'

I reached out my hand. 'I'll need your phone, Julie. Take care of your mother.'

While Julie comforted her mother, I used her phone to dial 9-1-1. 'There's been an accident,' I told the dispatcher. 'I'm afraid he's dead.'

When the paramedics arrived just five minutes later, all three of us were bawling.

TWENTY-ONE

t's wicked to say so, but it's the honest truth. I will not miss Scott.

In the twenty-five years he'd been married to my sister, I could count on the fingers of one hand the number of times we'd actually agreed on anything, other than our mutual fondness for rum raisin ice cream. I had to be there for my little sister, though. Her tortured face, red eyes and swollen lids still haunt my dreams.

Two days after Scott's murder, I let myself in through her mudroom door, set the casserole I was carrying down on the cluttered counter, and wandered into the living room where I found Georgina propped up with pillows on the sofa, staring at the television.

Georgina's hair was swept up and clipped into place with a black, rhinestone-studded claw. Soft tendrils damply framed her face. She wore black slacks and a black scoop-neck pullover. A gold and ruby cross hung from a chain around her neck, resting lightly in her cleavage. I have to say this about my sister: she looked stunning in widow's weeds.

'What are you watching?' I asked, for want of anything cleverer to say.

Georgina picked up the remote and aimed. The TV screen went dark. 'Something on the Nature Channel. Meercats, with cameras strapped to their necks. They're ridiculously cute. I'm trying to cheer myself up.'

I sat down on the sofa next to her. 'What can I do to help?'

The question resulted in an avalanche of fresh tears. I watched in respectful silence as her mascara bled into black smudges under her eyes and left telltale trails down her cheeks.

'I'm sorry, sis,' I said after a bit. 'I didn't intend to upset you.'

She snatched another tissue from a box next to her on the end table, used it to dab at her eyes, then crumpled it up. It joined a heap of used tissues on the carpet next to her feet. She flapped a hand. 'It's OK, really. It comes and goes.' She pressed her palms flat against her knees, took a deep, shuddery breath, then let it out slowly. 'There's just too much to do. I'm overwhelmed.'

'Where are the kids?' I asked.

'Julie's taken Colin to the movies and Dylan . . . Dylan, he's . . .' She grabbed another tissue. 'Dylan's at the funeral home.'

'What about Sean?' I asked after a few seconds had passed and there was no sign of fresh tears.

'Sean's meeting with the lawyers. I can't deal with the financial stuff, Hannah. Stocks, bonds, investment accounts, I'm clueless. Sean's like his dad. A good head for figures.'

After a moment she said, 'I don't know what to do, Hannah! The police took Scott's computer, so we don't have access to any of his important accounts.'

'Maybe Julie . . .' I began.

'Absolutely not!' She stood up so suddenly that it surprised me. 'That little miss has overstepped her bounds, big time.' Her eyes narrowed. 'I thought you'd have a moderating influence on her, Hannah. I didn't expect you to aid and abet.'

It was second nature to object, but I kept my mouth shut. Georgina was speaking the truth.

'Can I get you anything? Coffee, tea . . . sherry?' she asked cheerfully, as if her stinging reprimand had never happened.

'No thanks, I have to drive home, but don't let me stop you.'

I trailed after my sister into the dining room where she poured herself a generous tot of dark liquid from one of the bottles she kept on a silver tray on the buffet. 'Gonzalez Byass Sherry Polo Cortado Anada 1987,' she recited, toasting me with her glass. 'A gift from one of Scott's clients. Only 987 bottles produced.'

I grinned. 'Finest kind.'

'Scott was appreciated by his clients.' She carried the glass to the kitchen, wobbling a bit unsteadily, even in her low-heeled sandals. I suspected this wasn't her first sherry of the day.

'Are there any plans for the funeral?' I asked.

'Plans? Plans?' Georgina shouted. 'Of course I don't have any funeral plans! Nobody expected Scott to die!'

I tried again. 'I just want to help, Georgina!'

Georgina shrugged and sipped her sherry. After a moment she said, 'I'm leaving the funeral up to Dylan. He can slug it out with the church.'

'Slug?' I said.

'Let's just say that the meeting I had with Brother Bob yesterday didn't go well.'

Although I was dying for details, I knew from past experience that now was not the time to press her. 'Why don't I start by putting some of these casseroles in the freezer?' I suggested instead.

'Suit yourself,' she snapped.

I was losing patience. 'I didn't drive all the way up here from Annapolis to have my head bitten off, Georgina.'

'I'm sorry,' she said, sounding genuinely contrite. '"Take a pill, Georgina!" That's what Scott would say.' She turned her back on me and stared out the kitchen window.

I steeled myself. 'Did Scott have a will?'

'What?' She hadn't even been listening.

'A will, Georgina. Did Scott leave a will?'

'Yes,' she said, much more calmly. Maybe the sherry was doing its job. 'We both did. Remember? When I asked if you and Paul would take care of the children if anything happened to us?'

'Of course I do. I just wasn't sure you'd gone forward with it.'

Georgina slid onto a kitchen stool and took another sip of her sherry. 'Oh, yeah. Signed, sealed, advance directive and all that shit. Scott was very thorough.'

At least my brother-in-law hadn't died intestate. What a mess that would have been.

'I feel like I'm living somebody else's life,' Georgina said after a bit. 'Why would anybody want to kill Scott, Hannah?'

'I don't know,' I replied, 'but once the police figure out the why, I'm sure they will quickly get to the who, or vice versa. We'll just have to wait for them to finish their investigation.'

'Hah! What's the Baltimore solve rate? Fifty percent?'

Most of those victims, I knew from reading the *Baltimore Sun*, had been young, male and black; the solve rate for white victims was much higher. But, I knew better than to argue with her. The police had taken Scott's computer and business records,

Georgina had said, so they must be working on the theory that the crime was related to his business, or maybe his crazy club, or maybe both. Scott had been a social guy. There could be a lot of crossover.

Georgina set the wine glass down. It was empty. 'Besides, they're way too busy questioning Julie,' she said.

'But they questioned you and all your children, didn't they?'

'Two times,' Georgina said. She pinged her wine glass with a flick of her fingernail. 'Dear me. It seems to have sprung a leak.'

The police had questioned Julie twice? That was news to me. Then again, of all the Cardinales, Julie's alibi had been the shakiest. The medical examiner estimated that Scott had died on Friday afternoon between two and four o'clock. After his dental appointment, Colin had been back in school, Georgina zonked out on Imitrex, the twins hanging out at the ocean with six friends and a keg, while Julie was home alone. The fact that she'd recently clashed with her father was an open secret, yet I found it impossible to believe that she had bludgeoned her father to death in the afternoon, then calmly cooked up chicken nuggets for her little brother at dinner time.

'Did Scott have any enemies?' I asked, sounding, even to myself, like a standard issue television detective.

Georgina rolled her eyes. 'Are you kidding? Everybody loved Scott. You saw all the cards, flowers, food.' She swept her arm around the kitchen. Her expansive granite countertop was littered with baking dishes, aluminum foil pans and Tupperware canisters, including the blue and white Corning Ware dish that held my own famous turkey tetrazzini. I wondered why I had bothered. It was like carting sand to the beach.

'I don't know what I'm going to do with it all,' Georgina whined. She wrapped a hand around her wine glass and struggled to her feet.

I plopped a bag of somebody's homemade dinner rolls on top of my turkey tetrazzini and headed for the basement door. 'Deep freezing things before they spoil would be a good start.'

'Go for it,' she slurred, and disappeared into the dining room with her wine glass.

TWENTY-TWO

'm ashamed to admit that the first time I set foot in my sister's church, it was to attend Scott Cardinale's funeral. A lifelong Episcopalian, I preferred small parish churches like St. Catherine's in West Annapolis where my longtime friend, Eva Haberman, served as pastor.

Nothing prepared me for the Church of the Falls, an ultra-modern megalith that sprawled over a forty-acre site just north of the Baltimore beltway. Its spire, a twisted aluminum needle several hundred feet tall, seemed to pierce the sky.

'Jeesh,' said my sister, Ruth, sitting next to me in the back seat. 'It's even bigger than it looks on TV.'

Hutch glanced at his wife's reflection in the rear-view mirror. 'This guy's on TV? Like the "Hour of Power" or something?'

'Not that I know of,' Ruth said. 'I saw a show on PBS about the architect, some Swedish guy with lots of diacritical marks in his name. He's famous.'

I dipped my head, trying to get a better view of the spire out of the car window. 'So famous you forgot who he was?'

Ruth laughed. 'I remember he had a mustache and wore funny-looking square eyeglasses.'

'With a steeple like that,' Paul commented, 'they could broadcast Sunday services to Mars.'

'Maybe that's the plan,' I said.

Hutch steered his BMW off Padonia Road and into a paved lot the size of the satellite parking lot at BWI airport. An elderly gentleman carrying a clipboard and wearing an orange vest and matching ball cap greeted us at the entrance that was controlled by a turnstile sitting in the up position. The funeral home had provided us with a numbered card for our dashboard that said 'Family'. The attendant squinted at the permit, made a checkmark on his clipboard, then directed us to a parking place in a row of spaces marked *Reserved* nearest the sanctuary. 'Sorry for your loss,' he said, almost as an afterthought.

'What flavor is this church?' Hutch wanted to know as we joined a line of mourners in the antiseptic foyer, waiting our turn to file into the sanctuary.

'Evangelical,' I whispered. 'Where any liturgical tendencies come to die of neglect.'

Paul's elbow found my ribs. 'Shhhh.'

'Scott must have been popular,' Ruth mused as we accepted our programs from a young woman dressed entirely in white. Another young woman, identically clad, led us down the center aisle to our seats, our footsteps muffled by the dense blue carpet. With its raked, theater-style seating and overhanging balconies, I estimated the church could seat around a thousand. It was already half full.

Georgina and her children were seated in the left front row. Her glorious Titian hair hung long and loose, as I knew it would, 'the way Scott liked it'. Julie's stark black tresses, pulled back in a high, sleek ponytail, stood in sharp contrast to her mother's and the sandy, Scott-like heads of his three sons.

While the usher waited respectfully, we hugged our family one by one, shedding fresh tears, then slipped into our assigned seats in the row directly behind. A few minutes later, just as a female vocalist launched into a cringe-worthy rendition of something, as best I could determine, entitled 'I Will Rise', Emily, Dante and our three grandchildren arrived to occupy the seats just behind us.

Once at a family dinner, Georgina had given me an earful about music at Church of the Falls. It's fair to say that Georgina, a former church organist at All Hallows Episcopal in Baltimore's upscale Roland Park, was unimpressed.

'Honest to God, it breaks my heart,' she had said as she described a music program being led by a praise team that included a singer and an eight-piece band. 'I don't know where they've stashed the hymnals,' she said. 'They display the lyrics on flat screen Jumbotrons suspended from the ceiling.'

I looked up. Georgina had been right about the Jumbotrons. As the vocalist warbled and swooped her way through the song, its lyrics scrolled by on massive screens at the front of the church, flanking a colorful stained-glass window that depicted Christ's ascension into Heaven. 'Five years ago, a wealthy parishioner donated a brand-new Rogers Infinity pipe organ to the church,' Georgina had reported. 'It's got four keyboards and more than ten thousand pipes. Most organists would kill to play such an instrument. But that was before everybody was bashed over the head with guitars and pan flutes. It's hardly ever used, now.'

The vocalist had wrapped up her last Worthy-is-the-Lamb, when I felt a hand on my shoulder. I turned to see who it was and sprang to my feet. 'Daddy!'

I hugged my father, leaned back and mouthed a silent 'thank you'.

'Wrapped everything up as fast as I could,' Dad whispered. 'Had to put the birdwatching on hold, but Neelie thinks she can reschedule.' He released me, leaned across Paul to grasp Ruth's hand then focused his attention on Georgina, who nudged everyone over a seat to make room for him on the aisle. Dad sat down, slipped his arm around the back of her chair and drew his youngest daughter close. My heart lurched when Georgina rested her head on his shoulder.

Twenty years before, when her children were young and a decade before the happy surprise that was Colin, Georgina's sick fantasies had nearly torn our family apart. Scott had stuck with his wife, shepherding his family through the dark days until her recovery. If he seemed a little overprotective at times, well . . . Looking at my sister now, sitting strong and straight with her children around her, it all seemed worthwhile.

The praise band – guitar, electronic keyboard, flute, violin and drum kit – began to massacre the classic hymn, 'Old Rugged Cross'. In self-defense, I studied the program. The cover featured a color photograph of Scott lifted from the church directory. For his official mugshot as church treasurer, he'd worn a dark-blue suit and a yellow tie, which made him look more like your friendly, neighborhood real estate salesman than a highly-paid certified public accountant.

R.I.P. March 2, 1964 – August 18, 2018 was centered under Scott's picture. I swallowed hard. Just seeing the dates laid out in black and white made my brother-in-law's death seem more real.

As if I didn't need Scott's presence – in the form of cremains – to remind me that this day was no dream. Scott's ashes rested in an urn on a cloth-draped mini-altar centered just below the steps leading up to the chancel. Georgina certainly had good taste, I mused as I admired the ceramic Grecian-style urn. If Scott had been around to make the selection, it might have been a Tardis that launched his soul into time and space like Doctor Who.

I don't know who had written the memorial note – certainly not Georgina, who had told me she simply couldn't deal with it. I suspected one of Scott's two brothers – one older and one younger – who sat across the aisle from us looking shell-shocked, staring straight ahead. Scott had been born, according to the program, into a 'Catholic family of modest means' in Philadelphia, most of whom had predeceased him. I imagined his surviving brothers were having a hard time dealing with the vocalist, microphone in hand, who was roaming the aisle and plowing her breathless way through a tune called – according to the program – 'Just Save a Place for Me'. I felt nothing but relief when she wound it up and Pastor Robert Thomas Selden stepped up to the pulpit.

'My friends,' he began, 'I thank you and the family of Scott Cardinale thanks you for coming here today to celebrate Scott's life. I especially want to recognize . . .'

And the service droned on. And on. And on. As a general rule, Episcopalians discourage eulogies. If multiple speakers are allowed, they are usually limited to two or three minutes each, max. Apparently, no such rules applied at Church of the Falls. By the time two parishioners, a local businessman, three clients, the president of the local Rotary Club and one of Scott's brothers had finished eulogizing Scott, I pretty much felt like shuffling off this mortal coil myself.

My spirits revived when Dylan, the older of the twins by three minutes, stepped up to the pulpit. He stared straight into the congregation and recited, without notes and without fault, the Twenty-Third Psalm: *The Lord is my Shepherd, I shall not want* . . .

As the ancient prayer of comfort continued, Paul's arm snaked around my shoulder and pulled me close as I let the tears flow.

Ruth passed me a tissue from the packet she had half emptied herself.

After Dylan finished, I was astonished to see Julie ease out of her seat and exchange places with her brother in the pulpit. Taking her pitch from a single D from the instrumentalist sitting at the keyboard, my niece sang 'Amazing Grace' *a cappella* in a pure, high soprano voice.

The last note died away into total silence, broken only when a woman across the aisle, obviously overcome, exclaimed, 'The voice of an angel!'

I had no way of knowing whether Scott had gone to heaven or to 'the other place', but if heaven was his destination, I thought as I sobbed, he surely must have heard his daughter sing.

TWENTY-THREE

After the service ended, a white-clad usher escorted family members around a pink marble Baptismal font the size of a Volkswagen and out a side door. We followed the young woman down a long, glassed-in corridor that bisected a meditation labyrinth and a well-manicured courtyard abloom with seasonal flowers – coneflowers, asters and mums.

The corridor terminated at a pair of double doors that opened into a massive fellowship hall; a curtained stage dominated one end and a serious industrial-style kitchen the other. A wall of picture windows framed the neighboring woods like a mural in a budget hotel. Church ladies carrying trays bustled between the kitchen and a line of cloth-covered tables where volunteers busily arranged donations by basic potluck food group: salads, casseroles, breads and desserts with a token section, identified by tent cards, for diners of vegetarian or gluten-free persuasions.

A smartly-dressed woman – whether representing the church or the funeral home, I couldn't say – shook her head and silently tut-tutted, making it clear by gentle nudges that Ruth and I were meant to join Georgina and her four children in a receiving line.

I could think of nothing worse to ask of a grieving widow and her family. By some sort of sisterly telepathy, Ruth and I moved into protective positions flanking our baby sister. While I served as initial greeter, Ruth acted as relief pitcher, keeping well-wishers moving smartly along the line to Scott's two brothers and finally, to his bewildered children.

I was half listening to an over-caffeinated woman who had sung with Scott in the church choir – such a gorgeous tenor voice! – when Emily ushered her family into the room and, rather than joining the lengthening queue, sensibly shooed her ducklings toward the food. My stomach rumbled, no doubt in anticipation of the traditional green bean onion bake. I prayed there'd be some left by the time our ordeal was over.

I greeted choristers, musicians, ushers, flower arrangers, Bible study group members, sound technicians, janitors, cooks, gardeners and day care workers – was there anyone Scott didn't know? – until my hand throbbed. I had pretty much lost the will to live when a familiar face loomed into view. 'Dennis!' I kissed his cheek.

'I'm so glad to see you,' Georgina said, sounding completely sincere. 'It's been a long time.'

Chesapeake County police lieutenant Dennis Rutherford was married to Paul's sister, Connie. Although related to Scott only by marriage, they'd grown to know my sister and her husband well at family gatherings over the years. I was wondering what was keeping Connie when Dennis said, 'Connie sends apologies for not being here. She's got a sick calf.'

'I understand completely,' Georgina said with a wan smile. 'I hope the calf will be OK.'

'The vet's on the way,' Dennis said. 'Some sort of respiratory infection.' He kissed her cheek. 'I won't hold up the line, Georgina, but I hope to catch up with you later.'

'I'd like that, Dennis,' she said.

Dennis was followed by a succession of prosperous-looking businessmen – bankers, lawyers, restauranteurs and real estate developers, who according to whispered asides from Georgina, were members of Scott's 'stupid social club'. I wondered, briefly, why Cosmopolitan Forum members were coming through in a clump but gathered from casual chit-chat as they made their way past my duty station that they'd held some sort of pow-wow in the hallway following the service. As I smiled and greeted one bigshot after the other, I despaired. If everyone who attended the memorial service came through the receiving line, we'd be standing up shaking hands until Christ's Second Coming.

Fortunately, some parishioners were bypassing the queue hoping to get first dibs at the King Ranch chicken casserole or cheesy spaghetti bake. The praise band must have been particularly hungry after their performances because they sidestepped the line waiting to speak to Georgina and made a beeline for the pork sliders.

I was passing an elderly parishioner down the line and thinking I could kill for a pork slider myself when Emily materialized, seemingly out of nowhere. 'I'm probably breaking some sort of church protocol,' she announced, 'but this is silly.' So saying, she took ten-year-old Colin by the hand and snatched him out of the line. 'Let's get you something to eat, young man. After that, you can go outside and play with Timmy.'

I could see through the window that his cousin Timmy, my youngest grandson, was already swinging hand-over-hand from a piece of playground equipment that belonged to the church's day care center. Other youngsters were testing the durability of swings, slides, seesaws, spinners and spring riders. I wished I could join them, but at least thirty more people waited in line. I felt drained.

'Can you fake a faint?' I whispered to Georgina.

'I can do better than that,' she whispered back, and precisely on cue, burst into noisy, snuffling tears. Ruth, feigning concern, escorted Georgina in the direction of a round table near the stage, while I turned to those waiting in line and announced, 'So sorry, but Georgina's exhausted. I'm sure you understand.'

Unfortunately, the rules didn't seem to apply to the pastor and his wife. Five seconds after the receiving line disbanded, Pastor Robert Thomas Selden swanned into the room, aimed himself at my sisters and charged. Under the black robe he'd been wearing when he delivered the homily, Brother Bob wore a dark-blue silk suit, a pale-blue dress shirt and a red tie with a conservative blue stripe. His hair – a deep brown not heretofore seen in nature – was magnificently coifed, but suspiciously immobile. Was that a toupee, I wondered, or did his hair naturally grow that way? I tried not to stare too obviously at his forehead, searching for roots.

Clopping along behind him in sensible, low-heeled pumps was the minister's wife, Tamara, equally well turned out in a dark-navy suit and a white silk blouse. Her hair was styled in a no-nonsense chestnut pageboy that reminded me of my tenth grade Civics teacher. I hated her at once.

Target achieved, Tamara leaned in, her lips brushing Georgina's cheek, and said simply, 'Darling.'

'Georgina,' Brother Bob said, capturing Georgina's hand. 'We're so terribly sorry, uh . . .'

'For your loss,' Tamara said.

'If there's anything Tamara and I can do . . .'

'Please let us know,' his wife concluded.

I was sandwiched between a pair of talking bookends.

Ruth, the coward, took the opportunity to make her escape, heading for the food tables.

'The Women's Bible study group has organized a meal train,' Brother Bob began.

'With all you have on your mind . . .' Tamara continued.

'We don't want you to have to worry about shopping or cooking for a while,' Brother Bob said.

'They started the food deliveries two days ago.' Georgina smiled ruefully. 'Or maybe three. And they left such a helpful calendar saying who is bringing what on each day. My children and I can't thank you enough.'

'God never gives us more than we can handle, Georgina.' Brother Bob continued to pump Georgina's hand.

'You call us if you need any little thing,' his wife said.

Brother Bob leaned in, speaking close to Georgina's ear but loud enough for me to hear, 'What a blessing it is that Scott knew Jesus.'

After the pastor and his wife drifted away, I caught Georgina wiping her hand on her skirt.

Ruth waited until the coast was clear before returning with

a plate of food and a glass of pink lemonade. She set them down on the table and urged Georgina to tuck in. With Georgina in her capable hands, I went off to forage something for myself.

I ran into Julie and her brother Sean at the dessert table. 'I'm not really hungry, but if I'm stuffing myself with lemon bars I won't have to talk to anybody about Daddy,' Julie said, taking a bite.

I added a brownie and a cheesecake square to the chicken salad, green beans and cornbread on my plate. 'You look beautiful, Julie,' I said.

Julie shrugged. 'This dress? It's from my Goth period. Mom loaned me the pearls.'

'You ought to eat something other than sweets, Jules,' Sean scolded.

'You should talk,' she said, pointing out the assortment of desserts piled on her brother's plate.

My niece and nephew followed me back to their mother's table. In the few minutes we'd been gone, Daddy and Dennis Rutherford had also joined her.

'You're a cop,' Sean said to Dennis as he took a seat. 'Do you know what the police are doing to catch the sonofabitch who killed our dad?'

'See that guy over there, in the gray suit?' Still holding his lemonade glass, Dennis extended a finger and pointed. 'Dick Evans. Baltimore City homicide. He's leading the investigation. His partner's over there, next to the salads. Name's Pat Edwards. Wearing the black suit with the pink blouse.' He glanced at me. 'She kinda looks like you, Hannah.'

I followed his finger, squinting hard at the female officer. 'No, she doesn't.'

'Same height, weight, coloring, general build. Wears her hair the same way, too.'

I scowled. 'If I ever show up wearing a pussy bow like that, Dennis Rutherford, you will know that aliens have landed and taken over my body.'

'Hah!' He sipped his lemonade. 'She does, though.'

'Does what?'

'Look like you.'

'Poor thing,' I said.

'Do murderers often attend the funerals of their victims?' I asked after a bit. 'Like they do on TV?'

'That seems dumb,' Sean said. 'I'd sure as hell stay away.'

Dennis considered my nephew as if weighing his words. 'But what if the murderer is expected to be there? His absence would be a giveaway.'

'Do you mean . . .' Sean began.

'Murderers almost always know their victims,' Dennis said. 'That's why they are here.' By the tilt of his head, I knew he meant the Baltimore cops.

Julie said, 'Well, nobody's going to stand up, cackle like a maniac and say, "Ha ha ha! Glad he's dead! I did it!"'

'No,' Dennis said, glancing from Julie to Sean, 'but sometimes we get lucky.'

Dylan chose that moment to approach our table, head down, carrying a plate so heaped with food that he had to keep an eye on it. When he got close he looked up, frowned and veered away. Although two empty chairs remained at our table, he chose to sit down with some of the band members instead.

'Was it something I said?' Dennis asked of no one in particular. 'Has my deodorant failed?'

'What's up with Dylan?' I asked his twin.

Sean swallowed and waved a chicken wing. 'You'll have to ask him.'

'Where's your ever-loving?' Dennis asked me, suddenly shifting gears.

I pointed out Paul and Hutch who had their heads together with Dante over the industrial-sized coffee urn. I suspected by the way his arms wheeled about that Dante was holding forth on Spa Paradiso's latest acquisition: a hydrotherapy whirlpool.

'I'll just have a word,' Dennis said, and walked over to join them.

'Wait up,' Sean called after him. 'I need a cup of coffee.'

'Don't you want to join the boys?' I asked my father.

'Got some business to take care of first,' he said, reaching into his pocket. He pressed a key attached to a US Navy fob into my hand.

'What's that?' Ruth asked.

'Hannah said she wanted to look for something in the storage locker.'

My eyes slid to Julie and back. 'I'm hoping Grandmother Smith left some letters, diaries or something that might help solve the mystery of who our grandfather was.'

'That's a long shot,' Ruth said.

'Thanks, Dad,' I said. 'With all that's happened recently, the storage locker flew straight out of my head.' I slipped the key into my purse. 'Are you giving me carte blanche?'

'Keep the key as long as you need to, sweetheart. I'm glad you're going to sort through it, actually. After your mother died . . .'

I squeezed his arm. 'I know.'

Suddenly he smiled; his blue eyes twinkled. 'Besides, the rental is costing me a fortune. I'll have to clean the unit out eventually.'

A thought occurred to me. 'Are you back now for good, Dad? I'm thinking you might want to come along.'

My father shook his head. 'No can do. I'll trust you girls to take care of it.' He patted my hand. 'And now, I think I'll join the boys for some coffee.'

A few minutes after Daddy wandered off, Georgina said, 'See that woman over near the water cooler, talking to Brother Bob?'

I followed her gaze. 'Talking' didn't describe what I was seeing. 'Arguing' was more like it. Brother Bob stood nose to nose with a forty-something, bottle-blond, Botoxed woman dressed in a form-fitting gray sheath. She had the well-tended veneer I usually associate with third wives of aging billionaires. Brother Bob's face, on the other hand, had taken on a dangerously ruddy hue.

'Who is she?' I asked my sister.

'Judee McDaniel. Joo-dee with two Es, if you please.'

'Yes, but who is she?' I tried again.

'I know who she is,' Julie said. 'Director of the day care center.'

'Julie helps out in day care a couple of times a week,' her mother explained, favoring her daughter with an affectionate smile.

I stared at my niece. 'I didn't know that!'

Julie grinned. 'I try to keep a low profile.'

'What's day care got to do with Scott?' I asked.

'Oh, she's a church member, too,' Georgina said. 'And I don't like the way she manages . . . I mean, managed to sit next to Scott at Bible study. She always had the significance of the scripture reading down cold.' In a phony Southern accent, dripping with syrup, Georgina quoted, '"I've always thought that the book of Deuteronomy is structured as a series of farewell talks by Moses to the Hebrews as they prepare to end their years in the wilderness and claim the Promised Land."' She puffed air out through her lips. 'She probably looked it up on the Internet and practiced reciting in front of a mirror.'

Brother Bob ended whatever discussion he was having with Judee Two-Es by executing an abrupt about-face and stalking away.

'I really didn't think much of it at the time,' Georgina said, her eyes still on Judee, 'but Judee showed up a couple of weeks ago.'

'Showed up?' Julie squeaked. 'You mean at our house?'

Georgina nodded. 'One morning before lunchtime. I almost didn't recognize her. No make-up, and she was dressed in a fancy pink jogging outfit. Even her fricking shoes were pink. Said she'd stopped by to drop off an envelope for Scott from Brother Bob. Now I'm wondering . . .'

'Do you think Scott was having an affair?' Ruth cut in.

'No . . .' She paused. 'But . . .' She let the thought die.

My brother-in-law was smart enough not to be trysting with a woman in his own house, not with his wife likely to pop in at any minute. For a fleeting moment, though, I allowed myself to wonder how soundproofed Scott's third-floor office was.

As if reading my mind, Georgina said, 'If Scott had been having an affair, I would have known, Hannah. I would have known.'

'That's what Hillary Clinton thought, too,' I said.

Georgina suddenly ducked her head and muttered, *sotto voce*, 'Oh, oh, look out. Here she comes.'

Bearing down on us like a heat-seeking missile was Judee McDaniel. Target achieved, she leaned over the table and gushed, 'Georgina, I'm so sorry for your loss.'

'Thank you,' Georgina said in a small, flat voice.

'And you must be Georgina's sisters,' Judee said, glancing from me to Ruth and back to me again.

'Guilty,' I said. 'I'm Hannah and this is Ruth.'

'You girls look so different,' she said. 'If I hadn't seen you sitting together . . .'

'Oh, we're sisters, all right,' Georgina cut in dryly. 'And we have the DNA to prove it.'

Judee gaped like a fish, then plopped down in the empty chair between Julie and her mother. 'I understand you're taking a gap year, Julie. I was wondering if you'd be interested in taking a more active role in the day care center.'

While Julie described her plans, which in no way included the Church of the Falls Day Care Center, I had a chance to compare Georgina and Judee side-by-side. If Scott had preferred this sharp-edged, superannuated Barbie over my sister, he must have had rocks for brains.

Georgina abruptly stood, knocking the edge of the table with her knee, causing the drink cups to teeter. 'I'm done,' she announced. 'Time to go.'

'I'll rally the troops,' I said. 'Ruth? Julie? You ready?'

Both women looked relieved.

Ten minutes later, as we stood on the sidewalk outside the church waiting for Hutch who was driving us home, Georgina said, 'Now that Scott's gone, I'm never going to set foot in this horrible place again.' She linked arms with Sean on one side and Dylan on the other. Julie followed just behind, holding Colin's hand. And the little family walked to the waiting limo.

TWENTY-FOUR

Two days after Scott's funeral, I drove up to Baltimore to check on Georgina. When she didn't answer the doorbell, I walked around the back and let myself in through the mudroom door.

Georgina sat at the kitchen island nursing a cup of coffee,

leafing listlessly through a stack of sympathy cards. She glanced up when I came in, not seeming at all surprised. 'Sorry, Hannah. Was that you ringing the bell just now?'

I confessed that it was.

With a fluid sweep of her hand, she fanned the cards out on the counter like a deck of cards. 'I don't have to answer these, do I?'

'No, sweetheart, you don't.'

I hardly recognized Georgina's kitchen. Empty food containers littered the countertops; dirty plates and bowls teetered precariously in the sink; empty two-liter soda bottles were piled next to the recycling bin rather than in it. It looked like the morning after a New Year's Eve party when everybody slept in.

I opened the dishwasher, preparing to be helpful, but it was already full. I groaned silently. I pulled out the top rack and started putting glasses and cups away, making room for the next load.

'You don't have to do that, Hannah.'

'I know I don't, but your kitchen is usually so spotless. All this mess must be driving you nuts.'

'It's funny, but I just don't care.' She waved a card with a bouquet of lilies on the front. 'I hate lilies,' she said as she slid the card back into the envelope it had come in.

'With Scott not around to nag,' she said after a moment, 'I don't feel a pressing need to alphabetize the spice rack. Yesterday I put the basil away next to the poultry seasoning. It was surprisingly liberating.'

Georgina hopped off her stool and snatched the cereal bowl from my hand. 'I mean it, Hannah. Leave the dishes for the kids.'

'What's been wrong with the children up till now, then?' I asked, indicating the culinary detritus that surrounded us. 'Both arms broken?'

'School's back in session now,' she explained, 'and Julie's in and out interviewing. But they'll get around to it.'

'If you say so, but let me take the trash out, at least.' I peeked into the cabinet under the sink where Georgina kept the trash can hidden and wrinkled my nose. 'It's getting pretty ripe.'

Without waiting for permission, I tied up the reeking bag,

lined the can with a fresh one and began to fill a third bag with empty take-out containers, tinfoil pans, soiled plastic wrap, paper cups and balled up napkins. When the bag was nearly full, I stamped the trash down with my foot and added another couple of tinfoil pans.

'Do you recycle?' I asked my sister, indicating the accumulation of plastic soda bottles.

She picked up two bottles and handed them to me. 'Not today I don't.'

I added the bottles to the bag, pulled the plastic drawstrings and tied a knot. The rest could wait for the kids. Carrying the bags, one in each hand, I left through the mudroom door, heading for the garbage can in the back alley. As I passed the shed where Scott's body had lain for so long, I shuddered. No wonder nobody wanted to take out the trash. I scurried past the shed and escaped into the alley.

Baltimore City provides its residents with large green municipal trash cans on wheels. Using an elbow, I flipped open the top and tossed the bags in, jostling them around a little to make them fit.

Across the back alley, a Deepdene resident was doing the same thing. 'That's nice of you,' the woman said. She was dressed in khaki pants and a freshly pressed white camp shirt.

'I do what I can,' I said.

'Well, it's totally above and beyond the call of duty, I'd say.' She deposited her own, smaller bag into a trash can and let the lid fall with a hollow thud. She stared at me quietly for a while, as if waiting for me to say something, her gray eyes enormous behind thick lenses. 'You're here to collect the tape, I suppose.'

'Tape?' I repeated, thinking I'd misheard.

'From the security camera,' she explained.

Now that she mentioned it, I spotted the eye of a camera installed in the eaves of her house, aimed in our direction. 'Ah, yes,' I said. 'The tape.'

'Gordon installed the system himself,' she said, beaming with pride. 'As I told your partner, something has been getting into our garbage can and we were determined to catch it in the act. I never dreamed . . .' she began, then her face clouded. 'Didn't he tell you?'

Suddenly, the penny dropped. *She looks like you, actually,* Dennis had commented at Scott's funeral. Georgina's neighbor must be mistaking me for Pat Edwards, one of the homicide detectives working on Scott's case.

'It's always better to hear from witnesses directly,' I said, deftly sidestepping her question.

'I was on my hands and knees weeding my roses when I heard loud voices, so I looked up to see what was going on. We keep to ourselves, Gordon and I, and I don't like to stick my nose into other people's business, but after Mr Cardinale was murdered . . .' She paused, pressing a hand to her bosom. 'I saw one of the twins arguing with his father.'

My heart flopped in my chest and I struggled to keep my voice neutral. 'When was this?'

'On the very day the poor man died,' she said, wagging a finger to emphasize her words. 'I'm not sure of the exact time because I wasn't wearing my watch, but I'd just finished giving Gordon his lunch. Gordon has pimento cheese on wholewheat toast and a bowl of tomato soup every day at twelve-fifteen, so it must have been around one o'clock.'

I took a deep breath. My nephews had been one hundred and fifty miles away in Cape May, New Jersey on the day their father died. Or had they?

'Which twin?' I asked, trying to keep my voice steady. 'Sean or Dylan?'

She flapped a hand. '*I* can't tell them apart. But once you have the tape, I'm sure *you* can sort it out. Gordon transferred everything to a CD. Shall I get it for you?'

'No, don't do that, please,' I said, dismissing a totally insane impulse to grab the tape and make it disappear into the murky depths of the Patapsco River. 'An evidence technician will be around to collect it in due time. Chain of custody, you understand.'

'Oh, right, of course.'

'I was just . . .' I waved vaguely in the direction of my sister's house, then smiled. 'Guess I better get on with it.'

'I hope you catch whoever did this,' she said. 'Mr Cardinale was the *nicest* man. It's hard to believe that one of his children . . .' She shook her head.

'The investigation is far from over,' I said, hoping I was speaking the truth.

'Well, until they put that murderer behind bars,' she said, 'I'm sleeping with my doors double locked!'

'Always a good idea in the city,' I advised her over my shoulder as I trudged back to the house. When I got to the patio, I turned. She was still looking at me.

Back in the kitchen, Georgina had switched from coffee to wine. A bottle of Pinot Grigio, glistening with sweat, sat on the counter next to her elbow. Good. She was going to need it.

'When do the twins get home?' I asked.

She shrugged. 'They have different class schedules, but I expect them both for dinner.'

'Julie?'

'Who knows? Why do you ask?'

'We need to have a family meeting,' I said. 'And it needs to involve an attorney. Do you have one?'

'What the *hell* are you talking about, Hannah?'

'I was just talking to your backyard neighbor, and—'

'Claudia Turner?' she interrupted. 'Let me guess. Our dog's gotten into her garbage again.' She reached for the wine bottle and started to refill her glass. 'Buster has been dead for over a year. The woman's a kook.'

'Well, that kook just told the police that she saw one of the twins arguing with his father in the backyard on the day of Scott's murder.'

Georgina's hand began to shake. She set the wine bottle down. 'But that's crazy! Both of the boys were in Cape May that day. You know that. She's making it up.'

'The Turners have a security camera, Georgina. The police have a tape.'

Georgina stared at me, eyes wide and frightened. 'I don't understand.'

'Call your attorney, Georgina. And text the boys. They're needed at home. Now.'

TWENTY-FIVE

That evening, the Church of the Falls meal train ordered Pepe's pizza to be sent over to the Cardinale home. Pepe's pies are eleven on a scale of ten, but the funk I was in, even the Hawaiian Delight tasted like cardboard. I sprinkled hot pepper flakes on my slice. Result? Extra spicy cardboard.

The five of us perched uneasily on high stools around Georgina's kitchen island which was strewn with paper plates, plastic cups and half-eaten pizza. A sixth stool, still empty, was reserved for the family attorney, Tim Keane, one of Scott's Cosmopolitan Forum mates who specialized in tax law. He was running late. Neither was a good sign.

'Might as well get started,' Georgina said, officially bringing the family meeting to order. Skewering the twins with a penetrating, ice-green glare, she said, 'If what Claudia Turner told your aunt is true, the police already have, or are about to have, in their possession, a videotape of one of you arguing with your father in the backyard on the day he was murdered.'

Julie gasped. 'That's bogus! They were in Cape May.' She leaned into the island and addressed her brothers. 'You were in Cape May, right? Tell her, you guys.'

To my astonishment, the twins exchanged uneasy glances.

'OK,' I said, picking up on their body language. 'Which one of you was it?'

After a moment of nerve-wracking silence, Sean finally spoke up. 'We were *both* in Cape May, Aunt Hannah. An entire week, Saturday to Saturday. Sharing a condo. Partying at the beach with a bunch of fraternity brothers. That's what we told the police when they interviewed us last week, and it's the absolute truth.'

'But . . .' Dylan began, only to be interrupted by the jangle of the front door bell.

'Must be Tim,' Georgina said. 'Go let him in, please, Julie.'

Minutes later, Julie returned to the kitchen leading a dark-haired, stylishly-bearded man I guessed to be in his early forties dressed casually in deck shoes, chinos and a navy-blue V-neck sweater. He sported a bow tie spotted with *fleur de lis,* which in spite of the dark mood I was in, made me smile. 'Sorry,' Tim apologized as he joined us at the island. 'Parents night at my kid's school. Skipped out on Nora's study hall. Was the soonest I could manage. Blythe wasn't thrilled but agreed to cover for me.'

'Dylan was about to explain how he and Sean spent beach week,' Georgina said in a small, unsteady voice.

'What does it matter what we did?' Sean said, appealing to the attorney directly. 'What's important is we were in Cape May, New Jersey, not here.'

'Cape May's not that far away,' Tim Keane pointed out. 'You could get here from there in what, two and a half hours? I think we'll need to drill down a bit on your exact whereabouts on the afternoon your father died, don't you?'

'I can tell you what *I* was doing,' Dylan volunteered. 'Around ten, we hosted a kegger on the beach. Beer, barbeque from the Surfing Pig, the works.'

'Who is "we"?' Tim wanted to know.

'Sean, me, some frat brothers. Mike, Duke, Mac, Griff. Jeff was there for a couple of hours, too, but he had to leave early to go to work.'

'These guys have real names, I suppose?' Tim slid a small notebook out of his back pants pocket and extracted a slim, gold pen from its elastic pen loop.

'Sure.' Dylan scooped up his cell phone from the countertop and tapped the screen.

While Tim scribbled rapidly, copying down the twins' fraternity brothers' contact information as Dylan thumbed through the screens, Sean said, 'There were girls, too. But they weren't part of our usual gang, so we can't help much with that.'

Tim looked up. 'So, you were partying on the beach with a bunch of girls.'

'Yup. They just kinda showed up.'

'It's been a while since I graduated from college,' Tim said, 'but isn't the whole point of throwing a kegger on the beach that girls in bikinis will show up?'

'Busted,' Sean said.

Tim didn't smile. 'How long did this beach party go on?'

'Most of the day,' Dylan said. 'I left with Mike around three. A couple of the girls invited us to a poetry slam at The Magic Brain, so we went and hung out there until dinner time. I can't vouch for Sean.'

'Magic Brain?' Tim raised an eyebrow. 'Help me out here.'

'Awesome coffee shop,' Dylan explained. 'The kind of joint that whips up an oat milk iced dirty chai without breaking a sweat.'

'So, what's your story?' Tim asked, turning to Sean.

Sean shifted uncomfortably on his stool.

'He's about to lie,' Julie piped up unexpectedly. 'The tips of his ears are red.'

'Sean!' Georgina shrieked. 'This is important!'

Sean's face flushed the same color as his ears. 'I'm afraid I got wasted, Mom. I remember Dylan leaving the party, but it's hazy after that. There was this girl . . .'

'Says her name was Lacey,' Dylan supplied.

'Lacey, right. She'd remember me, but so would a lot of other people. What do you expect? We were out on the beach. There were a lot of party crashers.'

'Lacey who?' Georgina asked.

Sean shrugged, looking like a lost child. 'I don't know.'

Georgina's eyes narrowed dangerously. 'You don't *know*?'

Before the situation could escalate into full-blown war, Tim moved on. 'When did you last see your brother, Dylan?'

'He was there at noon, for sure, but after that . . .' His voice trailed off. 'As Sean said, the party attracted a lot of people.'

'Dylan! You have to vouch for Sean!' Julie cried.

'You want me to lie, Jules?'

'Of course not, but you *know* Sean didn't kill our dad.'

'All I *know*,' Dylan said, turning to address his twin, 'is that you disappeared from the party around noon and I didn't see you until the next morning when you staggered back to the condo, hungover and stinking of hops.'

'Jesus,' Georgina whispered.

'I'm sorry, Mom. I must have blacked out. I remember playing a couple of rounds of beer pong . . .' Sean rested his head in his hands, wagging it slowly as if still nursing the massive hangover he must have had that day. 'I woke up around ten in a motel room with this girl. She didn't seem in any hurry to leave . . .'

'So. What. Could. You. Do?' Dylan sneered.

Tim held up a cautionary hand, then turned to Sean. 'What motel?'

'Three stories, balconies overlooking the beach. Might have been blue. God, I don't know, Mr Keane! They all look the same!'

'No sign out front? In the lobby?'

Sean shook his head. 'I left out the back, via the beach.'

'If you show up on that surveillance tape, you'll need to beef up that alibi,' Tim warned.

'Wait a minute!' Sean said, his face brightening. 'How was I supposed to get here, huh? Walk? You can check out my car. It never left the parking garage. Check the EasyPass records. Any route you take, there'd be a toll. Interstate 95, the Bay Bridge, the Lewes ferry. All tolls.'

'Good point,' Tim said.

'Are we supposed to know about this security tape?' Georgina asked me, sounding eager to change the subject.

'Of course not,' I said. 'I didn't exactly lie to Mrs Turner, but I didn't correct her when she mistook me for a police officer, either.'

'It could be *anybody* on that tape,' Georgina insisted. 'Scott met lots of clients at the house. And Mrs Turner is blind as a bat.' She turned to me. 'You must have seen her glasses. And she mistook you for a woman at least twenty years younger.'

'Thanks, Georgina,' I said. 'I wonder where I stashed my cane?'

'If the Turner tape has any evidentiary value, and we're just guessing here, I'm sure the police will want to talk to you about it,' Tim said, moving on. 'But let's not jump the gun.'

'Mrs Turner told me her husband installed the security system himself. We can always hope he wasn't very good at it,' I said wryly.

'You need to alibi for each other,' Julie urged her brothers. 'Nobody can tell you apart, so if the tape shows one of you arguing with Dad, there's no way anyone could tell which one of you it was.' She managed a lackluster smile. 'I read that in an Agatha Christie novel once, or maybe it was Mary Higgins Clark.'

I wasn't so sure about that. Sean wore his hair parted on the left, his bangs swept casually to one side, while Dylan preferred a French crop, rocking that tousled, just-climbed-out-of-bed look. If they both opted for crew cuts, however, it would definitely take a family member to tell them apart.

Sean bristled. 'But, Jules! I don't care what's on the tape. I was nowhere near Baltimore when Dad died!'

'I can definitely prove where *I* was,' Dylan cut in. 'Sean needs to be held accountable for his own actions. Getting blind drunk and shacking up with a woman he doesn't even know . . .' He paused. 'What happened to your Virginity Pledge, Sean? Huh?'

Sean recoiled as if he'd been slapped.

'True love waits,' Dylan recited. 'I am making a commitment to myself, my family and my creator that I will abstain from sex before marriage. I will keep my body and my thoughts pure as I trust in God's perfect plan for my life . . .'

'Total bullshit,' Sean growled. He picked up a piece of pizza, considered the cheese congealing on top like a sheet of blistered plastic, frowned and dropped it back on the paper plate.

'"Flee from sexual immorality",' Dylan sputtered, rising from his stool. 'First Corinthians. "Every other sin a person commits is outside the body, but the sexually immoral person sins against his own body".'

'"He that is without sin among you, let him cast the first stone",' Sean shot back. 'John eight seven. Remember Kayla Mills? Senior prom?'

Georgina pressed her palms flat against her ears. 'La, la, la, la, I can't hear you!' she sing-songed.

I snatched my sister's hand away. 'Not listening isn't going to help, Georgina.' I turned my attention away from Georgina long enough to give the evil eye to my nephews. 'And hurling Bible verses at one another like rival evangelicals isn't going to help either, dammit.'

Aunt Hannah's curse seemed to have a sobering effect on the twins.

'I have a rock solid alibi,' Dylan said after a moment of quiet reflection.

'And I don't,' Sean said, finally admitting the truth.

'Unless we can find Lacey,' I said.

'Facebook?' Julie suggested.

'Did anybody take pictures at the beach party?' I asked the twins.

'I imagine so,' Dylan said. 'Everyone has a cell phone.'

'Do either of you have a picture of Lacey?'

'I do!' Sean said, bending over to retrieve his cell phone from the backpack at his feet. 'I can't believe I forgot about that. We took a selfie at Uncle Charlie's Ice Cream.' While Sean brought his cell phone to life, I turned to his brother.

'Did any of your friends – Griff, Duke, whoever – hook up with any of the girls in Lacey's group, Dylan?'

'Maybe. Dunno.'

'Here it is!' Sean said, rotating the screen of his cell phone so we could all see the photo.

The young woman glancing sideways at the camera – lush lips puckered, caught in the act of planting a kiss on my nephew's cheek – wore her dark blond hair in a tousled, jaw-length bob. The straps of a flowered, halter-style bikini top were tied loosely around her neck. The waffle cone she held out – two scoops of chocolate topped with a rainbow of sprinkles – loomed gigantically in the foreground.

'Lacey's cute,' I observed.

Sean flushed. 'I thought so, too.'

'Email that photo to your pals,' I said.

Sean cradled his cell phone in his left hand. 'What am I supposed to tell them?'

'Don't mention the police, that might scare them off,' Tim suggested. 'Say that you met this girl, Lacey, you really liked her, but because of what happened, yadda yadda, you forgot to get her contact information.'

Head down, Sean's thumbs began to dart over the tiny screen. Suddenly he paused and looked up. 'You actually believe me, don't you, Aunt Hannah?'

'I do.'

'Then who the hell could be on that surveillance tape, arguing with Dad?'

'I don't know, Sean,' I said, 'but if the police take the tape seriously, and if we're allowed to see it, maybe we'll be able to figure it out.'

'That's a lot of ifs,' Georgina said.

'And here's another if for you,' Tim said, rising to his feet. 'If the police come around asking questions about the tape, you're going to need a criminal defense attorney, and that's not me.'

'Bite your tongue,' Georgina said.

Tim scribbled in his notebook, tore the page out and handed it directly to Sean. 'Just in case. Call this number. Ask for Sydney Foster.'

Sean stared at the slip of paper, looking sad and vulnerable. 'But how can I afford—'

'Hush, Sean,' his mother interrupted. 'We'll pay for it somehow.' She slid off her stool. 'Thank you for coming, Tim. I can't tell you how much we appreciate your advice. Let me know how much we owe you.'

Tim waved the request for payment away. 'No charge, Georgina. It's the least I can do for Scott. He sent a lot of business my way. I'm going to miss him, in more ways than one. Scott was one hell of a bocce player.'

Georgina escorted Tim out of the kitchen. When she was out of earshot, Dylan laid a hand on his brother's arm.

'Sorry I lost it back there, bro. Just want you to know that I've got your back. Blood is thicker than water, as they say.'

'Damn right,' Julie said.

TWENTY-SIX

Several days went by. No homicide detectives knocked at the Cardinales' front door and I began to wonder if I'd dreamt up the whole conversation with Claudia Turner. Nobody mentioned it, but the specter of the neighbor's videotape hung over our heads on the slenderest of threads, like the sword of Damocles.

Yet our lives went on.

Through daily text messages, I learned that the twins were throwing themselves into their graduate work at Hopkins – Sean in Economics and Dylan in History – while Julie was busily applying for volunteer positions with AmeriCorps, teaching internships in East Asia, as well as exploring missionary opportunities in poverty-stricken Central American countries sponsored by Church of the Falls. At the moment, she was leaning in favor of an international organization that would send her to teach computer skills to children in the Dominican Republic, but according to Julie's latest Tweet, 'The jury is still out.'

Meanwhile, nobody had been able to track down Lacey.

Nope, sorry. Good-looking chick, though.

Sweet! But no clue.

Good luck, dude. She's hot.

Hey, babe! You can grab me a beer any time!

Is she the ice maiden who came with Brie?

Sadly, Brie had no clue either.

To keep my mind off looming disaster, I threw myself into work on our family tree, an exercise that I'd sadly neglected in the aftermath of Scott's murder. I signed up for GedMatch, the most scientific of the publicly available genetic databases. It had been created in 2010 by a Florida grandpa and a transportation engineer from Texas who had no idea that their little 'side project' would eventually become the go-to destination not only for serious genealogists, but for investigators across the country to solve the coldest of cases.

Nick had recommended the site during a FaceTime chat from a state park in Iowa, one of several stops they'd made on their long drive home. He'd recently contributed his own family data to the database, a consolation prize, he soberly claimed, for having to leave town before they'd had a chance to meet the rest of the cousins. In the heartbreak and confusion following Scott's death, however, it seemed the proper thing to do.

Nick had warned me that GedMatch was barebones and utilitarian. After I uploaded Julie's and my raw data and selected the One-to-Many analysis, I could see what he meant. I was presented with a multi-columned table with cryptic headings that went on for screen after screen after screen. The meaning of kit number, name and email were transparent, but the remaining columns? Something only a rocket scientist could love.

Back in the day, my technical support team at Whitworth and Sullivan had an abbreviation for it: RTFM. As I puzzled over my search results, I decided I'd better Read the F-ing Manual myself.

I watched the YouTube tutorial three times. I downloaded the GedMatch Absolute Beginners Guide and read it from beginning to end.

SNP, IBS, IBD and MRCA? The manual lost me at single nucleotide polymorphisms. And the red, yellow, green and blue bars that compared individual chromosome strands like disk fragmentation charts on my old PC made my eyes roll back in my head.

We had another abbreviation at Whitworth and Sullivan: KISS. Keep it Simple Stupid.

Did I need to know what haplogroup I belonged to? Probably not, but the number of shared centimorgans (cM) seemed key. The more centimorgans you have in common with someone, the closer you are related. Julie's name topped my match list. My niece and I shared approximately 1700 cMs, or about twenty-five percent of our DNA. No surprises there.

The GENerations column was critical, too. Using the One-to-One option, I compared Julie's results with Nicholas's and Mai's. The GEN column for each read four. Roughly translated, according to the tutorial, the cousins' MRCA – most recent common ancestor – was four generations away. Thus they shared a great-great-grandparent. When I compared myself with Nick and Mai, the GEN value was 'three' – my great-grandparent, their great-great-grandparent. Who could that be but John Otaktay 'Kills Many' Johnson? If Hawk had been our most recent common ancestor, the values would have been two for me and three for them, respectively.

Proof positive, at least to me, that White Bear was my biological grandfather, and not his brother, Hawk. My heart beat a little faster just having my suspicions confirmed.

Seeking more information about my new family, I Googled 'American Indian census' and was directed immediately to the website for the National Archives and Records Administration in Washington, DC. The Indian Census Rolls 1885-1940 were archived on six-hundred-and-ninety-two rolls of microfilm, but, sadly, not indexed. Further complicating my research, the pages were displayed sideways, and the view could not be rotated. After half-an-hour's scrolling with my head tipped sideways, I stopped, massaged the crick in my neck and muttered aloud, 'There has to be a better way.'

Fortunately, there was. Google informed me that Ancestry. com, bless their generous hearts, had uploaded the microfilm records from the National Archives and (hallelujah!) indexed them. I logged on to their website.

In 1913, Otaktay, his wife Ehawee and their children Matoska, age two and Tahatan, age zero, lived together on the Pine Ridge reservation. Wasula joined the family in 1916. By 1936, Tahatan had married Kimimela and baby Takoda joined the tight-knit family unit, but Wasula, then around twenty years old, had moved on.

Had Wasula married? I added the question to the list I had for my cousin Nick the next time we had a FaceTime conversation.

Extrapolating from the census information, White Bear had been born around 1911. When, exactly, had he died and, thinking about Wasula's belief that her brother's death had been no accident, more importantly, how?

Finding the 'when' was easy. According to the South Dakota death index, grandfather Joseph White Bear passed away on September 4, 1932. No birth date or cause of death was listed on the digital record, though – a scan of a printout so old it had holes at the sides for feeding the paper through a dot-matrix printer.

Wasula had mentioned that White Bear had been a rodeo star. I wondered if his skills had attracted the attention of any contemporaneous newspapers. If he'd been famous enough, his death would surely not have gone unreported.

Deadwood, South Dakota must have been a happening place in the 1930s. Of eleven South Dakota newspapers publishing

between 1920 and 1932, five were located in Deadwood. And
Joseph White Bear himself had been a busy boy. Beginning in
1927, his name began popping up in lists of rodeo performers
all over the Mount Rushmore State. By 1930, his appearance
would be a headliner for the annual Days of '76 Celebration
held in Deadwood every August.

The August of 1932 was no exception. According to the
Deadwood Pioneer-Times, my grandfather had won the cham-
pion bucking contest and a purse of $800.

I sat back. $800 would have been a fortune back then. I
minimized the newspaper and brought up a new search window.
Adjusted for inflation, $800 in 1932 would equal $13,508.16
in today's dollars. White Bear was a rock star, indeed.

From the *Pioneer-Times* several weeks later, though, came
this distressing news:

> *Saturday, September 3. Yesterday this newspaper received
> advices from John Kills Many in Pine Ridge stating that
> his son Joseph White Bear, who was injured recently in a
> rodeo accident at Rosebud when a bucking horse fell on
> him, had suffered similar injuries in a rodeo performance
> at White River. Reports first received in Pine Ridge stating
> that he had been fatally injured later proved to be exag-
> gerated. His son resumed participation in different rodeos
> in that section. Riding again on Wednesday of this week
> a bucking horse again fell with him and he sustained
> injuries from which recovery is quite doubtful. He is at St
> Mary's hospital in an extremely critical condition from a
> fracture to the skull. Many friends and acquaintances in
> this section of the Hills will regret to learn of his
> misfortune.*

Although I paged forward looking for it, there was no formal
announcement of his death or any funeral.

The newspaper's account of White Bear's accident didn't
dovetail with the story Wasula had been told, that he'd been
trampled to death by his horse in its stall. Had she been inten-
tionally misinformed, or had the *Pioneer-Times*? Being fatally
trampled by one's own horse would have been an ignominious

way for a rodeo star to die. Had John Kills Many invented a rodeo accident in order to salvage his son's reputation? Or had he invented the story to cover up his murder, as Wasula clearly believed?

When Nick called several days later, his hair sticking out in spikes as if he'd just stepped out of the shower, I told him what I had found out about his great-great-uncle, my grandfather. 'He died on September 4th,' I said. 'According to the newspaper, it was a rodeo accident.'

Nick's dark eyes flashed. 'He didn't die, Cousin Hannah. White Bear walked on.'

'That's a lovely way to put it,' I said. 'Walking on. Where do the Lakota believe people go after they die?'

'To Wakan Tanka, the spirit world in the sky.'

'We'd say heaven.'

'Exactly.' He grinned. 'So would the priests at our school.'

'Can you tell me where my grandfather's buried?' I asked. 'One day, I'd like to visit his grave.'

'That's a more complicated issue,' Nick said. 'These days, we bury our dead in cemeteries and mark the graves with decorated crosses just like everyone else. Back then, though, White Bear would have been dressed in his best clothes and placed on a scaffold, along with his possessions. Food would have been set out for him as if he were still alive. There'd be a wake, too, and it might go on for two or three days. Then his body would have been taken down and buried in the ground under a big pile of rocks. It's hard to say where the grave would be now.

'Wasula kept his soul bundle,' Nick added.

I must have looked puzzled because Nick went on to explain how it was customary for a lock of hair cut from the deceased to be held over burning sweetgrass to purify it. Then it would be wrapped in a piece of sacred buckskin while mourners smoked the Sacred Pipe. 'The buckskin bundle would be kept in a special place for about a year, then carried outside and released,' Nick said. 'Wasula was the keeper of her brother's soul.'

'Golly,' I croaked, overcome by the image. I swallowed, took a deep breath and asked, 'Did Wasula ever marry?'

'Oh, yes,' Nick said. 'A cantankerous old fellow from what I understand, named Jesse Has Horns. He died long before I was born.' He paused. 'Have you ever heard of code talkers?'

'Of course,' I said. 'The Navajo code talkers were famous for stymieing the Japanese.'

'Little known fact. There were more than sixty Lakota code talkers, too,' Nick said. 'Jesse Has Horns was one of them. He spoke three Sioux dialects. Served in the South Pacific. His skills were so critical he had two bodyguards. I gather the Japanese knew about the code talkers and sent snipers out to get them. Jesse came home safely in 1946, but the bullets, mortars and bombs really got to him. He died of alcoholism in the early fifties.'

'What a shame,' I said.

'Alcoholism is a sad fact of life on the reservation,' Nick said.

I simply stared at Nick's image on the screen, not sure what to say.

'Father once told me that White Bear was buried with Wakinyan,' Nick said after a moment.

I searched my memory banks. 'Wakinyan?'

'Wakinyan. Thunder Spirit, his horse.'

A wave of sadness washed over me. Two senseless deaths: first the talented young man, my grandfather, then his magnificent, spirited horse.

'Was that because they believed that Thunder Spirit killed him?'

'It's hard to say, Hannah. I know that the horses of some Lakota, particularly warriors, were sometimes sacrificed at the grave and their tails tacked up on the scaffold.'

I shivered. 'I hate that custom.'

'Needless to say, we don't do that any more.'

'I'm glad to hear that.'

'So, what's happening with the investigation into your brother-in-law's murder?' Nick asked, deftly turning the conversation from two senseless deaths to a third.

I told him about my conversation with Claudia Turner and about the possibility that one of the twins had been home on the day of the murder and had lied about it.

Nick whistled.

'Although it's been days now,' I added, 'and we haven't heard a word from the police about any tape, so maybe . . . well, knock on wood.' I reached out and tapped my solid oak bookshelf three times.

But I guess I didn't knock hard enough.

TWENTY-SEVEN

The telephone rang just after nine a.m., jolting me out of the *New York Times* crossword puzzle. I filled in B-A-L-D for 'barely-there tires' and picked up.

'They've arrested the twins!' Georgina cried.

'Just now?'

'Yes!' she wailed, sounding desperate.

'Miranda warning, handcuffs, the whole bit?' I asked, starting to feel panicky myself.

Georgina took a deep breath. 'Well, no. That detective, what's his name, Evans, and that officer who looks like you. Said they were taking Sean and Dylan downtown for questioning.'

'She doesn't look like me,' I insisted, emphasizing every word.

'Are you listening to me?' Georgina said. 'They. Took. The. Twins.'

In my experience, when the cops *really* come to get you, they arrive at the crack of dawn while you're still in your jammies. No time for phone calls. No time for coffee. Grab you when you're most vulnerable – *Yes, yes, I did it! Now please may I have a cup of coffee?*

'Relax,' I told my sister. 'It's not serious until they get out the handcuffs.'

'I told the twins not to say anything until the attorney got there,' Georgina said.

'Tim?'

'No. I called that guy that Tim recommended. Sydney Foster. I think we need the big guns, don't you?'

'Wouldn't hurt. Is he going to meet the boys at the station?'

'I don't even know where that is!' she whined.

'East Fayette Street,' I said, speaking from personal experience, 'but the attorney will know that.'

'I didn't actually talk to him,' Georgina said, 'but I left a message with his service.' I heard a sharp intake of breath. 'What if he doesn't get there in time?'

'Don't worry, Georgina. Sean and Dylan are not stupid.' After a moment I added, 'Do you want me to come up?'

Georgina heaved a sigh. 'Would you? I don't want to be alone.'

'You're alone?' That surprised me. 'Where's Julie?'

'Working at the day care center. She'll be home around three.'

'Maybe the twins will be back by then, too,' I said, trying to sound reassuring. 'And I'll be there as soon as I can.'

After I hung up, I filled a travel mug with coffee, doctored it with half and half and extra sugar, texted Paul to say where I was going and set out.

I'd driven to Baltimore so often in the previous month that my car could probably navigate there on its own. To keep the drive interesting, I like to vary the route every now and again. That day, I decided to skirt the Inner Harbor and head straight up Charles Street, a slower trip by five minutes or so, but less stress-fraught than the beltway.

I stopped by Eddie's to pick up a continental breakfast tray before heading around the corner to my sister's. Fueled by coffee and Danishes, I helped Georgina address thank you notes while we waited for news, good or bad.

All the mini-Danishes were gone by the time Dylan texted: *Hey! Don't worry. On our way home.*

Georgina collapsed over the countertop, limp with relief.

'Sit down,' I said, when the twins wandered into the kitchen twenty minutes later, looking glum but not suicidal.

'Who pigged out?' asked Dylan, eyeing the half-empty platter.

'Hush up, young man,' I said. 'I'm on a sugar high and could be dangerous.' I shoved the platter in his direction. 'Help yourself. Sit down. Then talk.'

'Did the lawyer show up?' Georgina wanted to know as she watched her sons tuck into the pastries.

'Ms Foster? Yeah, she was super,' Dylan said.

That caught my attention. 'She?'

Dylan shrugged. 'Tall, brunette, around forty wearing wicked don't-mess-with-me glasses.'

I'd forgotten Sydney could be a girl's name, too.

'You were right about the videotape, Aunt Hannah,' Sean mumbled around a mouthful of croissant. 'They questioned Dylan and me separately, but afterwards, Ms Foster got us together and the cops showed us the video.'

'Jesus, Mary and Joseph!' Georgina blurted. 'So? So? Don't keep us in suspense, dammit! Who was it?'

Instead of answering his mother, Sean turned to me. 'It was surreal, Aunt Hannah, like looking in a mirror. My God, it *is* me, I thought. Maybe I drove home in a blackout?'

My heart did a somersault. 'You mean you *lied* to everyone earlier about your whereabouts, Sean?'

'No, no!' He swiped at his bangs, clearing them out of his eyes. 'I was at the beach, like I said. The guy on the tape? He looked exactly like me, but he couldn't have been.'

On the next stool over, Dylan nodded. 'I thought it was Sean, too.' He turned to his brother. 'Sorry I went off on you like that, bro, but when I saw the tape, I thought you'd been shitting me.'

'We asked them to run the tape again, and there was something not quite right about it.' Sean wiped his hands clean on a napkin, balled it up. 'Whoever the guy was, he was wearing a light-blue windbreaker. I don't even *own* a windbreaker, let alone a light-blue one,' he said with a tone of distain, as if owning such a garment would be a fashion *faux pas.*

'But if he looked like you, Sean, why did the police let you go?'

Dylan answered for his brother. 'Because the tape doesn't prove anything, Mom. Let's say, just for the sake of argument, that it was actually Sean on the tape. All it proves is that Sean talked to Dad around one-fifteen and that he lied about it for some reason. There can't be any physical evidence connecting Sean to Dad's murder or Sean would be sitting in the slammer as we speak.'

'Sydney Foster asked if I was being charged with a crime, and they said, "Not at this time". She told me there's a possibility they'll come back to me later, so I shouldn't get too complacent.'

'What does the tape actually show?' I asked. Sean had just bit into another croissant, so I aimed the question at Dylan.

'It was really hard to watch,' Dylan said, his voice choked with emotion. 'I really miss him, you know?' His Adam's apple bobbled as he swallowed hard. After a moment, he said, 'Dad walks down the driveway with this guy who looks like Sean, they talk a bit over by the trampoline, then Dad walks down the lawn toward the shed.'

'The guy follows him,' his brother continued without missing a beat.

'Did either man seem angry?' I asked Sean.

'No, they were just talking. But Dad has this body language, you know, like he wishes the fellow would just go away.'

'Then Dad gets out his cell phone,' Dylan continued. 'Looked like he was taking a call. Anyway, he turns his back on the guy.'

'After Dad finishes the call,' Sean went on, 'he sticks the phone back in his pocket, turns around, looking surprised the guy is still hanging around. Then the guy takes a piece of paper out of the pocket of his windbreaker, unfolds it, and shows it to Dad.'

'They talk for a couple of minutes, then the guy walks away,' Dylan said.

'Which way did he go?' I asked.

'Back toward the house and down the driveway,' Sean said.

'And your dad?'

'Went into the shed and came out with the hedge clippers, then . . .'

'Fade to black,' added his brother.

Georgina, who had been listening silently while her sons told their story, finally spoke up. 'What I don't understand is this. If your father was killed in the shed, how come the actual murderer didn't show up on Claudia Turner's videotape, later on when it actually happened?'

'You're not going to believe this,' Dylan said, 'but a pigeon flew up and perched on the camera, skewing it down. All it recorded after that was Mrs Turner weeding her mint patch.'

'Then they shouldn't be bothering my children,' Georgina huffed. Turning to the twins, she asked, 'Does that mean you're both off the hook?'

Sean shrugged, his face turned serious. 'They told us not to leave town.'

Georgina snorted. 'I thought cops only said that on television.'

'I'm not going anywhere anyway, Mom. I'm working on a team project and they'd kill me if I ran out on them.'

'What kind of project?' I asked, genuinely curious.

Sean made quote marks in the air. 'Land Use, Parking, and Post Internal Combustion Settlement Patterns.'

Dylan grinned. '"If this young man expresses himself in terms too deep for me, why, what a very singularly deep young man this deep young man must be".'

Quoting Gilbert and Sullivan, I thought, smiling to myself, was a refreshing change from slinging Bible verses about like weapons.

I had opened my mouth to ask Sean what in blue blazes his project was about when, correctly reading the puzzlement on my face, he clarified, 'Urban planning. We're looking for cures for Parkageddon.'

'Ah,' I said, trying to sound wise.

'We're not quite finished here,' Sean said, reaching for his cell phone and tapping it to life. 'The cops isolated a frame from the videotape, enhanced it and made a still. They gave the still to our attorney, but she let me take a photo of it after we got into the cab.' He hopped off his bar stool, walked around to our side of the counter and set his cell phone down between his mother and me.

I stared at the image on the screen. My nephew, Sean Cardinale, stared right back.

Next to me Georgina gasped and grabbed my arm. 'No way!'

I leaned closer, squinting at the tiny screen.

Like looking in a mirror, Sean had said earlier, and yet . . . I flicked my fingers to enlarge the image. 'This isn't Sean,' I said, trying to keep my voice calm. 'Take a look.' I circled my hand in the air until I had everyone's undivided attention. 'Sean parts his hair on the left. This guy, whoever he is, parts his hair on the right.'

'Maybe the image's reversed?' Georgina suggested.

'Nope,' I said. 'The numbers painted on the garbage bins are right way round.'

'It's not Sean!' Georgina whooped.

'No, it's not.'

'Then who the hell *is* it?'

'That's a very good question.' I looked up at Sean. 'I think you better call Ms Foster, don't you?'

'They say everyone has a doppelgänger,' Dylan mused. 'Someone who looks exactly like you, down to that annoying mole you've been meaning to have removed.'

'Story of my life,' Sean snorted.

'I didn't mean twins, obviously,' his brother said.

'Time out, boys,' I said. 'One of you call Sydney Foster now. Let her know what we've discovered about the guy in this picture. In the meantime, keep looking. I think Lacey will be easier to find than doppelgängers.'

TWENTY-EIGHT

Several days later, I met Georgina for lunch at Atwater's Belvedere Square Market, a popular eatery featuring home-made soups and artisanal sandwiches. After picking up our order at a counter inside the sprawling market, we managed to snag one of the sidewalk tables, shaded from the noontime sun by a green and white awning.

The police had been strangely quiet, and we hadn't heard anything more from the twins' attorney, but rather than feeling relieved, our nerves were humming with unresolved tension.

'I think we need some time away. Just us sisters. You, me and Ruth,' I said after we sat down, emphasizing my point with a spoon of corn chowder.

Georgina harrumphed. 'Remember how well our last sister trip turned out?'

'All the more reason to try again,' I said.

Georgina nibbled on her avocado toast, apparently mulling it over.

'How long has it been since you visited our place on the Eastern Shore?' I asked.

Four years previously, Paul and I had purchased a fixer-upper on Chiconnesick Creek near Elizabethtown, Maryland. We'd repaired, renovated and laid its ghosts to rest and now spent almost every summer weekend enjoying our cottage retreat.

Georgina sipped her chai latte. 'Honestly, Hannah, I can't remember. A year ago maybe?'

'I rest my case,' I said, sliding the soup bowl aside and reaching for my grilled ham muffaletta. 'Ruth cleared her schedule for this coming weekend. Say you can, too.'

'I thought you and Ruth were going to tackle Dad's storage unit this weekend.'

'We were, but Dennis called and needed his truck so we had to postpone. It's not like there's any rush. Nobody's touched anything in there for years.'

'You'll probably run up against rust, mold and mildew,' she grumbled.

'Climate controlled,' I told her. 'Stop changing the subject. Are you coming or not?'

Her brow furrowed. 'Gosh, Hannah . . . I don't know. What about the kids?'

'What about them? The twins are in school, Julie's filling out job applications . . .'

'Aren't you forgetting about Colin?' she cut in.

'Colin can stay with Emily. I've already checked with her. A little cousin time with Timmy will be fun for both of them.'

She still looked skeptical. 'Ganging up on me again, are you?'

I confessed that we were. 'The older kids are grownups, Georgina. And they won't even have to cook. You have more casseroles than they could eat in a month of Sundays. I know, because I stowed them in your freezer. Thaw and bake. Easy peasey.'

She dredged up a smile from somewhere. 'OK, Hannah, you've talked me into it.'

'Great!' I said. 'So, here's the plan. If we're going to avoid weekend traffic on the Bay Bridge, you'll need to bring Colin down to Emily's early on Friday morning.'

'Wait a minute!' she said. 'He's got school!'

'Missing a day or two of fifth grade will not screw up Colin's chances of getting into Harvard, Georgina.'

She laughed, the first genuine laugh I'd heard from her since before Scott's death. 'OK, you win!' And she tucked into her lunch with enthusiasm. Both the laugh and the appetite were promising signs my sister was coming back from the dark place where she'd been living lately.

Mid-afternoon on Friday, after a provisioning trip to Harris Teeter outside Easton, Ruth, Georgina and I arrived at the cottage we'd named *Our Time*. I'd phoned ahead to give Laurie, our caretaker, a head's up. She'd put out clean towels, made up the beds with fresh linen and opened the windows to the balmy, late summer breeze. When we arrived, Laurie's husband, Rusty, had just finished cleaning the barbeque grill. He greeted us with a breezy, 'Have a great weekend, ladies,' tossed his tools into a compartment on the back of his Harley and took off in a shower of gravel.

After stowing the groceries, I kicked off my shoes and padded barefoot out onto the deck that overlooked the creek. A great blue heron posed at the end of our dock as flocks of geese honked noisily overhead. 'Ah, that's what I'm talking about,' I said.

Georgina came up behind me, carrying a tall glass of iced tea. 'Thanks for talking me into this, Hannah.' She settled into a deck chair, turned her face toward the afternoon sun and closed her eyes.

'What room do you want me to take?' Ruth shouted from an upstairs window.

'Either one,' I yelled.

'I have dibs on the yellow room,' Georgina shouted back without even opening her eyes.

I would be sleeping in the master suite I usually shared with Paul in a wing addition just off the living room.

After cheeseburgers on the grill, we relaxed in chairs on the deck listening to the keening of the frogs. Ruth unearthed a second bottle of Oyster Bay merlot which paired perfectly with the dark chocolate-covered caramels I'd picked up at Trader Joes. I'd been hiding them from myself in the cottage pantry.

'When it comes to religion and politics,' Georgina said, breaking the companionable silence, 'I have nothing in common with Church of the Falls people, but they couldn't have been kinder to me and the kids after Scott died.'

'"Freely you have received, freely give",' Ruth quoted. 'Book of Matthew, I believe.'

Georgina smiled. 'Scott would know. He could quote chapter and verse.' After a moment she added, 'The Johnsons sent a beautiful peace lily in a pot and the nicest handwritten note.'

'The Johnsons?' Ruth asked.

'Our Native American cousins,' Georgina reminded her. 'I'm sorry I didn't get to meet them.'

This was a welcome, one-hundred-and-eighty-degree turnaround from her previous attitude.

'I'm kicking myself, too,' Ruth said, 'but at least I have an excuse. I was out of the country. Have they gone back to South Dakota, then, Hannah?'

'They've been home for a couple of weeks. Everyone had to get back to work.'

'Do you think they'll ever come back?' Georgina asked.

'They hope to,' I said. 'But until then, there's no reason you couldn't visit them.'

'Julie's talking about going,' Georgina said. 'She's rather taken with the twins, I gather. Mai and Nick.'

'They're great kids,' I told her. 'Properly brought up.'

Thinking about the mystery surrounding the death of our common ancestor – Joseph White Bear – I reminded my sisters that I still had the key to our father's storage unit. 'I'm looking for a good time to reschedule the work. Ruth, are you still in?'

Ruth raised a lazy hand.

'Georgina, do you want to help us look through it for clues?' Ruth turned her head. 'Come on, Georgina. Be a sport.'

'I just can't right now,' Georgina said. 'Just about everything sends me off on a crying jag. Looking at old family photos will do me in for sure. Maybe later?'

'Wasula's a hundred and two,' I reminded her, 'so I'm not inclined to dilly-dally.'

'No worries,' Ruth said. 'I'm all in. Name the day, and I'll be there, as long as it's not Thursday. That's my yoga day.'

A buzzer rudely rent the air. I excused myself to transfer a load of sheets from the washing machine to the dryer. When I returned, Ruth was silhouetted by the setting sun, leafing through the *Tidewater Times*, a purse-sized booklet that included feature articles, tide tables and a monthly calendar of local events sandwiched between ads for local businesses.

'Here's something I'd like to see,' Ruth said. 'It's an exhibition at the Blue Crab Art Gallery in Elizabethtown.' She glanced up from the page. 'Have you ever been there, Hannah?'

'Yes, once. It's lovely,' I said. 'They bought an old pharmacy and converted it.'

'What kind of show?' Georgina asked lazily.

'It's called "Arts by the Shore",' Ruth said, referring to the booklet. 'Showcasing over fifty regional artists and craftsmen. Maybe I'll find some merchandise to sell at the shop.' She closed the booklet over her thumb, marking the place. 'How about we have lunch somewhere in town, then check it out?'

'Cool,' Georgina said, looking more relaxed than I'd seen her since the August we'd spent at Rehoboth Beach shortly before her marriage to Scott. 'I'm in.'

My wine glass was halfway to my lips when a silent alarm brought me up short. Scott and Georgina's wedding had been in early September. They had an anniversary coming up soon. I drained my glass and reached for the wine bottle, thinking *Beware: Dangerous Shoals Ahead.*

Around ten o'clock, with dishes done, my sisters having retired for the evening and a last load of sheets and pillowcases tumbling in the dryer, I set about the routine of putting the cottage to bed for the night. As I flipped on the nightlight in the upstairs hallway, I noticed that Georgina's door was open and her bed hadn't been slept in. I poked my head in the doorway. 'Georgina?'

Her room was empty.

She wasn't in the bathroom, either.

No need to panic, I thought as I hustled downstairs to search for my sister.

I found her outside, dressed in her nightshirt, sitting at the end of the dock, dangling her bare feet in the water. Moonlight glistened off the tears that streamed down her cheeks.

'Keep that up,' I said as I settled down next to her, 'and you'll raise the water level in the Bay.'

Georgina swiped tears away with the back of her hand, and then surprised me by laughing.

Grief affects people in unique and mysterious ways, I'd found. I wrapped my arm around my sister and drew her close. 'I know you loved him, Georgina.'

Surprisingly, she began to giggle. 'But that's just it, Hannah! Do you want to know why I'm crying? It's not because I miss Scott, it's because for the first time in my life I feel truly *free!*'

If I had been sitting any closer to the end of the dock, I might have tumbled straight into the water. 'What?'

'Shocks the hell out of me, too, just saying it out loud.'

'But tears?' I said.

'Because I feel guilty about it.' She turned to me, eyes wide. 'Am I a terrible person?'

I assured her that she wasn't.

'You won't tell anybody, will you?'

'Don't be silly. Of course not.' After a moment, I asked, 'Are you going to be OK, Georgina? Financially, I mean.'

'Scott took good care of us, Hannah. He had a huge life insurance policy and some sort of mortgage insurance that paid off the house. Turns out Scott was worth more to us dead than alive.' Georgina's voice quavered. 'I feel horrible about that.'

Georgina scissored her legs, splashing water over her calves, sending mini-waves rippling into the creek. 'Can I share something else?'

'If you think my heart can take it.'

'It's good news,' she said. 'I got an email upstairs just now. In October, I'll be playing the organ again at All Hallows.'

'I thought you couldn't stand the warden there, Lionel Streeting?'

'It's not nice to say, but Lionel had a stroke and had to retire, thank God. The new church warden is a woman, someone I know from before, in fact. She sought me out when their organist moved to Seattle. I'd told her no at first, but after Scott . . .' She let the thought die.

'That's fabulous, Georgina,' I said, meaning it.

'It is, isn't it?' Another tear slid down her cheek. 'I'm *so* happy.'

I bumped her arm with my elbow. 'Little Sister, you are hopeless.'

TWENTY-NINE

The next morning, I awoke early. I poured myself a mug of coffee, stirred in sugar and a splash of half and half and carried it out to the end of the dock to watch the sun rise.

Ruth and Georgina slept in. When the aroma of fresh-brewed coffee didn't lure my sisters downstairs, I tried the nuclear option: frying bacon. Twenty minutes later, still dressed in our nightshirts, we were enjoying breakfast on the deck and planning our day.

At ten thirty, casually dressed in jeans, T-shirts and sensible walking shoes, we piled into the Volvo. With grass *swish-swishing* under the car, I drove cautiously down the rutted track that led from the cottage to the main road. Five miles of corn and soybean fields later, we reached civilization – the colonial town of Elizabethtown.

Carefully avoiding jaywalking Saturday shoppers, I steered the car down High Street, through the town's single traffic light where High intersected with King and parked on the town square between the war memorial and the gaily-painted bandstand. Retracing our route down High Street on foot, we found the Blue Crab Gallery where I was pleased to note that the new owners, out of respect for the building's history, had retained the 'Wm Chase & Son' spelled in black and white tiles on the sidewalk out front.

When Ruth pushed the door open, a bell jangled, announcing our arrival. 'Wow!' she said as we stepped inside.

Wow, indeed. For the 'Arts by the Shore' event every square inch of floor and wall space had been given over to local artisans.

To our right, panels of painted silk fabrics undulated like Salome's veils in the breeze wafting in through the open door, complementing the stained-glass mirrors that Alison Young had on display in an alcove just beyond.

Ruth, immediately taken by Susan Woythaler's whimsical blown glass ornaments, stopped to chat with the artist about them. When the discussion turned to consignments and invoicing, Georgina and I drifted away. I deserted Georgina at Deborah Kelchner's jewelry stall where she decided to purchase a necklace crafted of silver, polished shells and fresh water pearls, but was having a hard time selecting a pair of matching earrings, and refusing to take my advice anyway. Let Deborah deal with Georgina, I thought.

I was inexorably drawn to a section near the back of the gallery by the torso of a mannequin decked out in a bikini made of vegetables. The area beyond the mannequin had been dedicated to low-brow pop art, including colorful Cinco de Mayo-style skulls painted on a recycled skateboard deck. Two large wooden panels, mounted on the wall, depicted surfer dudes captioned with graffiti-style puff lettering: Amped! Froth! Goofy Foot! My taste in decorating was eclectic, but not so eclectic as to include surfer dudes. I wandered on, past the artist who specialized in dog portraits and the mustachioed gentleman who crafted fish out of wine bottles and twisted metal, heading instead for a separate room marked Fine Photography.

Yes! This was more my speed. Roger Miller's vibrant, color photographs of Fourth of July fireworks over the Annapolis skyline, the Chesapeake Bay Bridge at sunset, and the Thomas Point Lighthouse decorated a moveable partition to my right. Black and white photographs by Pete Souza of Naval Academy men and women going about the serious business of being midshipmen hung on a similar partition set at right angles to Miller's work. The wall to the far left, however, had been dedicated, not to photographs, but to a special long-term exhibit of seven beautifully matted and framed etchings, each signed by the artist, James A. Earl.

I had never heard of James Earl, but the man was talented, no doubt about that. I was particularly taken by an exquisitely detailed etching of plovers skittering in the surf entitled 'Can't Catch Me!'. I noted the price – affordable – and decided it would be perfect for the blank wall over my desk at *Our Time*, then moved on to the next etching.

A great blue heron dominated the foreground of 'Ready for My Closeup', its every feather meticulously executed. The magnificent bird had a rapt audience of two: a middle-aged couple shared an Adirondack loveseat in the background. For some reason, the couple looked familiar. I stared at the etching for a long moment, then stepped closer, hoping I wouldn't set off any security alarms. If the couple in the etching hadn't been holding hands, I would have sworn I was gawking at a portrait of Pastor Robert Thomas Selden and Judee McDaniel. No, don't be silly, I told myself. You saw them only that one time, at the reception following Scott's funeral. You're probably mistaken. I needed to consult an expert.

Georgina was no longer at the shell jewelry booth. Deborah Kelchner had last seen my sister heading in the direction of Beaded Magic. I wandered through the maze of exhibits looking for her, but when I got to Beaded Magic, she'd already moved on.

If I were correct, and both married-to-other-people Brother Bob and Judee Two-Es had been caught by an artist canoodling on Maryland's eastern shore, it would be important to know when. It was impossible to tell from the etching itself; the only assumption I could make from the shorts and flip-flops the couple wore was that it was summertime. I'd need to consult the artist.

Earlier, I'd noticed a forty-something guy wearing an oxford button-down shirt belted into a pair of chinos, holding forth near the front of the gallery. Since he stood behind a table smiling, greeting and dispensing champagne in three-ounce paper cups to all comers, I assumed he was one of the owners.

'Those amazing etchings in the back room?' I asked as I accepted a cup of champagne from the man's outstretched fingers. 'What can you tell me about the artist?'

'Jim Earl? He's one of our favorites. Retired a few years ago from the University of Maryland. He was a physics professor.'

'I'm thinking about buying the plovers,' I said truthfully, 'and I'd like to know a little more about him.'

He reached for a loose-leaf notebook on a shelf behind him and laid it on the table in front of the ice bucket. 'This has information about each of our artists.'

I chug-a-lugged the champagne then tossed the empty cup in the wastebasket near his feet. 'Thanks,' I said, reaching for the notebook. 'I'll take a look.'

'It's got Jim's CV and contact information in it,' the owner said, 'but why don't you go talk to him yourself? He's over there, by the display window.'

Sometime in my youth or childhood, I must have done something good.

James Earl sat at the front of the store in a tall-backed wicker chair, sipping from a cup of coffee that I knew from the logo had come from the High Spot Café directly across the street. He seemed to be sketching in a small, leather-bound book.

From the information in the gallery's notebook, I learned that Earl had a degree from MIT and had earned a second degree in studio art, one semester at a time, while teaching Astronomy at the University of Maryland. Blessed by a financially conservative father and a mother who was a canny investor, Earl's family foundation generously supported music and the arts as well as local environmental causes.

If the information in the notebook was correct, the philanthropist was ninety-three years old, but from where I stood, about ten feet away, he didn't look a day over eighty. I returned the notebook to its place on the shelf and walked over to introduce myself.

'Hi, I'm Hannah Ives. May I talk to you about your work?'

Earl looked up from his sketchbook – a leather-bound book about the size of a paperback – and holstered the pen between the leaves. 'Always delighted.'

I got straight to the point. 'I love your etchings, Mr Earl. I'm planning on buying the plovers, but one of the other etchings caught my attention. I think you've drawn a couple of my friends. The couple in the Adirondack loveseat? With the heron?'

'Could be,' he said.

'Do you know who they are?' I asked.

'I thought you said they were your friends.'

I smiled ruefully. 'They *look* like my friends,' I said, but from the twinkle in his dark eyes, I knew he was teasing me.

'I didn't ask them,' he said. 'Frankly, I was more interested in the heron, the way he stood still for so long, like an artist's model, posing for me.'

'Do you work from photographs?' I asked.

He frowned and shook his head, as if suggesting such a thing was sacrilege. 'I draw from life. You probably noticed me sketching just now. There was a pretty redhead looking at jewelry a few minutes ago . . .'

He had to be talking about Georgina. 'She's my sister,' I told him.

He opened the sketchbook to the page he'd been working on. In the short time Georgina'd been standing in front of the jewelry counter, Earl had captured her perfectly, down to the details of the claw that held up her hair, the flowered design on her T-shirt and the fact that her left shoestring was untied.

'You're very good,' I said.

'Thank you.'

'May I have a closer look?' I asked, holding out my hand for the sketchbook.

With a smile, James Earl placed his sketchbook in it.

Earl had sketched Georgina on the right-hand page, and on the left side, facing it, Earl had written, 'Redhead, Blue Crab Gallery, Elizabethtown, Maryland, September 2, 2018.'

I started to turn back a few pages before thinking to ask permission. 'May I?'

'Of course.'

He'd drawn each of his sketches in the same format – a drawing to the right with the subject, place and date documented on the facing leaf to the left. 'Did you do a preliminary sketch for the heron etching?' I inquired.

'I always do preliminary sketches,' he said.

'Would it be in this sketchbook?'

'I'm not sure,' Earl said. 'It was some time ago, but you can check. I run through sketchbooks fairly quickly, but if it's in this one, it will be toward the beginning.'

Sometimes you get lucky. The preliminary sketch for 'Ready for My Closeup' appeared on the third page: Great Blue Heron, Chesapeake Bay Hyatt, Cambridge, MD, July 29, 2018.

'Here it is!' I announced triumphantly. 'I see it was done in Cambridge this summer.'

The Cambridge Hyatt's full name was a mouthful: the Hyatt Regency Chesapeake Bay Golf Resort, Spa and Marina. It was also an upscale conference center. In a picturesque setting overlooking the Choptank River, it attracted groups from all over the country who could afford the costs.

'Refresh my memory,' he said, holding out his hand for the sketchbook.

He studied his work, brow furrowed. 'Ah, yes. I was speaking at a physics symposium in Cambridge that weekend. There was a golf tournament going on, and the place was crawling with visitors.' He paged forward. 'Here's a sketch of some kids playing giant chess near the Grand Fireplace, and another one of seagulls at the bar on the Breakwater Pavilion.'

I checked out those sketches, too, just to be polite. Wearing what I hoped was a disarming smile, I said, 'Do you mind if I take a photograph of the heron sketch? To show my friends?' I added hastily.

'Not at all.' Earl paged back to the heron. Using both hands, he held the sketchbook open in front of my iPhone.

'Thank you,' I said as I aimed, framing both pages on the screen, and touched the button to capture the image. 'My friends will appreciate it.'

After I finished, James Earl closed his sketchbook and slipped it into his breast pocket. He smiled up at me from his chair. 'But I'd rather they bought the etching.'

I tapped my temple. 'I'll see what I can do about that, Mr Earl.'

'It's Bob and Judee, for sure,' Georgina said when I finally tracked her down and dragged her to the back room to view Earl's etchings first-hand. 'See that butterfly on the woman's

ankle? Judee's got one just like it.' She took a deep breath, then
let it out slowly. 'Well, I'll be *damned!*'

'Not you,' I said reasonably. 'It's Brother Bob who needs to
be worrying about damnation. Last time I looked, *Thou Shalt
Not Commit Adultery* was still on the list of Ten Commandments.

'One problem. I checked out the date with the artist,' I told
her. 'July 29th was a Sunday. Wouldn't Brother Bob have been
in church?'

'Not necessarily. One of the assistant pastors takes over
when Bob is away. But, there's a way to find out. Church of
the Falls posts their sermons online. It'd be easy to see who
was preaching that Sunday.'

Prompted by Georgina, I logged onto the Church's website
on my iPhone. A search of the sermons revealed that Brother
Bob's slot on the 29th had been filled by Brother Vernon
speaking on 'Storm-Proofing Your Life'.

'If Brother Bob was doing what we think he was doing that
Sunday, he might need a bit of storm-proofing himself,' I said.
'Tamara didn't strike me as the Live-and-Let-Live type.'

'Tell me about it,' Georgina snorted. 'Ever wonder why the
church secretary looks like your maiden aunt? Tamara hired
her.'

I had to laugh.

'Click on the pull-down menu for News,' Georgina suggested,
leaning in close. 'Let's see what Bob *said* he would be doing
that weekend. There should be a newsletter for July.'

'What's KidMin?' I asked after the newsletter filled the
screen.

'It's short for children's ministry.'

I turned the iPhone screen in her direction. 'According to
this, he and Judee were attending a KidMin conference in
Cambridge that weekend.'

'Let me see that.' Georgina practically snatched the phone
out of my hand. As I watched speechlessly, she initiated a fresh
Safari search and tapped a few keys. 'Then he's a big, fat liar.
The KidMin Conference was in Dayton, Ohio this year.'

We exchanged glances.

'Do you suppose Scott discovered they'd lied about where
they were that weekend?' Georgina said. 'And if he knew

about their affair, my God, was Scott killed to keep him quiet about it?'

'That seems extreme,' I said, 'especially in this day and age. Was Scott bothered when a serial adulterer married a nude model and moved into the White House?'

Georgina snorted. 'Not particularly. He even voted for him.'

'Then it's possible he wouldn't have been troubled by learning that his pastor was having an affair with a co-worker,' I said. 'Perhaps something was going on here that had nothing to do with Scott.'

'Better safe than sorry,' Georgina said. 'Open your email, attach that photo and type what I tell you.'

A minute later, my email swooshed. If Dick Evans, the homicide detective in charge of the investigation into my brother-in-law's murder was on top of his inbox, a copy of James Earl's sketchbook and what Georgina and I knew about it would soon be in his hands.

THIRTY

I'd been so busy providing the police with suspects in my brother-in-law's murder that I was barely able to keep up with my email via iPhone let alone any heretofore unknown relatives who might be trying to connect with me through Gen-Tree. And I'd completely forgotten about my custodial arrangement with Julie's family tree, until a message popped up on the email account I'd linked to it.

Dear JLC2000.

Twenty-five years ago, my mother underwent in vitro fertilization at the Great Lakes Center for Fertility and Women's Health in Chicago and became pregnant with sperm from Donor #7135. Through Gen-Tree DNA testing, I have located fifteen half-siblings, also children of Donor #7135. Your DNA results indicate you may be a donor sibling, too. Were you a child of Donor #7135? Hope to hear back from you soon. DavidM23

I sat back, stunned, trying to take that in. When I could breathe again, I clicked back through the Gen-Tree menus to Julie's test results. In the weeks since I'd first uploaded her data, DavidM23 and at least ten other individuals were showing up as 'close family' with 'high probability'.

Scott was definitely Julie's father: you had only to look at her to figure that out. Her glorious hair came from the Drew side of our family, true, but her green eyes and the dimpled chin were pure Cardinale.

I explored some more and discovered that while I shared DNA with Julie, as expected, none of her donor sibling matches shared anything with me.

For Julie and her donor siblings, then, Scott had to be the common denominator.

Where had Scott been twenty-five years ago – I counted backwards – in 1983? Nineteen years old, studying for an undergraduate degree in Economics at the University of Chicago, that's where. We'd all heard, time and time again, 'poor me' stories of how he'd worked his way through college waiting tables. No surprise he failed to mention that he'd supplemented the income from his part-time job in a campus dining hall by selling his sperm.

No wonder Scott had been so squirrelly about Julie being tested. Despite all privacy assurances that presumably had been given by the clinic at the time, Donor #7135 had just been outed to at least one person: me.

I felt like a bomb had gone off in the basement. Fifteen matches and counting. Donor #7135 had apparently been a bestseller. How many other little #7135s were out there? How many children did my late brother-in-law have?

And what's more, what was I going to do with this information?

Do I answer DavidM23?

I decided to leave that up to Julie. 'Do you want to tell your mother or shall I?' I wrote, attached David's email and hit send before I could change my mind.

'Let me get this straight,' Julie said when she phoned, 'because this is totally freaking me out. I have sixteen half-brothers and sisters, all around twenty-five years old.'

'So far,' I added helpfully.

'What if I had married one of them?' she wailed.

'Now you won't,' I said.

'So I emailed the guy and he got right back. They're planning a reunion.'

'Reunion!' Georgina shrieked in the background. 'That's a funny way to put it.'

'I'm putting you on speaker,' Julie said. 'Mom's really pissed.'

'Pissed is putting it mildly, Hannah. If Scott weren't already dead, I'd kill him.'

'I warned you,' Julie said, lowering her voice.

'You tell that David person that I have absolutely no interest in joining his sister-mom club, either, Hannah. I got my sperm donations the regular way, thank you, by cutting out the middle man.'

'Oooh, that's harsh,' her daughter said.

'Georgina, stop sputtering and listen to me. Do you think Scott knew that his donor kids had connected?'

'If he did, do you think he'd tell *me*?'

'I'm worried that one of them may have tracked him down. Think about it. Somebody was seen in the backyard talking to Scott on the day he died. Somebody who looked exactly like Sean.'

'It wasn't DavidM23,' Julie cut in. 'He sent me a photo. He's got masses of dark hair.'

'Are you thinking that one of Scott's donor sons tracked him down and Scott blew him off?'

'Oh, Scott would deny it if confronted, that's for sure,' Georgina snarked. 'Sixteen kids out there, maybe more? Shit!'

'Dad could deny it all he wants, Mom, but DNA doesn't lie.'

'Maybe the kid couldn't deal with rejection,' I said.

To me, Julie said, 'Should we tell the cops?'

'I think you'd better.'

'That'll take their mind off Sean,' Julie said.

'We can hope so,' I said.

'OK, Aunt Hannah,' Julie said, her voice unnaturally loud. 'I'll get that number for you now. Let me put you on hold.'

What on earth? But I was dealing with Julie, so hang on for the ride.

After a brief silence, my niece returned to the call. 'Hi, I'm back. Had to get rid of Mom.'

'What did you do with her? Lock her in the bathroom?'

'Ha ha, I wish. No, I wanted to talk to you about something. In private.'

'Why do I have the feeling I'm about to be sorry you called?'

'I want to go to that reunion,' she said without preamble.

'Then go,' I said. 'What's stopping you?'

I figured Julie was going to ask me for money, but she surprised me by saying, 'I want you to go with me.'

'Julie!'

'I do, I'm completely serious, Aunt Hannah. I'll even pay your way.'

'Don't be ridiculous. You don't have that kind of money.'

'Do, too. I've been saving up from my day care job.'

'Well, I wouldn't accept it.'

'Then you'll go?'

'I didn't say yes, Julie.'

'But, you didn't say no either.'

'What does your mother say about it?'

'She says those children have nothing to do with her, and that I should do whatever I want. And what I want is to go to that reunion. Besides, maybe this guy who looks like Sean will be there.'

'Where is it?' I asked, feeling my resolve weakening.

'A place in Illinois I've never heard of called Des Plaines.'

'Bummer,' I said. 'If you'd said Honolulu . . .'

'Please?' Julie begged. 'If you were in my situation, wouldn't you need moral support, too?'

I had to agree that I would, and I was curious about the Sean lookalike, too.

Which explains why three hours later I found myself on the American Airlines website booking two flights to Chicago. On my VISA.

THIRTY-ONE

O'Hare Airport: the tenth circle of Dante's hell. Four terminals, nine concourses and a complex so large that it spans both Cook and DuPage counties. You need wizardry, not moving walkways, to get from one concourse to another.

I had planned on a rental car for our trip to Des Plaines until DavidM23, the organizer whose last name turned out to be Moody, told us about the Best Western courtesy airport shuttle, so I signed us up for a round trip.

After a forty-minute drive, the shuttle pulled under the portico of a Best Western by the BP Station, just past Mr Pup and directly across the street from Burger King. Modest accommodation to be sure, but clean and comfortable, and the seventy-nine dollar rate suited my pocketbook just fine.

Julie didn't want to be seen until she'd had a chance to freshen up, so we checked in at reception and hustled up to our room on the second floor.

'Which bed do you want?' I asked as the door clicked shut behind us. 'I'm not particular.'

Julie dropped her rucksack and fell backward, like a tree, onto the bed nearest the window. She bounced up and down a bit, testing out the mattress. 'This is cool,' she said. After plumping up several of the pillows and propping them behind her back, she opened the Welcome Envelope we'd been given at the front desk.

'What's in the envelope?' I asked as I unzipped my carry-on and removed my toiletry bag.

Julie shuffled several pages. 'There's a schedule of events.' She looked up from the page. 'We're due in the conference room at four for a meet and greet, followed by cocktails at five and dinner at six at a restaurant called the Silver Stallion.'

'It's practically next door,' I said. 'We drove by it on the way in.'

Julie looked up. 'Sounds like a gay bar.'

I laughed. 'It's a family place, I think. Steak, chicken, chops.'

'A vegetarian's delight,' she said.

When I returned from hanging up my toiletries on a towel rack in the bathroom, Julie said, 'Here's a list of my known half-siblings with contact information. The ones with an asterisk are supposed to be here,' she said, starting to count. 'Six boys and five girls, including me. None of these people live anywhere near Baltimore,' she said. 'And look! I have a half-ling in Australia! I've never been to Australia.'

'When do you want to go downstairs?' I asked my niece.

'A little after four, maybe?' She grinned nervously. 'I plan to be fashionably late.'

'If it's all right with you, then, I'll put my feet up for a little while.'

'Go for it,' Julie said. 'I'm going to wash my hair again. There's a hair dryer in there, I hope.'

After repeated shampooing, Julie's hair had nearly returned to its natural apricot color, but another washing couldn't hurt. 'Go for it,' I said.

Two hours later, my niece and I, both freshly showered and smelling like Best Western's Aromae Botanicals bath bar, presented ourselves at the door to the hotel's single conference room. Julie vibrated with excitement.

'Welcome!' David Moody said. While he beamed at Julie, I searched his face for a resemblance to my late brother-in-law, but with the exception of his ice-blue eyes, David had the dark-haired, olive-skinned good looks of his mother, Karen, who stood next to him behind the table.

'Welcome,' Karen Moody said, handing me a 'Hello, my name is' stick-on name badge and a Sharpie. 'You must be one of the sister-moms.'

'I'm with Julie,' I told her, neatly side-stepping the question.

Karen peeled a gold star off a roll of stickers and pressed it onto the upper right-hand corner of my nametag. Since she wore a similar gold star, I figured the star identified me as a sister-mom whether I liked it or not.

'Take off a shoe,' Karen said after I'd finished writing 'Hannah' on my nametag and returned the Sharpie.

'I beg your pardon?'

'It's an ice breaker.' She grinned, revealing a row of impossibly even, improbably white teeth. 'Take off your right shoe and throw it in that pile in the middle of the room. As soon as everyone gets here, we'll have some fun.'

Swell.

Julie and I did as we were told.

About two dozen chairs had been arranged around the sides of the small conference room. Julie and I limped over to claim two chairs next to a small table set with a tub of ice studded with small, eight-ounce bottles of water.

'Diddle-diddle-dumpling,' I muttered.

'What?'

'Never mind, Julie,' I said. *Doesn't anybody read nursery rhymes to their children any more?*

As we waited for the 'fun' to begin, Julie and I sat quietly, observing as her half-siblings and their sister-moms arrived and the pile of shoes in the center of the room gradually grew.

'So far, nobody looks the least bit like me,' Julie said, sounding disappointed.

'That's because you're the image of your mother,' I reminded her. 'But, look. The Cardinale genes are pretty strong. Check out all the dimpled chins.'

Julie touched the dimple in her own chin and smiled. Suddenly, she grabbed my arm. 'Oh my god, that guy over there?' She nodded in the direction of the door. 'He looks just like Colin, but all grown up! Like one of those pictures of missing kids on milk cartons all, um, what do you call it?'

'Age progressed?'

'That's it.'

As the room filled up Julie pointed out the various traces of Scott she detected in his offspring. The blue-gray eyes, the sandy hair, the fair skin, the square-shaped ears and the dimple, always the dimple. 'And that guy over there with the buzz cut? Jeesh! He looks just like Sean and Dylan the summer they went whitewater rafting with Outward Bound!' After a moment, she added, 'I'm getting seriously weirded out, Aunt Hannah.'

In truth, I was, too.

'How can I connect in any *real* way with so many siblings?' she whispered. 'I feel like I'm part of a *herd*, not a family.'

'It gives a whole new meaning to the concept of family, doesn't it, Julie?' I said, reaching out for her hand and squeezing it affectionately.

Nearly every chair had been taken by then: half-lings and sister-moms sitting in a ring, eyes darting about, sizing up one another. Eventually, Karen Moody strolled to the center of the circle and clapped her hands for attention. 'Welcome, diblings and sister-moms!'

Julie turned to me and mouthed, 'Diblings?'

'Ugh,' I muttered.

Karen continued to *clap-clap-clap* which we took as a sign we were to join her, as if applauding ourselves for turning up.

'OK, now,' she said after the applause died away. 'When I say "go", everybody run to the center of the room and grab a shoe. Then, you have to find the owner of that shoe and get acquainted!'

I'd played this game before, back in my corporate days, so I'd already set my sights on the turquoise and gray Keens of a sister-mom who came in with her daughter and retreated shyly, like Julie and I had, to a corner.

Karen shouted 'Go!' and the scramble began. After everyone had been reunited with his or her shoe, I found myself back in the corner near the ice tub with Gloria, owner of the Keens, and her daughter, Nevada. Gloria, far from being shy, turned out to be a cheerleader for the Donor Sibling Registry.

'Next game!' Karen announced.

'I'll sit this one out on the sidelines, if you don't mind,' I said.

'Me, too,' Gloria agreed. 'I have enough of touchy-feely HR exercises back at the office. I once had to convince a co-worker to drink blue buttermilk.'

'Bleah!' I said. It made my toes curl just thinking about it.

I did not regret my decision: the next ice breaker involved a jar of M&Ms and a game of twenty questions.

'My favorite food is nachos!'

'The cartoon character that describes me best is Superman!'

'Describe my personality in one word? Oh, that's so hard . . . bubbly!'

While that went on around us, Gloria turned to Julie and asked, 'Have you signed up at the DSR?'

'No, I haven't,' Julie said. 'David found me on Gen-Tree. com. Tell me about DSR.'

'Sixty-thousand members strong and counting,' Nevada explained. 'You put in your donor number and get matched up with half-siblings who share the same donor number. Donors can register, too,' she added. 'If they want to, of course. Our donor, Number 7135, hasn't gone online yet.'

Julie's eyes grew wide and she turned to me as the significance of what Nevada had said sank in. No way Scott would have gone online, Julie knew that. And no wonder he had acted so negatively when he learned about Julie's DNA test kit.

'The largest half-sibling group match they've found so far is two hundred,' Gloria informed us, her face serious. 'The guy keeps track of his kids on an Excel spreadsheet.'

'That's creepy,' Julie said.

'Donor 7135 lived in Chicago, or so I assume because that's where the clinic was,' I said. 'Julie noticed that a lot of her half-siblings still live in the Chicago area. Doesn't anybody worry about incest?'

'Part of my sex education has always been knowing my donor number,' Nevada said, looking directly at Julie.

'I've only just found out,' Julie said, sounding defensive.

Nevada shifted her steely-blue gaze to me. Clearly I'd come up short in the sister-mom department.

'Well,' Julie said, moving on. 'That'll certainly take the zing out of a first date. Hi, I'm Julie and my father was sperm donor number 7135. How about you?'

I was still mulling over the ego maniac sitting in his office and keeping track of his offspring on an Excel spreadsheet. 'Isn't there any law to limit how many kids a donor can father?'

'In my opinion,' Gloria said, 'there should be a cap on sales, but so far, nada.'

'But the sperm banks keep track of everything, right?'

Gloria wagged her head. 'Here's the scary thing: less than

half the women who come to a sperm bank end up reporting
their pregnancy back to the bank.'

'Well, there ought to be a law,' Julie said.

'I agree, but the Food and Drug Administration doesn't. We
tried to get a law passed that would limit the number of times
an individual donor's sperm could be used. It would also
mandate the reporting of donor conceived births and require
post-conception medical updates about the offspring, you know,
in case there turned out to be medical issues with some of the
donors.'

'That sounds like a no-brainer,' Julie said. 'What happened?'

Gloria smiled grimly. 'You're gonna *love* this. The FDA
determined that such a law would infringe on the right to privacy
and the right to procreate, giving the government control over
who has children and with whom.'

I'm afraid I laughed out loud. 'Sorry,' I said, feeling everyone's eyes turn from their M&Ms to me. 'And this is coming
from the same government that wants to tell women when and
how they can have access to birth control, or to a legal
abortion?'

'God Bless America,' Nevada said.

The M&M game eventually drew to a close and we were
herded into the lobby for drinks. In the area where the hotel
normally served breakfast, the reunion organizers had set up
cartons of Box-o-Wine – both red and white – a frosty pitcher
of margaritas, and a bowl of fruit punch. They'd whipped up
onion-herb dip for the potato chips and cut up veggies, and
someone had put small bowls of mixed nuts out on each of the
little, square tables. I lost track of Julie as I grazed among the
hors d'oeuvres; I hadn't eaten since the pretzels on the plane.

When I caught up with Julie again, she and Nevada were
giggling over something another one of their half-sisters, a girl
named Beth, had said.

'Brothers!' Julie hooted. 'I should know. I have three of
them.' Julie didn't add that they would be half-siblings to the
others, too. I'd leave it to her on when, and if, to blow Scott's
cover.

'Come with me,' Nevada said to her sisters. 'You need to
meet Andy Zimmer. We've known about each other for a couple

of years. He's been trying to track our donor down, and he's so close.'

Leaving me to nurse my Pinot Grigio in relative solitude.

Andy turned out to be the Outward Bound version of Sean and Dylan who Julie had singled out earlier at the ice breaker. I watched from a distance as he was backed into a corner near the fireplace by the trio of half-sisters who fluttered around him like groupies.

I studied Andy's profile, so eerily like that of my nephews. If I painted a full head of floppy, Sean-style hair on his short-cropped head, Andy could easily have passed for the lookalike captured on Mrs Turner's video. And if he *were* the donor son who had confronted my brother-in-law in his own backyard on the day he died, Andy would have to know from her nametag that Julie was Scott's standard-issue daughter. How many Cardinales can there be?

'He's close to tracking our donor down,' Nevada had said. If only she knew how close.

I managed to catch Julie's eye by waving my plastic wine glass in a please-fetch-me-another kind of way. When she returned with a refill, I shared my suspicions about Andy.

'No way,' Julie said.

'Way!' I said. 'Turn around and take a good look at him.'

Julie squinted in Andy's direction. 'Maybe from a distance,' she said. 'But if you're right, Aunt Hannah, how can we prove it?'

'Maybe one of us can corner him at dinner,' I said, just as Karen Moody appeared in the lobby ringing a small handbell.

'Better you than me,' Julie said as we joined the parade heading next door to the Silver Stallion, where I was dismayed to see that Karen had arranged assigned seating for our dinner. Tented name cards decorated with the DNA helix placed me at the far end of a long community table and Julie at the other. Andy was seated near the middle, next to Nevada's mother, Gloria, and I ended up with bubbly Beth. If there was a method to Karen's madness, it totally escaped me.

By the time dessert rolled around (homemade rice pudding!) even Beth's wild-and-crazy stories about growing up with a succession of five stepfathers failed to keep my eyelids from drooping, so I excused myself from the table. 'Over to you,' I whispered in Julie's ear as I left. 'You can tell me about it in the morning.'

THIRTY-TWO

Sunday morning, an hour before the shuttle that would take us back to the airport, I parked my luggage next to a square, marble-topped table not far from the fake fireplace in the hotel lobby and headed for the breakfast bar. While I waited for Julie to shower, dress, finish packing and join me, I filled a bowl with corn flakes from a dispenser, grabbed a cup of blueberry yogurt from a mini-fridge, snagged a cup of coffee and sat down.

About five minutes later Julie managed to find me. She'd stopped at the make-your-own waffle machine and was carrying a banana and a chunky Belgian waffle swimming in syrup, topped with a generous swirl of whipped cream. 'How do you stay so thin?' I asked, eyeing her breakfast and silently calculating the calories.

Julie scooted her chair forward, leaned over her plate and whispered, 'Hardly any of Dad's children are fat, did you notice?' Wielding a plastic knife and fork, she sawed a corner off the waffle, popped it into her mouth, closed her eyes and chewed appreciatively. 'High metabolism must run in the family,' she said, waving her fork. 'Thank you, Dad.'

I dumped the yogurt onto my cereal, stirred and dug in with a spoon. 'Sorry to run out on you last night, but I just couldn't keep my eyes open. Did you get a chance to talk with Andy?'

'No such luck,' she said. 'He bugged out shortly after you did.'

'Darn,' I said. 'Maybe he'll show up for breakfast.'

'It still feels totally surreal,' Julie said. 'I keep wishing my brothers were here, the ones I grew up with, I mean.'

Because of his age, Georgina had decided not to tell Colin. Dylan had zero interest in meeting his extended family; he'd expressed anger at his father, in fact. Sean had been keen, but even if he hadn't been warned to stick around town by Baltimore's Finest, his class schedule would have kept him away from Des Plaines.

'I hope they come around,' I said, remembering the fury with which Dylan had greeted the news that his father had been a sperm donor, treating it as an act of betrayal.

Julie must have been thinking the same thing because she said, 'You'd think Dad had been unfaithful to Mom the way Dylan carried on. But, Dad hadn't even *met* Mom yet!'

'Give them time to . . .' I began, and then I spotted Andy Zimmer, carrying a duffle bag and looking spiff in slim jeans and a long-sleeved polo shirt that brought out the blue in his eyes.

'Julie!' I whispered. 'There's Andy. Go ask him to join us.'

Rather than leap to her feet as I would have done, Julie unfolded herself casually, stood and wandered in Andy's direction, waylaying him just short of our table.

'Mornin', Andy.' Julie's smile dazzled. 'Would you like to sit with us?'

Andy grinned and dropped his duffle bag next to her chair. 'Thanks. Watch that for me, will you?' With a glance at Julie's plate he said, 'There's a waffle over there just calling my name.'

Julie sat down and scooted her chair forward, nudging Andy's bag with her foot to make room. Her brow furrowed. She reached into her pocket and grabbed her cell phone. After a quick glance around the room, she ducked her head under the table. As I watched, mystified, I heard the distinctive sound of a shutter closing.

When her head surfaced again, I whispered, 'What the heck are you doing?'

Instead of answering, she handed me her cell phone and refocused attention on her waffle.

I studied the screen. Julie had photographed the checked baggage tag wrapped around the strap of Andy's duffle. I raised an eyebrow. Julie made a flicking motion with her thumb and forefinger, indicating I should enlarge the image. I did.

BWI to MDW.

Midway is the airport in downtown Chicago, and BWI . . .

My heart did a quick *rat-a-tat-tat* as my eyes focused on the date. On August 18, the day that Scott Cardinale was murdered, Andy Zimmer had flown from Baltimore back to Chicago on Southwest Airlines Flight 2097.

'He told me he'd never been to Baltimore,' Julie said. 'Liar.'

'I wonder what time that flight was?' I said, calling up the Safari app and doing a quick search. 'Six p.m.,' I told her.

'Time enough . . .' Julie began, then, 'Shhhh. He's coming back.'

'Let me handle this, Julie.'

Her eyes narrowed, but she nodded.

'So, tell me about your family, Andy,' I said as he joined us at the table. 'We didn't get much time to chat last night.'

'I had two moms, never a Dad. My moms were great, don't get me wrong, it's just . . .'

He smiled. 'Mom always said I was conceived on the corner of Drexel and 57th during her lunch hour. No man involved.'

'Did you miss not having a dad?' Julie wanted to know.

Andy shrugged. 'Sometimes, like if there was a father-son event at school. People should be more sensitive, you know? But mostly my father was like a relative who died before I was born.'

Julie's smile turned from disarming to dangerous. 'Donor number 7135 was my father.'

'The father of us all,' Andy said.

'No, I mean my actual father, Andy. My dad. First tooth, first communion, first don't-you-dare-keep-my-daughter-out-late kind of dad.'

Andy sat back abruptly, feigning shock.

'I guess the secret's out now,' Julie said, skewering him with her eyes, 'but you knew that already, didn't you, Andrew?'

'W-what are you talking about?' he stammered.

'The date on your baggage tag, Andrew Zimmer,' she said, her voice dripping acid. 'You were in Baltimore, Maryland. You met my dad.'

Andy's eyes flicked to the duffle at his feet, then back to Julie. He melted into the back of his chair, looking defeated. 'Yeah, it's true. Ever since my mother died, I felt like half of me was a big question mark. I decided to look for my donor. I wanted to see his face. Is it like mine? I wanted to hear my donor laugh, see him smile, you know? I hoped to be able to shake his hand.'

I tried to imagine what it would have been like never to have known my own father – the smart, big-hearted, funny scientist I called Dad. My heart ached for what Andy had missed.

Andy paused for a sip of coffee, his hand shaking. 'I put my DNA up early on. Every time there was a match, I'd think, this might be it, but the matches always turned out to be donor kids, too. So I decided to try another tack.'

'Which was?' I asked after several long seconds of silence.

'There was this lab tech at the clinic. I don't want to get her into trouble, so all I'll say is I got a name. Once I had the name . . .'

I filled in the blank. Unlike Smith, Brown or Jones, Cardinale wasn't exactly your garden variety family name. It must have been easy after that. And it was.

'I did a search on Google,' Andy said, addressing Julie. 'There was a picture of your dad up on that church website. Once I saw the picture, I knew.'

'Yeah, spitting image,' Julie said dryly. 'Well, I hope you got to shake his hand.'

He smiled. 'I did.'

Julie attacked without mercy. 'Because he died. A month ago.'

Andy fell back in his chair as if he'd been shot. 'My God, no!'

Julie let him mull that over. I think we were both surprised when a single tear rolled down Andy's cheek. He swiped it away. 'Sorry,' he sniffed. 'I don't know how I can miss someone I never really knew.

'He's dead?' he repeated, as if he'd misheard. 'I simply can't believe it. All those years of wondering, then searching and I get to spend fifteen minutes with him, now . . .' His eyes misted over. 'Shit. Dead.'

'Murdered, to be exact,' I said.

His head jerked in my direction so quickly I thought he'd get whiplash. 'I think I want to go back to Chicago and start this weekend all over again. Murdered?'

I nodded, deciding to skip the details.

Andy turned to his half-sister, his eyes pleading. 'I didn't kill him, Julie. When I left your house he was definitely alive.'

'We saw that,' Julie said, letting him off the hook inch by painful inch. 'You were caught on a neighbor's security camera.'

'I see. Well, if that's the case, then you know I had nothing to do with it.'

'Somebody did,' I said. 'What can you tell us about your visit, Andy? It might help track Scott's killer down.'

'OK.' He pushed his breakfast, now stone cold, aside. 'I got there around one. Your dad was pulling weeds out of the flower bed in front of your house, Julie. I just walked up to him and introduced myself.'

'That must have been difficult,' I said.

Andy managed a smile. 'I'd practiced it for years, Hannah. Hi. My name is Andrew Zimmer. Twenty-five years ago my mother became pregnant with the sperm you donated to a clinic in Chicago.'

I was trying to picture Scott's face when confronted so baldly, but failed.

'So, what did Dad say?'

'He was really nice about it, Julie. He invited me into the backyard. I told him about my background and he seemed genuinely interested. Then he asked me for time to break the news to his family, in other words, you.'

'And he honored that commitment, Julie,' I said, thinking she'd been a bit brutal with him. 'Andy could have revealed Donor 7135's identity to everyone this weekend, but he didn't.'

'I kept thinking I'd hear from him,' Andy said, sounding lost.

Julie nudged him gently. 'What happened after that?'

'He got a call on his cell, answered it, then told me he had to go.'

'What time was that?' I asked.

'I don't know – one thirty or so.'

'Did he say who was calling him?'

'No, why should he? He just apologized for cutting our talk

short. Said it was business.' Andy reached into his back pocket and pulled out a thin plastic case. 'I gave him my card, and he told me he'd be in touch after he'd had time to think things over.'

He handed Julie one of his cards and waited while she studied it.

'You're an accountant,' she observed.

He flushed. 'Yeah. The apple doesn't fall very far from the tree, does it?'

'My brother, your half-brother, Sean, he's working on a masters in Economics at Hopkins.'

'Brigham Young for me,' Andy said.

Julie wrapped her hand around Andy's wrist. 'You need to talk to the Baltimore police, Andy. They think my brother, Sean, might have killed our dad.'

'You say I'm on tape?'

'Yeah. Looking exactly like my brother.'

'I am your brother.'

The remark made Julie smile.

Something was still puzzling me. 'We mistook you for Sean on the tape because of the floppy hair.'

'I got a haircut,' Andy said simply, rubbing his hand over his fuzz.

Julie cocked her head. 'How do we know you didn't come back later?'

'I took an Uber, Julie, both coming and going.' He reached for his cell phone, tapped the screen and called up the Uber app with the record of his past trips. 'See?'

'OK, then,' Julie said, after studying the screen. 'I believe you.'

'You want to freshen up your breakfast?' I asked, indicating his long-neglected plate.

'Not really hungry just now,' Andy said.

'Let me show you something.' Julie reached into the knapsack hanging off the back of her chair and pulled out a thin paperback photo album. *The Cardinale Family Summer, 2018* was scrawled across the cover in elegant calligraphic script. 'I had it printed at Shutterfly,' Julie explained.

I had to hand it to my niece – she'd come to the reunion

prepared. At least four additional copies of her family album remained in her bag. I wondered who she planned to give them to.

Julie pushed the paperback across the table and watched silently as Andy opened it and began to leaf slowly through. 'It's like looking in a mirror,' he said.

'You can keep it,' Julie said.

Andy wagged his head sadly. 'I have so many questions.'

'And I'll do my best to answer them,' she said.

Suddenly she popped up from her chair. 'I know we did a group shot last night, but Aunt Hannah, will you take our picture?' She looked at Andy. 'Do you mind?'

'Not at all.' Andy stood up, too, wrapped his arm around Julie's shoulders.

'How do you take such wonderful pictures?' I'd once asked my artist friend, Naddie Gray. 'Stand as close to the subject as you think you need to be,' she'd advised, 'and then step closer.'

Brother and sister smiled as I framed the shot, stepped closer, then pressed the button.

'Will you email it to me?' Andy asked.

Julie took the phone from my hand and, referring to the business card he'd given her, did so on the spot.

'I'm grateful to your dad, Julie,' he said, tucking the photo album carefully into his duffle. 'It bears repeating that I wouldn't be here without him.'

'I don't know why my dad decided to donate his sperm to the fertility clinic,' Julie said. 'Maybe he needed the money? But, one thing I know for sure. When guys donate their sperm it's not like slam-bang you're done. They need to understand that they're actually making people.'

'Will you give me permission to tell our diblings?'

'Hell,' Julie said, 'tell the *New York Times*, if you want, but promise me one thing.'

'What's that?'

She screwed up her face. 'Don't *ever* call me a dibling.'

THIRTY-THREE

The Saturday after Julie and I returned from Des Plaines, Illinois, I invited Georgina to join me at *Our Time* on the Eastern Shore. I told her I needed help washing, drying and rehanging the curtains, which was true in a way, but the Housekeeping Police wouldn't have shown up to give me a citation if I'd put off the task until Spring. I felt Georgina needed a break from Baltimore, is all, and she readily agreed.

With Andy Zimmer almost certainly out of the picture, we'd stayed up late that night drinking red wine and mulling over our only other suspects in Scott's murder – Bob and Judee. 'But what was their motive?' I'd asked my sister.

'They were having an affair,' Georgina said flatly, waving her wine glass.

'The only proof of that is the sketch,' I said.

'But we saw them arguing at Scott's funeral, remember?' Georgina said.

'Neither would hold up in a court of law, Georgina. Besides, just because they'd been having an affair and Scott got wind of it, isn't much of a reason to murder him.'

'Well, they were fighting about *something*,' she insisted.

'That could have been about anything,' I told her, pouring myself another glass. 'Maybe Judee needed more money for playground equipment and Brother Bob was being stingy about it.'

So we'd gone to bed a little tipsier and no closer to a solution than the moment we walked through the cottage door.

When I wandered out for coffee late the following morning, I was astonished to find Julie sitting at the kitchen counter.

I pressed a hand to my chest. 'You nearly gave me a heart attack,' I teased. 'What are you doing here?'

'I think I found the smoking gun,' Julie said, her voice quavering with excitement. 'It was hidden in plain sight,' she rattled on, 'tacked up on Daddy's bulletin board the whole time.

It wouldn't have meant a thing to the police, of course, so that's why they didn't take it.'

I held up a hand. 'Whoa! What on earth are you talking about?'

'It's the roster of kids attending day care at the church,' Julie explained. 'The monthly report the Day Care Director submits to the pastor and the pastor sends to the treasurer.' She hoisted her backpack onto the counter, unzipped a pocket and pulled out a wodge of pages. She plopped them on the counter, smoothed out the top sheet, then stabbed at it with her finger. 'This is total bullshit!'

'Bullshit is a two coffee problem,' I said as I headed for the Keurig machine. 'Can I make you a cup?'

'No, thanks,' Julie said. 'I stopped at Starbucks on the way over.'

While I waited for water to gurgle through the coffee machine, I studied the roster over my niece's shoulder. It looked like a perfectly ordinary list of children, arranged alphabetically by last name, followed by a grid of seven dated columns with checks to mark attendance.

When the coffee was done, I dosed it quickly with cream and sugar and then gave my full attention to Julie.

'Explain,' I said.

'How many children do you see there?' she asked.

That was easy. The list was numbered one to twenty-five. Twenty-one lines had names after them. 'Twenty-one,' I said.

'Look at the next sheet down,' Julie instructed.

'Nineteen,' I said.

'And the next?'

'Twenty.'

'I work part-time in the day care center,' Julie reminded me. 'And we always have at least twenty-five kids. Always!' She slapped the top of the pile. 'According to these reports, we didn't have a single week with more than twenty-two children.'

'Maybe I need more coffee, Julie, but I'm not sure where you're going with this.'

'OK. When I first saw the roster, and it didn't add up, I looked at the individual names. Where's Jamie? Where's Declan?'

'Maybe they were away that week?' I suggested.

'No way! Declan's a little monster. He kicked me in the shin.' She tugged on her pant leg, revealing a convincing bruise. 'See that?'

'If I understand you correctly, there were usually twenty-five children in day care, but only twenty on that week's report.'

'Five children unaccounted for,' Julie interrupted. 'You got it. The day care isn't free, Aunt Hannah. They may be a church and all, but they're not that charitable.

'So, I decided to look into it,' Julie continued. 'The teacher has a contact list for all the parents, for emergencies and stuff, so I called Declan's mom.'

'To complain about the kicking?'

'Fat lot of good that would have done,' Julie huffed. 'Anger management issues? Not her little darling.'

'So what *did* you tell her?'

'I said that the church was planning to offer parents the opportunity to pay day care tuition by direct deposit, and if so, would she be interested. Then I asked her how she paid tuition now – cash, check or credit card – and she said, "the usual way".' At this point, Julie paused, drawing the story out, keeping me in suspense.

'Which was?'

'Judee McDaniel told Declan's mom that since she runs the day care center, the church had set up a special account in her name, so the checks should be made payable directly to her.'

'Ah, the light is dawning.'

Julie slapped the countertop. 'It's unbelievable! I called Jamie's mom, too, and Justin's, and Ashley's. Same story.'

'So, the roster that Judee submitted to the church didn't include the names of the children whose tuition she stole.'

'Yup.'

'How much does the day care cost?'

'They charge thirty-two dollars a day, which works out to $972 a month, more or less. The way I figure it, Judee had to be skimming close to five thousand dollars a month off the top.'

'Do you think someone at the church tipped your father off?'

Julie flushed. 'I think I did. I told him about Declan kicking me. Declan's an unusual name. When he didn't see it on the roster, maybe he got suspicious. I mean, why else would Dad have the day care rosters tacked up on his bulletin board?'

'Julie?' Georgina shuffled into the kitchen, rubbing sleep out of her eyes. 'I thought I heard your voice. What the hell are you doing here?' Her eyes grew wide. 'Has something happened . . .?'

'Everyone's fine,' I assured her. 'Sit down. Let me get you some coffee while Julie explains.'

After Julie finished telling her mother about Judee McDaniel's day care scam, Georgina said, 'Scott had introduced best practices at the church. They were about to conduct their first external audit, and everyone had until September 30 to submit their reports.' She pointed at the pages Julie had brought with her, still spread out on the counter in front of us. 'That must be one of them.'

'Do you think Brother Bob knew that Mrs McDaniel was stealing from the day care center?' Julie wondered.

'I think it's a question the police are going to want to ask him, Julie, especially since he seems to have been sleeping with her.'

'You are shitting me! They were having an *affair*?'

'Julie! Language!'

'Sorry, Mom, but eeeuw! Can you imagine having sex with Brother Bob? Gross.' After a moment of apparent reflection on the nastiness of sleeping with the pastor, she said, 'Are you sure?'

I fetched my iPhone from the charging station and showed Julie the photo I'd taken of the sketch of Brother Bob, Judee and the heron.

'That's them all right,' she said, pointing out, as Georgina had, Judee's distinctive tattoo. 'Damn!'

'This is serious,' I said. 'If Scott confronted Judee about the embezzlement, she certainly had a motive to kill him. And if Scott knew about Judee's affair with Brother Bob . . .' I paused. 'Not exactly career-enhancing for an aspiring televangelist, is it? He'd fall from grace faster than a skydiver without a parachute. Maybe Brother Bob wanted to shut him up.'

'Maybe both,' Georgina said.

'What are we waiting for? Somebody needs to make the call.'

Julie shot from her stool, my cell phone in hand. 'I said I never wanted to talk to that detective again, but this time, I'm going to enjoy it.'

THIRTY-FOUR

A t six o'clock the following evening, in the middle of dinner, Georgina called me back. I got up from my chicken piccatta to take her call.

'Scott's biological minions can rest easy,' she began.

'So Uber confirmed Andy's story?'

'They did. Are you sitting down?'

'No,' I said.

'Detective Evans just called. They're charging Judee McDaniel with Scott's murder.'

'Hallelujah,' I said. 'How'd they catch her?'

'Anyone who works with kids in Maryland needs to have a background check,' Georgina explained. 'They tracked down the security firm that did the work and matched her prints to a partial the FBI lifted from the handle of the garden shears.'

'And the money she stole?'

'Oh, it's perfectly safe, wherever she and her duffle bag are.'

'She's not in custody?'

'Flew the proverbial coop. Judee's husband, of course, has no idea, which I totally believe, by the way. She'd been squirreling the money away in an offshore account. Nobody knows what she was planning to do with it.'

Thinking about the incriminating etching, I asked, 'What about Brother Bob?'

'Threw Judee completely under the bus. That man in the picture? Not him, no way. There wasn't enough evidence for the police to charge him with anything, but there was plenty of evidence for Tamara. She kicked him out. Last I heard, Brother Bob is camping out in his office.'

'Amen,' I said.

'Exactly.'

'Are you OK, Georgina?' I asked. 'You sound exhausted.'

'I'm fine, Hannah, really, but I'll really perk up when that bitch is behind bars.'

Twenty minutes later, Julie called. 'They took me, Aunt Hannah, they took me,' Julie bubbled.

'Who took you where?' I teased, although I could guess. Julie'd applied to AmeriCorps, a kind of domestic Peace Corps that sent volunteers out to do good work in impoverished communities.

'I've been accepted into AmeriCorps. I filled out my wish list, now I just have to wait for an assignment.'

'What's your first choice?' I asked.

'Secret,' Julie said coyly. 'I don't want to jinx it. Oh, I forgot to tell you that Lacey turned up,' she rattled on. 'Lacey confirmed Sean's story, not that he needs an alibi now.' She paused to take a breath. 'Lacey doesn't do Facebook, can you imagine? One of her friends told her Sean was looking for her. I'm afraid we're going to be seeing her around.'

'Is that a bad thing?'

'Well, his Virginity Pledge is toast, so what's to lose?'

'Good night, Julie,' I said firmly, but I was smiling.

'Goodnight, Aunt Hannah,' Julie said, but I could tell that she was smiling, too.

THIRTY-FIVE

Dressed in our grubbiest work clothes, Ruth and I drove north on Route 2 in an elderly Ford F-150 pickup truck we'd borrowed from my brother-in-law, Dennis Rutherford. Just north of the South River Bridge, I rattled and jolted into the parking lot of the commercial storage facility where Daddy had been keeping the household contents of his former home. Once inside, I used the key Daddy had given me to open the padlock on his unit.

Ruth raised the roller door. 'Good Lord!' she said.

We faced a daunting wall of furniture, boxes and storage containers, stacked six feet high. 'I don't know where to begin,' she added.

'One step at a time,' I said as I pulled a folded aluminum lawn chair with a broken plastic seat strap off the top of a charcoal grill and set it aside in the hallway.

Ruth grabbed a blue bicycle by the handlebars and eased it out of the locker. Both tires were flat. 'This used to be mine,' she said, 'until I got the ten speed for my birthday. I can't understand why he kept it.' The kickstand was missing, so she leaned the bike against the door of the adjoining locker. 'Why didn't he have a garage sale?'

'Too busy, I suppose. Besides, after Mom died, you remember how he couldn't be talked into parting with anything. "Save it for another day", he'd say.'

Ruth hauled out a second lawn chair and the cushions that matched it and piled them next to the bike, followed by the charcoal grill. 'I guess another day has finally come.'

For the next ten minutes, my sister and I relocated furniture and household items from the storage unit to the hallway, gradually clearing a path through the center of the unit. It was like an episode of *Storage Wars*, except that nobody was bidding on the contents.

'What are we looking for exactly?' Ruth asked.

'I'm not sure,' I said. 'If we're lucky, it will be a box labeled "Charlotte's Things".'

'Hah,' Ruth snorted. 'Do you ever remember seeing anything like that in Mom and Dad's attic?'

I had to admit that I hadn't, primarily because I'd never been in my parents' attic except one time accompanying the pest control man who had been hired to check out a squirrel invasion.

'Maybe there'll be something that will help solve the mystery surrounding White Bear's death,' Ruth said.

'Here, take these,' I said, handing two kites – a dragon and a bird of paradise – over to Ruth.

'Ah, these bring back memories,' she said. 'Remember flying them on the beach that summer before I went to college?' She set the kites carefully aside. 'Maybe your grandkids would like them now.'

'Into the truck, then,' I said.

Stacked to my right, in two columns five high, were cardboard boxes labeled: 'Books'. I eased between the books and a drop leaf table that had once been in our mother's kitchen. It, too, was stacked with boxes marked, appropriately, 'Kitchen'.

What was I looking for? A vintage trunk, maybe? A carved wooden hope chest? An antique safe?

A handle protruded from under the kitchen table. I moved a floor lamp in order to kneel down and check it out. 'Oh my gosh,' I said, 'it's my Chatty Cathy doll!'

Blue-eyed Cathy sat bolt upright in a miniature baby stroller. She was still dressed in the bright yellow gingham dress she'd worn when I last played with her, and a ruffled crinoline with lacy bloomers underneath. Her blond ponytails were tied with matching yellow ribbons. I reached under her dress, grabbed the plastic ring I knew I'd find there and pulled the string. 'Please brush my hair,' Cathy said. I laughed. 'I don't remember her being that whiney.' I pulled the string a second time. 'Give me a kiss,' the doll said. I kissed the top of her head, smoothed her dress and settled her back into her stroller. 'This is a keeper,' I said as I rolled it out into the hallway on its miniature wheels.

On a pair of stacked end tables just beyond the kitchen table I found three boxes marked 'Ruth', 'Hannah' and 'Georgina'. While Ruth wrestled with a Queen Anne chair, I ripped the packing tape off the top of the box marked 'Hannah' and looked inside. In neatly labeled folders Mom had saved my juvenile artwork and every report card and school photograph from kindergarten through twelfth grade. Records of my immunizations, too, and a packet of letters postmarked Oberlin, Ohio, held together by a rubber band that disintegrated when I touched it. In the days before the Internet took over our lives, I wrote home from college once a week.

Tears pricked at my eyes.

Ruth noticed. 'Hannah?'

I looked up helplessly. 'There's a box here for you, too. And one for Georgina.'

Ruth eased the box gently out of my hands. 'Why don't we save these for later?'

'All those memories,' I said, feeling defeated. I eyed the upholstered chair, longing to curl up in it as I had when it sat in the corner of our living room, next to the fireplace.

'You're the one who set us off on this fishing expedition,' Ruth scolded. 'You can't wimp out now.'

'Right.' I took a deep breath, let it out slowly, squared my shoulders and waded back in bravely.

'If I were Grandmother and I wanted to keep personal things private,' Ruth called out, 'I'd keep them in my bedroom.'

'I'm remembering a cedar chest that sat at the foot of Mom's bed,' I said.

I stood on tiptoe, peering over an ancient television – with rabbit ears! – toward the back of the unit. 'I see a four-poster back there, but it will take me a while to get to it.'

With Ruth's help, I moved a mattress and box springs to one side and carted a headboard and footboard out into the hallway so we could gain access to an oak chest of drawers that had once been my grandmother's. The two small drawers at the top held nothing but flowered shelf liner, a paperclip and two blond bobby pins. Except for shelf liner, the three large drawers below them were equally empty. Two bedside tables that were part of the same bedroom suite held no surprises other than a desiccated trap-door spider.

While I was disposing of the spider, Ruth uncovered two oversize plastic storage containers of sheets and towels. 'Didn't Daddy take anything with him?' she complained, shoving the containers, still stacked one atop the other, aside.

'I think Neelie was fully stocked with linens,' I said. 'I know he took his Navy memorabilia.'

'What about his desk?' she asked.

'That, too,' I said, venturing deeper into the unit.

'It's always the last place you look!' I yelled in triumph.

I'd found Mother's cedar chest, resting on top of an upholstered loveseat and covered with a quilted shipping blanket. By the time Ruth joined me, I'd already raised the lid and was pawing through its contents. I found my parents' 1952 wedding album and a square box about the size of a dinner plate containing the wedding bells from the top of their wedding cake. A Lord & Taylor shirt box held a christening gown, ivory with age, wrapped in tissue paper. My sisters and I had worn it, each in turn, for our baptisms. 'I wondered where this gown had got to,' I said, folding the tissue paper back around it again. 'They were moving when I needed it for Emily.'

'Look at this.' Ruth had unearthed a red leather-bound book with 'Autographs' embossed in gold script on the cover. She flipped the book open to the flyleaf. 'It was Mom's in seventh grade.' She chuckled, then paged forward. 'Oh my gosh, listen! Someone named Polly wrote:

> *Lois and John,*
> *Sitting in a tree,*
> *K-I-S-S-I-N-G.*
> *First comes love,*
> *Then comes marriage,*
> *Then comes Lois with a baby carriage.*

'I wonder who John was?' I laughed out loud at the silliness of the verse.

'I don't think we need to know,' Ruth said, setting the autograph book aside in the pile destined for the truck.

The cedar chest was too heavy for Ruth and me to carry out to the truck on our own, so we systematically sorted through its contents. At the bottom of the chest, under a garment bag containing my mother's wedding suit, was an oversized padded mailer marked KEEP. The mailer was sealed.

I glanced up at my sister who was looming like a vulture.

'What are you waiting for?' she said. 'You don't need my permission.'

So I seized the string tab and tore the mailer open.

'If we're lucky,' I had quipped to Ruth earlier that morning, 'it will be a box labeled "Charlotte's Things".'

We'd been incredibly lucky. Nestled inside the mailer I found an old-fashioned scrapbook, its manila pages pre-punched to fit over posts in a black cover which was fastened on with shoestring, tied in a neat bow.

'Charlotte: Her Book' was written on the title page in Gothic letters using India ink. Charlotte had been practicing her calligraphy.

My sister and I stared at each other, then at the scrapbook in reverent silence. I turned to the first page. 'It seems to start in mid-high school,' I said, noting a corsage flattened between the pages next to a booklet titled, 'Spring Formal'. Charlotte had been a popular girl. Every slot on her dance card was filled, but the first and last dances of the evening had been claimed by the same young man, S. Smith.

'That has to be our grandfather,' Ruth said.

I closed the scrapbook carefully and held it close to my chest. 'Let's take this out where the light is better.'

A few minutes later, my sister and I sat side-by-side on folding lawn chairs, watching our grandmother's early life scroll by. Tickets to a concert by Ben Pollack and His Californians. Postcards from Quechee Gorge near her home in Vermont as well as places farther flung like New York City and Niagara Falls.

Charlotte had graduated from high school in June of 1928 and almost immediately bought a train ticket from White River Junction, Vermont to Pierre, South Dakota, with a stopover in Chicago (during the height of Prohibition). Matchbooks and ticket stubs suggested she'd stayed at the Allerton Hotel and attended a showing of 'A Mysterious Lady' with Greta Garbo at the Biograph.

She'd owned a camera, too. At some point Charlotte climbed to the top of a building on Wacker Drive overlooking the Chicago River and the massive construction works that had been required to straighten it. Further on in her journey, blurry photos captured Midwestern towns from her window as the train sped through.

She'd saved a menu from the dining car. Oyster stew cost seventy-five cents, deep dish blueberry pie (baked on car today!) was thirty cents and a special prime rib dinner with all the trimmings would have set Charlotte back just a dollar ten.

Eventually she documented her arrival in Pierre, moving into the boarding house on North Huron, a sprawling Victorian with a front porch large enough to hold all the residents who posed for a group picture there in the summer of 1929. I spotted Charles Keene at once, lounging casually on the steps, straw boater in hand. Dressed in a lacy white frock, Charlotte stood directly behind Charles, leaning against a pillar. The ample, apron-clad woman to the far right had to be their landlady, Mrs Lumley. If I referred back to the 1930 census data, I might be able to sort the others out eventually, too.

Charlotte had chosen to wear a short jacket and wide-legged pleated slacks for a photo while standing on the running board of a Model T, her head cocked to one side, smiling shyly for whomever held her camera. 'She looks so like Amelia Earhart in that shot,' Ruth observed.

I agreed. 'A kindred spirit.'

Some Lakota lived in teepees then, we learned from Charlotte's photos, and as Wasula had told me, rodeos had been big, with a capital B. It's hard to capture a bucking bronco, but Charlotte had tried: she'd dedicated four pages of her scrapbook to action-packed rodeo scenes.

I turned the page and uncovered a treasure – Joseph, Henry and a teenaged Wasula posing against a split-rail fence. At Wasula's feet sat a black and white dog. Everyone was smiling, even the dog, except for Henry who had turned his face away from the camera and seemed to be glowering at something beyond the frame.

'Thank goodness she labeled everyone,' Ruth said. 'What kind of dog is Scout, do you know?'

I squinted. 'Some sort of mixed collie, I guess.'

'So, which brother did Charlotte favor?' Ruth asked. 'Joseph or Henry?'

'Joseph, for sure,' I said. 'Henry looks like a sourpuss, wishing he were anywhere else but.'

After turning to the next page, however, the answer to Ruth's question was obvious: Joseph alone, posing before the same fence, Stetson pushed back on his head.

Joseph grinning broadly, showing off his trophy, a silver belt buckle.

A newspaper article on the Calgary Exhibition and Stampede where Joseph White Bear had won the saddle bronc event. Charlotte had underlined his name three times.

'She was sweet on him,' Ruth said.

Tucked between the next two pages we found a slim packet of notes, written on notebook paper in what I assumed was Lakota, with the exception of a thank you note in English from

Mrs Two Knives who was grateful for Charlotte's help with a school fair. 'I'll have to ask Sam or his aunt to translate these for us,' I said, setting the packet aside for the time being.

The rodeo clipping was followed by several from the *Burlington Free Press* held together by a rusted paper clip. Someone must have mailed them to Charlotte because, 'See what you missed!' was written across the article on top in barely legible pencil.

Wednesday, August 31st, 1932

The curtain will rise on Burlington's great celestial drama – the sun's total eclipse – at exactly 2:16 p.m. today.

The following day's paper reported:

Celestial show races through skies filled with big, slow-moving clouds. Some gazers see corona as a color spectacle, others as a yellow glow. Haze will probably ruin many a plate of scientific photographers. Spectators fared better than astronomers, for the eye was better than the camera in this eclipse, and much that the plates missed excited the admiration of millions.

My eye had been caught by another headline: 'Girl, smoking glass to witness the eclipse, nearly burned to death' when Ruth reached across and ran a finger over the masthead. 'September 1, 1932,' she read aloud. 'Didn't you reckon Mom was conceived around that time?'

My heart did a somersault. 'Ohmahgawd.'

'Dee-dee-do-do, dee-dee-do-do,' chanted Ruth, making 'Twilight Zone' noises. 'I wonder . . .' She turned the pages. Blank, blank, and blank again. The article about the solar eclipse was the last thing Charlotte had pasted into her scrapbook.

'It's as if her life ended with that eclipse,' Ruth said.

I looked my sister squarely in the eyes. 'Act One had come to an end, at least. A little more than a month later, she would start life over as a married woman.'

'A pregnant married woman,' Ruth said.

I closed the scrapbook carefully. When I picked up the padded mailer intending to return the scrapbook to it, a five by seven inch photograph slithered out and fluttered to the concrete floor. I stooped to retrieve it.

A man sits astride a white horse. While the horse seems transfixed by the camera, the man stares into the distance, giving me a clear view of his chiseled, noble profile. He wears dark trousers, a jacket with fringed leather cuffs and a black Stetson hat. The hand resting on his thigh holds a cigarette. He is Joseph White Bear.

I turned the photo over. 'My Knight,' Grandmother had written.

THIRTY-SIX

As my mother was fond of saying, 'You can't get there from here.'

Although I plugged BWI to PIR into every travel website known to the modern Internet, no airline flew direct from Baltimore to Pierre. In the end I accomplished the trip piecemeal, booking a flight to Denver then catching a California Pacific flight to Pierre which, for some reason, didn't fly on Wednesdays and Fridays.

The plane landed at 12:45. I had no checked luggage, so it took only minutes to make my way to the Budget Rental Car counter and pick up my car.

Interstate 90 runs west out of Pierre, straight as a ruler, for mile after hypnotizing mile. I found myself nodding off. I was minutes from pulling off to the side of the road for a catnap, when the interchange with SD73 at Kadoka came into view along with a welcome cluster of gas stations, restaurants and a budget inn.

I purchased a large coffee at the gas station which made the endless miles of widely spaced farms, pastures and ponds south of Kadoka less soporific.

At a stop sign at a cross roads in the vast prairie of nowhere,

I gained an hour when the time zone changed from Central to Mountain time. SD44 eventually merged with the Big Foot Trail on the outskirts of Kyle, a rather soulless sprawl of widely-spaced, one-story buildings.

'Your GPS will do you no good,' Sam had emailed when giving directions. 'When you get to Little Wound School in the center of town, turn left on Allen Road. At St Barnabas Episcopal Church, check your odometer. The dirt road that leads to Wasula's house is exactly one point two miles past the church, on the right.'

Little Wound School, a massive, multi-storied red block of a building, was impossible to miss. St Barnabas Church? Not so much. I'd driven past the barn-like structure twice before I saw it and got myself back on track.

Wasula's modest ranch-style home sat one hundred yards off the road, surrounded by acres of fenced pastureland where a half-dozen cows, two horses and a buffalo grazed in contented harmony.

Mai answered my knock. 'Hannah, so good to see you.'

We exchanged hugs.

'Did you get Julie's message?' she asked in a rush.

'What? No. I haven't had any cell phone service since Pierre.'

'Sucks, doesn't it?' She gave me a what-are-ya-gonna-do kind of shrug. 'Julie's been accepted in an AmeriCorps program.'

I set my overnight bag down on the carpet and shrugged out of my jacket. 'I knew that, actually. She told me she'd applied just before I left to come here.'

Mai grinned slyly. Something was up. 'But you haven't heard the best of it. I don't know how Father did it, but he must have pulled some strings because Julie's been assigned to the Red Cloud Indian School here on the rez.'

Deep down in her DNA, Julie carried the genes of another pioneer woman, venturing out into Indian territory to help better the lives of others. Like her great-grandmother before her, would Julie find her knight? I prayed that unlike Charlotte, Julie's fairy tale would have a happily ever after.

'That's wonderful,' I told Mai, meaning it. 'What will she be doing?'

'Teacher's aide, I think, for the Head Start program.'

'Ah, Julie loves working with toddlers,' I told her. As long as they're not named Declan, I thought to myself.

'She'll homestay with a Lakota family near the school,' Mai babbled on. 'It'll be so cool.'

The reservation, I knew from driving only a part of it, was huge. 'How far away will she be?'

'Only sixty miles.' She dismissed the distance with a wave of her hand. 'I drive more than that to work every day. Speaking of which, I gotta go or I'll be late.' She snatched a fleece hoodie from a peg on the wall. 'Bingo waits for no man . . . or woman.'

Before Mai breezed out the door, slamming it behind her, she pointed me in the direction of the living room where I found Aunt Wasula perched on a loveseat, hands folded in her lap, waiting patiently. She wore her usual uniform – a flowered dress and cardigan – but this time, she'd slipped her feet into a pair of fur-lined slippers.

I wasn't certain of the protocol, but I took her hands in mine and planted a light kiss on her cheek. 'You look well,' I said.

She smiled. 'Every day is a blessing.'

Wasula inquired about my trip, then asked if I wanted anything to drink.

'No, but thank you. I had some coffee earlier.' I grinned. 'Mostly, I could use a bathroom.'

When I returned, carrying my overnight bag, Wasula said, 'You have brought some things to show me.' She moved her feet off the ottoman, indicating that I should sit there.

'I have, and I also need your help.' I dug Charlotte's scrapbook out of my bag, laid it on Wasula's knees and opened it to the first page. I watched silently as she leafed through Charlotte's life, using her hand to smooth each page as she came to it.

At the photograph of Charlotte on the Model T, she paused. 'That's Lottie.'

'Yes.'

'Wasn't she lovely?'

I agreed that she was.

'I found some notes, too,' I said, reaching again into my bag. 'Most of them are written in Lakota.' I handed the first one to her. 'I didn't know my grandmother spoke Lakota.'

Wasula's old eyes sparkled. 'Lottie was very smart. She picked up our language quickly while tending to patients on the reservation, especially the elder ones who did not speak English. By the time she left us, she was almost fluent.'

I called attention to the note, in case she'd forgotten she was holding it. 'Can you tell me what this says?'

Wasula's eyes strayed to the paper. After a moment she said, 'It's from White Bear. He's asking Lottie to bring extra flour when she comes. He tells her he will pay for it.'

'How about this one?' I handed her the next note in the little pile.

'White Bear is arranging to meet Lottie to see a movie when he comes to Pierre with two horses to sell.'

'And this?' I handed her the longest of the notes, written on a single sheet of notebook paper, White Bear's bold capital letters covering both sides.

As Wasula read, her face clouded, her eyelids drooped. At first I thought she'd dozed off. I reached out to nudge her gently awake when her eyes flew open and, startled, I drew my hand back.

'After the rodeos became successful,' she began, 'the Lakota decided to manage the money themselves. One year, after the rodeo was over, the cash receipts went missing.' She turned to me, her face serious. 'You can guess which year that was.'

'1932?'

She patted my hand and nodded. 'One of the young bull riders, Red Shirt, was accused of the crime. Nothing was ever proven, but he left the reservation in disgrace. White Bear is telling Lottie that he knows it was Hawk who stole the money. He's asking her what he should do.'

The room grew quiet as we let the significance of that fact sink in.

'I know what Grandmother would have said,' I told her. 'She would have advised him to talk to his brother, convince him to give the money back.'

'Yes,' Wasula said. 'And I fear that's exactly what White Bear did.'

'Do you believe that Hawk murdered your brother, to keep him quiet about the money?'

'Sixty-three dollars and seventy-six cents, that's all it was,' she said. 'My brothers never got along, but I never thought . . .' Her voice trailed off.

It's all about the money, I thought, thinking about my brother-in-law's murder. It's always about the money.

'A newspaper in Deadwood claimed it was a rodeo accident,' I said, 'that White Bear was injured while riding a bucking bronc.'

'Ah, yes,' she said. 'Father thought it was better that way.'

'What happened to Hawk?' I asked, seething quietly over the cover-up.

'He married, had children, a normal life,' she said. 'Hawk died in 1990. Whatever actually happened that day was a secret he kept all those years and took to the grave with him.'

There was one final note in the pile. 'This is the last one,' I said. 'Can you translate it for me?'

Wasula studied the single page for what seemed like an eternity. 'It's a love letter,' she told me at last. 'White Bear's words to Lottie are private, not meant to be shared.'

'But . . .' I protested.

'I will tell you this, Hannah,' she said, as if to soften the blow. 'White Bear writes this letter to *wínyan-mit-áwa*: my wife, my lover.'

My throat grew tight; I suppressed a sob.

'White Bear won some money at the Celebration rodeo,' Wasula said. 'He could afford to marry. But, after my brother died, I never saw Lottie again. I kept asking myself, why didn't she come to say goodbye?'

A single tear, that of a heartbroken sixteen-year-old girl, rolled down her wrinkled cheek.

'She must have been devastated by his death,' I said. I turned to the back of the scrapbook, to the newspaper article describing the eclipse. I pointed out the date on the masthead. 'She was still in South Dakota then,' I said, 'but this article must have been important to her.'

Wasula closed the scrapbook and laid both hands protectively on the cover. 'In Lakota culture,' she explained, 'a total solar eclipse is the physical manifestation of the sacred union of the Divine Masculine, represented by the sun, and the Divine

Feminine, represented by the moon.' She patted the seat cushion next to her. 'Come, sit by me. I will tell you a story.'

Like an eager toddler at storytime, I moved from the ottoman to the loveseat and sat.

'You may have heard of the peace pipe?'

'Yes,' I told her, 'but everything I know about it comes from movies and television so it's probably not very accurate.'

'Whenever the white men and the Indians got together to talk about treaties, the Indian way was to smoke a pipe first, so the negotiations could be witnessed by the Great Spirit. White men usually associated the pipe with the discussion of peace, so they are the ones, like in the Western movies you saw, who named it the peace pipe. To our people, however, it's always been called the Sacred Pipe because when we smoke it, we are communicating directly with the Creator.

'You are a Christian, Hannah?'

'I am, yes, of the Episcopalian persuasion.'

She nodded, looking wise. 'Think of the Sacred Pipe as a portable altar. Our great Lakota holy man Frank Fools Crow once described praying with the Sacred Pipe as having the same significance to our people as if you, a Christian, prayed while holding Jesus Christ in your arms.

'So, you can understand that the Sacred Pipe was a great gift to the Lakota Nation.'

'You say gift?'

'The Sacred Pipe was brought to us by the White Buffalo Calf Woman. Many have heard the legend of the White Buffalo Calf Woman, but this part of the story is often left out. The Sun and the Moon are husband and wife and they had one daughter: the Morning Star. And it was the Morning Star who came down to earth as the White Buffalo Calf Woman and brought the Sacred Pipe to the Native people.

'So the sun and the moon joining together in a solar eclipse can be a time of Creation,' she said, reaching for my hand. 'Your mother is the Morning Star.'

I rested my head against Aunt Wasula's comforting shoulder and wept.